Bridge Jumping

A Novel

Bridge Jumping

A Novel

Kathleen Ready Dayan

ROUNDFIRE
BOOKS

Winchester, UK
Washington, USA

JOHN HUNT PUBLISHING

First published by Roundfire Books, 2022
Roundfire Books is an imprint of John Hunt Publishing Ltd., No. 3 East St., Alresford,
Hampshire SO24 9EE, UK
office@jhpbooks.com
www.johnhuntpublishing.com
www.roundfire-books.com

For distributor details and how to order please visit the 'Ordering' section on our website.

Text copyright: Kathleen Ready Dayan 2021

ISBN: 978 1 80341 352 5
978 1 80341 353 2 (ebook)
Library of Congress Control Number: 2022914886

A CIP catalogue record for this book is available from the British Library.

Design: Lapiz Digital Services

UK: Printed and bound by CPI Group (UK) Ltd, Croydon, CR0 4YY
Printed in North America by CPI GPS partners

We operate a distinctive and ethical publishing philosophy in
all areas of our business, from our global network of authors to
production and worldwide distribution.

Contents

This one is for my father, the original feminist. Thank you, Dad, for empowering all of us.

Christian, Jew, Muslim, shaman, Zoroastrian,
stone, ground, mountain, river, each has a
secret way of being with the mystery, unique
and not to be judged.

—*Rumi*

Chapter One

Paige, *the Heretic*

There is no death. Only a change of worlds.
—*Chief Seattle, Suquamish Chief*

It was a perfect day for a funeral. The sun was bright and warm, there was a gentle breeze off the harbor and cotton-like clouds were gliding overhead. It was exactly the way it would have looked had Paige painted it with her own hand.

"I wouldn't be caught dead in a casket," she'd teased Gabriel months before. The joke had fallen flat with her boyfriend, but nonetheless, he vowed to follow every one of her instructions, which included not being memorialized in a church.

"How 'bout the gazebo?" he'd asked, and she'd tugged her eyebrows together, considering.

They had lived together in a rented cottage in the village of Onset in Wareham, Massachusetts, a town known as "the Gateway to Cape Cod." Not far from their home, the weather-worn gazebo sat on a hill that overlooked Onset Harbor. It wasn't big enough to seat all of Paige's family and friends, but it would make a nice platform for the speakers. He could arrange chairs on the grass, and guests would be able to view the gorgeous backdrop of Onset Harbor, the sandy beach and the periwinkle sky stretched above it, dotted with sea birds.

Paige's voice was wistful when she'd replied, "Yeah, that's the place."

Now the day had arrived, and he was waiting for the service to begin, to walk through her wishes, like he'd promised her he would. He kept imagining that any moment Paige would wake him up and tell him it had all been a nightmare. A sick distortion his brain created while he slept. Terrifying and believable, but not real.

1

He was standing in the parking lot near Kenny's Saltwater Taffy shop watching seagulls dive for French fries when his parents' silver Audi pulled in. Gabriel ran his fingers through his hair, creating an inadvertent mohawk. He'd used gel to tame it for the service, but now it stuck out wherever it pleased. Paige never liked it neat anyway. "You're a musician, not a businessman," she used to say.

His mom reached him and enfolded him in an embrace. She was wearing a bright red, floppy hat, exactly what her son expected her to wear to his girlfriend's funeral.

"Did you sleep?" his dad asked as soon as he caught up.

"A bit," he lied and led his parents up the brick walkway toward the small crowd. At the top of the hill, he paused near a bronze statue of a Native American woman gazing at the harbor, as if she were listening to the waves from her cross-legged perch. Admiring the statue was something Gabriel had always done with Paige. Now he felt a kinship with the bronze woman. She sat alone on that hill year after year.

His mother straightened his tie, an electric blue Jerry Garcia print, before they approached the group gathered near the gazebo. Gabriel's sleeves were rolled to his elbows and a string of black beads was wrapped several times around his wrist. It was a mala from Tibet, used during his meditations. A postmortem gift from his girlfriend.

The gazebo steps were lined with colorful arrangements of flowers. Flanking the top step, where the speakers would stand, were two enormous vases filled with sunflowers, which created the illusion that a marriage ceremony was about to take place, something Gabriel hadn't anticipated. The only hint that it was a memorial service was a box next to the podium containing twelve glass vials filled with cremation ashes.

"I think we're on this side," his mother suggested when they reached the white wooden chairs placed on the grass in neat rows with an opening between the two groups that resembled an aisle.

"It's not a wedding," Gabriel replied. "There aren't any sides."

"We'll follow your lead," his dad patiently replied.

He led them to the front row. "I'm Gabriel," he said and offered his hand to Joe Junior, Paige's baby brother, who lived out of state. With his golden hair and silvery-blue eyes, Joe looked like he'd stepped off the cover of a magazine, but there was a timidity to his expression that revealed his discomfort with his own image. He'd be happier without all the attention. He got plenty of it, right now from Paige's college roommates, Julia and Kim, who were sitting behind him with Paige's ex-husband, Christopher. Gabriel had never met any of them, although he recognized Christopher from a wedding photo. In the front row between Joe and his sister, Abigail, there were three empty seats. The space between them struck Gabriel as odd, but not unexpected.

"Would it be alright if we sit here?" he asked Joe.

"Yes, of course," Paige's brother stammered. "Listen, I'm sorry I didn't come sooner."

"It's okay," Gabriel softly replied. "Paige didn't want you to see her sick."

He waited for his parents to get situated in their chairs, and then sat down between his mother and Abigail. Joe was nibbling fiercely on a fingernail, on the edge of his seat.

"Hello, Abigail," Gabriel offered. She was wearing a dark blue suit with pumps in contrast to the majority of attendees, who were dressed in brightly colored clothes, at Paige's request. "Screw a funeral," she had said. "Make it a bon voyage party."

Abigail was a slight woman who took up little space in her chair. Her golden hair was held tightly by a turquoise barrette that used to belong to Paige, the only bright color adorning her body. Unlike Paige, Abigail's hair and eyes were fair, but to Gabriel she looked remarkably similar to Paige before the diagnosis, except that their facial expressions were different.

Paige had been as open and welcoming as a golden retriever, whereas her sister bore a dignified sense of controlled emotion, like one of the Kennedys during a family crisis. She was a closed book.

"Good morning," she replied without looking at him. Gabriel grinned when he noticed *Where the Sidewalk Ends*, a collection of children's poetry, clutched in her fingers. It was one of Paige's favorites. There was a dog-eared copy on the night table next to their bed. She used to read it out loud to him and had once told him that she was hoping to track down Shel Silverstein when she got to the "other side." She'd need someone to make her laugh, she'd said.

Next to Abigail was her husband, Jim. He was a criminal prosecutor, and twice the size of his wife. "How are you holding up?" he asked gently.

The concern in his voice made Gabriel's throat freeze. He felt like one of those toy dogs in the back of cars, his head shaking, but no words escaping. He liked Jim, though. Even now, bobbing his head like a plastic puppy, he felt comfortable in his presence.

Jim was the softer, more introspective side of his marital relationship, even though he was supposed to be a pit bull by profession. Abigail worked hard on her tough exterior, and only revealed her true feelings on rare occasions — like now, clasping the children's poetry book so she could read a poem one more time for her little sister. Paige used to say that Abigail was like a coconut, her outer shell nearly impenetrable, but only because her insides were as soft as milk.

Paige's dad, Joe Senior, sat across the aisle, with his second wife, Evelyn, and another couple, friends from their church. Evelyn was conversing politely with them, her hand protectively on Joe's. His eyes were on the harbor, a tranquil smile on his lips. Dementia had infiltrated his once brilliant mind. Gabriel wondered if he knew he was at his daughter's funeral.

Bon voyage party he corrected himself, as if Paige was whispering the words in his ear. *Don't use the "f" word,* she'd insisted.

Gabriel turned in his seat to introduce himself to her college roommates. He extended his hand to Paige's ex-husband as well, but Christopher turned away without taking it. It was overwhelming, meeting all the people who had been part of Paige's life, all of whom he'd heard about, but most never met. He felt like an outsider, even though he was her partner. Until today, for the most part, life had been just the two of them.

"Why all the sunflowers?" Julia asked him. Her brown hair spilled from under a sun hat with a bright pink band around it to match her suit. A large gap between her two front teeth made her smile uniquely beautiful, and her energy was warm, which helped to ease the unexpected awkwardness between Gabriel and Christopher.

"We have friends who are Spiritualists," he replied. "I'm guessing the flowers are from them. Sunflowers are the symbol of their religion."

"What's a Spiritualist?" Julia further inquired.

"Uh, basically, it's someone who believes that life continues after death and that communication with them is still possible."

"Oooh, how interesting!" Julia cooed.

"How strange," Kim piped in, and Gabriel turned back around in his chair. He didn't feel the need to defend the Spiritualists, or anyone else. Besides, the Spiritualists weren't responsible for the sunflowers. Paige's ex-husband was, although he didn't admit it, even though he was listening to the conversation. Christopher's exterior created the illusion that he was coolly waiting for the service to begin. Every hair was in place, and he was wearing a new expensive suit. But behind his Wayfarers, his eyes were red and swollen. It was, by far, the hardest day of his life.

Abigail spun in her chair to face her sister's friends. "Just ignore him," she hissed. "Apparently, he thinks he's some kind of psychic."

"How old is he?" Kim asked.

"Shhh!" Julia intervened.

"Twenty-eight," Abigail whispered anyway, although Gabriel heard every word. He was sitting right beside her. "He didn't go to college. He's a construction worker."

The resentment in her comments stunned Gabriel. Abigail wasn't his biggest fan, as far as he knew because Paige had moved out of her house and into his, but he wasn't expecting her to be mean-spirited. He willed away the negativity and let his head fall back with his eyes on the sky. A large white bird was flying over him. His mother noticed it, too, and squeezed his hand.

"Paige's crane," she gasped.

"Paige's crane," he repeated. He'd been waiting for that crane since the morning she passed over. Had he taken the time to carve out a comeback to Abigail's bitter words, he might have missed it. It wasn't until the bird was almost out of view that he noticed others in the group were watching it, too. Joe Junior was smiling at the sky and Gabriel heard a female voice say, "Paige would love that." *Ah, no,* he thought, *she would orchestrate it.* Only Abigail appeared annoyed by it. The funeral she'd envisioned for her little sister didn't include wild animals.

"Sometimes I think the people closest to Paige didn't know her well," Gabriel said.

"You said the same thing when Billy died," his mother reminded him.

His eyes moved to the couple sitting across the makeshift aisle—Billy's parents. "I can't believe they came," he said. Billy had been his lifelong best friend until his sudden death five years prior. Now Billy's mother was dressed in a floral sundress, trying to look festive for Paige's sake. Her Irish eyes winked beneath the brim of a sun hat as they made contact with Gabriel's. He forced a smile and lifted his hand in greeting.

The first speaker was taking her place behind the podium when Gabriel's mother said, "If they don't understand Paige, maybe you could help them." Her suggestion gave him an idea. "Or maybe she could," he replied. A statuesque woman wearing a turquoise dress, known in her native Nigeria as a kaba, gracefully stepped forward and introduced herself. "My name is Arica," she began. "My fiancé and I have been friends with Paige and Gabriel for the past year. Paige asked me to read this poem today. It's called *Fiddler Jones* and was written by Edgar Lee Masters." She took a breath and began to read:

> The earth keeps some vibration going
> there in your heart, and that is you.
> And if the people find you can fiddle,
> why, fiddle you must, for all your life. . .

Gabriel turned toward the bronze statue on the hill. He had a photograph of Paige sitting cross-legged beside it, with braids in her hair, too, as if she were the living version of the bronze woman. It was easier to think about that than the poem's message, which Paige apparently chose specifically for him. *Fiddle you must, for all your life* he chanted silently and leaned into Abigail to whisper, "After the service there's something I'd like to lend you. It's in my truck." She gave a quick nod without looking at him.

Abigail stepped forward as soon as Arica moved away from the podium. She didn't address the crowd only opened the book and started reading "Forgotten Flowers" out loud. When she finished, she explained, "This is the first book I read to Paige when we were little girls. I guess she still liked it because, according to her boyfriend, even as a forty-year-old woman she was still carrying it around."

People laughed because it was characteristic of Paige's playful personality to be fascinated by a children's poet, and that broke the emotional tension created by businesslike Abigail reciting a children's poem to her dead sister. She took her seat, and one by one, family members and friends took turns telling their favorite Paige stories. Yara and Davi, her friends from yoga class, ended the service with a Portuguese lullaby.

Arica, who started the service, once again claimed the podium and explained that there were twelve vials containing ashes from the cremation of Paige's body, and that it was Paige's wish that those closest to her scatter the ashes in a place that would honor the relationship they shared.

After claiming their vials, Gabriel and Abigail walked together down the brick path that divided the grassy hill. A bench carved out of stone and bearing the words *Live, Love, Laugh, Dance, Fish. Life is Short* caught Gabriel's eye as they passed it. In the parking lot the seagulls swarmed over the cars. And there was something in the air.

"It's almost here," he muttered.

"What is?" Abigail asked.

"The first day of summer."

Abigail made a scoffing sound. It was only May. And why was Gabriel thinking about summer when her sister was dead? Paige was always saying how thoughtful and sweet he was. Abigail might have called him attractive if his hair was cut shorter, but thoughtful? Paige, she assumed, was never able to see past his big brown eyes. His insensitive comment encouraged her to say what was on her mind, even though she knew it would sound cold. "Paige had a fairly sizable retirement account."

"I know," Gabriel replied. "I have no interest in it."

"Exactly."

He stopped walking. "What I meant is that I want no part of it."

"I thought you might want compensation," Abigail stated without emotion.

"For what?" he challenged. "Taking care of her? I took care of Paige because I loved her. Because I *love* her."

Gabriel started across the parking lot again, but at a quicker pace so that he arrived at his old Chevy pickup truck ten feet ahead of Abigail. He yanked off the suffocating tie and tossed it onto the seat. A moment later she caught up and he handed her a book.

"It's Paige's journal," he explained.

"She kept a journal?" Abigail sputtered. God only knows what she might have written, she was thinking. Paige always had too much to say.

He was holding it out, so she took it from his hand. It was dirty. There were smudges of red paint on the cover and it had a strong odor, like some kind of Indian spice. She wasn't sure she wanted to touch it, let alone read it, but then it occurred to her that Gabriel was assuming it belonged to him and was only allowing her to borrow it. That seemed an outrage and stirred in her the resentment she felt over his control of Paige's ashes. She didn't believe that Paige chose to have her cremation ashes separated. Surely, she would have expected them to go to her family.

"You want the journal back?" she asked.

"Yes," he answered politely. "Because Paige gave it to me. They're our memories mostly. But there's stuff in there about your family, too. Just—" He took a breath, and the movement of his upper lip revealed a chip on his left front tooth. It reminded Abigail of a comment she'd once made to Paige about the broken tooth. *It probably happened in a bar fight.* Paige had been furious. "Make sure you read it all the way to the end," Gabriel continued. "Paige changed a lot in the last year."

"Because she was dying!" Abigail railed, finally giving her anger an outlet.

Her energy knocked him backwards a step, as if she had pushed him. "Because she was living," he softly countered.

"I'll mail it to you when I'm finished with it," she snapped. She was several strides away when she heard his voice behind her.

"Hey, Abby," he called.

"Abigail," she corrected as she turned on her heel to face him. Only family members had the privilege of calling her Abby. Gabriel was not—and never would be—part of the Delaney family.

"For the record, and because I don't know if I'll see you again, I'm not a construction worker. I'm a house painter. And I do have a degree. From Berklee College of Music."

She threw her arms out to intimate *whatever* without having to say it.

"I'm twenty-nine," he continued. "I'll be thirty in July. Oh, and I'm not psychic. I'm clairvoyant, which means I can see people after they pass out of their bodies—your sister and your mother, for example. They're together in case you were wondering."

The word *liar* spun through Abigail's mind, and she barely resisted the urge to throw it at him. She turned and left him alone with his dirty pickup truck, resentment brewing like poison in her chest. If Paige could make herself known after death, wouldn't she appear to Joey or herself? Why to some guy who barely knew her? He was a con artist, she believed, who'd seduced her sister into spending the last year of her life with him. Had Paige taken her advice to stay in the marriage with Christopher—the person who probably loved her more than anyone, she could have spent that time with her real family. But no, her impulsiveness had prevented it.

Before she returned to the gazebo where the remainder of Paige's family and friends were mingling, she opened the journal for a quick peek. The inside cover had the words *started on March 23, 2009* scribbled in Paige's familiar fat script. That was almost six months before the diagnosis. Even before she met Gabriel.

Underneath the date, Paige had written something else.
Who are we to each other? The human race is like an immense
spiderweb. If I were to draw it, it would look like an enormous
mandala, a great wheel spinning slowly, untraceably. In my
mind's eye, I see us all bumping up against each other with our
arms and legs reaching. On one outstretched hand, my index
finger touches my mother's, my middle finger my father's and
my ring and smallest fingers, Abby and Joe. With my other
hand I reach for Gabriel, his mom and dad, Arica & Ben.
But at my feet there are more connections: Christopher, Kim &
Julia, Yara & Davi, and people that I've left behind, but still
carry in my heart, friends from the old neighborhood and high
school. And they are connected, too, some to each other, and
to even more people who I do not yet know. Where would I
put God in my imaginary drawing, at the center of the wheel,
or surrounding the parameter? Maybe God is the
"in between," the energy that binds us to each other.

A sob escaped Abigail's mouth. She quickly covered it with her
hand and her cool gray eyes scanned her surroundings to make
sure she was alone. She could see the taillights of Gabriel's truck
moving down Onset Avenue in the direction of his cottage and
hear music pouring irreverently through the truck window. She
should close the journal until back home. But curiosity had her.
She turned the page.

*March 23, 2009: Today the divorce is final and
the whole ridiculous fifteen months of squabbling
over every little thing is finally in the past. Even
after all that's been said and done, I don't hate
Chris. I've just been angry at him for so long that
I've forgotten how much I like him. But it's time
to let go of the anger before it consumes our entire
relationship. Here's the plan.*

1. To quit my job and live off my savings until I find something I like.
2. To work on my Masters' thesis in Theology.
3. To move out of Abby and Jim's house as soon as I decide where I want to live.
4. To practice yoga every day.
5. To ask my Higher Power to help me reclaim my life because—obviously—I need help.
6. To journal faithfully, so that I can check my progress by reading back in time. As an aside, I will try my hardest to write only positive thoughts.

This is a journal of empowerment. The book of my rebirth.

March 24, 2009: Have you ever considered that nearly everything in our lives is subjective? It all relies upon interpretation.

For example, I love alternative rock music, but let's say you don't. While watching a performance, I see a group of creative sorts walking along their spirit paths, whereas you might see a group of misguided bohemians. When you hear ear-splitting noise, I hear emotion-filled vocals. You say "outrageous." I say "inimitable."

Who, then, is right?

Neither of us. Judgment is a faulty device. I cannot perceive what you're perceiving, and vice versa, even when we're party to the same event, because all our past experiences and expectations influence us.

Life is like a game of pin the tail on the donkey, except the donkey keeps moving. And so we wander through life with our blindfolds on, still 100% sure that we are right. Ego is a lying voice disguised as truth. Why then are we all so willing to listen to it?

March 25, 2009: Thinking about my "subjective universe" theory that I wrote about last night, I thought of a metaphor. Here goes.

A man—let's call him Jack—was driving home. He'd just been fired from his job and was ashamed to tell his wife. As he neared his neighborhood, one of his tires blew. He was a mile from home, had no spare in the trunk, and it was January. As he stepped out of the car in his suit, a passing car blasted its horn. Jack yelled an obscenity at the driver and walked straight into a puddle of slush. Now his Italian leather shoes were ruined, and his feet were cold.

A dog from a neighboring yard timidly made its way toward him. Jack shouted, "Go away!" and it did. As he walked home, he noticed that every mound of snow was tarnished with dirt and car exhaust. The sun's glare was giving him a headache. Not even the blue sky was beautiful. To him, it echoed the coldness of the winter air. From Jack's perspective, life was a series of difficulties.

An hour later, a school bus pulled up to the very same spot where Jack's car had been before it was towed, and an eight-year-old boy, Oliver, stepped out of it right into the puddle that had ruined Jack's shoes. It made a satisfying sound, so the boy jumped up and down in it until the bus driver prompted him to cross the street in front of the bus. As he did, he noticed the shivering dog.

"Here boy," he said, and the dog wiggled over to him with his tail wagging. Oliver dropped to his knees and hugged the dog to warm him. He noticed his soft fur and how the dog seemed to smile. The sun glittering like diamonds on a snow pile drew his attention. He ran to it with the dog trotting joyfully beside him and climbed it. To the boy, it was a snow castle, and he was the ruler, King Oliver. The dog was his knight and above them, the sky was velvety blue, a perfect ceiling for his kingdom. From the boy's perspective, all of life was magical, laid at his feet like jewels.

My point? Two souls heading down the same path at virtually the same time don't share the same reality, and they don't necessarily arrive at the same conclusions.

March 26, 2009: When I awaken in the morning to the melodic voices of birds in the backyard, the sheets cool and silky against my legs, I don't feel old or less than. I'm not thinking about the body that contains me. I am pure consciousness taking in the sights, sounds, smells and sensations of the universe. I am just me. Me, and that is more than enough.

But soon I see my reflection in the bathroom mirror and immediately notice the flaws. The crow's feet and forehead lines are creased with sleep, and my eyes wear the heaviness of the past year. I'm about to turn forty, which is a futile time to focus on appearance, but I can't help noticing. I have medium brown hair, thanks to Clairol, and clear skin compliments of Neutrogena. On my counter are the following items: mascara to lengthen my lashes, blush to color my cheeks, collagen gloss to plump my lips, under-eye concealer to cover the dark semi-circles, moisturizers for day and night, even toothpaste to whiten my teeth.

It makes me wonder, why in this culture do we place such importance on a woman's face? And why am I buying into it?

But perhaps most importantly, why am I so hard on myself?

Chapter Two

Joe Jr., *the Dissident*

Both read the Bible day and night, but thou read black where I read white.
—William Blake

Joe was holding the vial of ashes in his hand when he walked away from the memorial service and ducked into his brother-in-law's Toyota Prius. The escape vehicle.

"What the fuck?" he vented loudly to no one but himself.

He dropped his head onto the steering wheel and closed his eyes, the first moment of peace he'd felt all day. Thank God he'd taken Jim's car, or he'd be riding home in Abigail's SUV right now listening to her complaints about the service. Somehow, despite numerous phone calls about the funeral, she'd not once mentioned that the ashes were being divided. She'd been so keenly focused on the fact that the service would not be in a church, that she seemed to have overlooked everything else. And everything she'd forgotten—the speakers, the flowers, the chairs—had been arranged by Gabriel. Not that it would occur to Abby to thank him for it.

Joe had assumed Gabriel would be tending to her ashes, as well. He was obviously the person closest to Paige, even if he wasn't technically family. But Abigail would never agree to that. Maybe that was why the ashes were separated, so that no one's feelings would be hurt. As for Joe, he'd feel more at peace leaving the funeral without carrying a piece of his dead sister with him. Arica, Paige's friend, made a huge point of saying that people should only take a vial if they felt comfortable with it, but he was her brother. How could he leave it to someone else? That would be beyond rude. It felt almost, well, sacrilegious. But what the hell was he supposed to do with them?

Paige's childhood, like the rest of her life, had been loud and bold. Shout it from the rooftops. Wave your freak flag. His sister had been an eccentric, and a personable one. She leapt into life in a way he could never understand. As a boy, he'd been like a spider in a hole. Hiding was his childhood superpower. Paige had a way of finding him, though, and softly urging him back into the world. *Don't be scared, Joey. I'm right here. Everything's okay, Joey. You're my favorite brother.* Even as children, she'd loved him deeply, and he never really understood why. How was it that she easily grasped his worth when he'd never been able to?

Still, the vial was in his hand, sweaty from being clasped too tightly. At least he hadn't dropped it in the parking lot, like he'd imagined. It was a gut-wrenching visual, his sister's cremation ashes scattered on the asphalt, mingled with sand and cigarette butts. Abigail would never forgive him for that, although if it was possible in some other realm, he knew Paige would be laughing.

Since moving to D.C. he'd only known his sisters through phone calls and short holiday trips. He'd opted out of their lives because it was easier than facing them with the truth. Joe was a grown man, yet whenever Abigail was nearby, he felt like a little kid. She was always right about everything, even when he figured out later that she was wrong. Her attitude emanated righteousness, and how could anyone argue with that?

Of course, Paige had, and that was part of the reason he felt guilty. Paige never took crap from Abby. And she didn't opt out either. Judging by her boyfriend, a good ten years her junior, even at the end of her life, she'd refused to let anyone tell her who she was supposed to be. God damn, he admired her. Still, the contrast made him feel weak.

He patted the stopper on the vial to make sure it was properly closed before he laid it down on the passenger seat and reached for the hand sanitizer, which made him feel like he was washing his dead sister off his hands, and that triggered another guilty thought. He hadn't traveled home to see Paige when she was sick, and he wasn't sure he would ever come to terms with that. Joe considered himself the black sheep of the family. His sisters were opposites, but equally strong. He never dared to take on either one of them in an argument. Instead, he kept his mouth shut, but he felt like his exterior betrayed the fact that he wasn't an equal opponent. He had his mother's curls that still made him feel like the second grader he was the first time he took scissors to them. Golden blonde ringlets, like a cherub. He had his father's gray eyes, but his mother's black lashes, which made it look like he was wearing eyeliner. As kids, his sisters nicknamed him "Panda." To Joe, it wasn't only about his eyes, but his passive nature. If he was a panda, Abigail and Paige were grizzlies. And nobody fucks with grizzly bears.

He was still in the parking lot, sitting alone in Jim's Prius, watching his sister's eclectic friends move past him as they left the service. Apparently, Paige still collected companions like other people collect seashells. Two women walking together looked familiar. One of them, the brunette, smiled in his direction and the space between her two front teeth triggered his recall. They were Paige's college roommates. Back then, they'd struck Joe as ridiculous with their big hair, midriff T-shirts, and arrogant assumption that he was lusting over them. That was twenty years ago. Now they were dressed in business suits, even if they were hot pink and lime green, choices no doubt inspired by his sister's request. When Joe first arrived, the scene had looked more like a luau than a funeral. Paige would have loved it. She'd been one of a kind, his sister. A gypsy who'd fallen from a caravan and somehow landed in the twentieth century. Confident to the point of crassness, but funny, too, and always kind. Was she beautiful? Not really. But she was unforgettable.

He wondered now as he watched her old roommates step into a convertible in the parking lot if they had changed at all, or if they were still the pair he had seen slugging down beer in his sister's bedroom and blowing hash smoke out the window. He suddenly remembered that Kim was the name of the bleached blonde in the driver's seat. She had once debated gay rights with his father over Sunday dinner, one of the few issues Joe Delaney Senior had been closed to discussing.

"Homosexuality is a perversion," he used to say, "an intentional act against God." Of course, he hadn't known at the time, and still didn't know, that his only son was gay.

Listening to his father's words was like hearing the voice of God himself. *There's something wrong with you. You're not like the rest of us. You're unnatural, twisted.*

This was the person he had been named after, as if it were presumed, even at birth, that he'd grow up to be just like him. An imprint of the last generation. Joseph Junior. There was too much expectation in that name.

Did his father understand the power of his judgment? For Joe, it brought to mind Michelangelo's Jesus sitting on a cloud, showing mercy for fortunate souls, but forcing others into eternal damnation. In the painting, Michelangelo's own skin hung from St. Bartholomew's hand, and that was the image Joe identified with. He'd never be one of the blessed who rose like Phoenixes above the flames. Even his father had unknowingly said so. Those declarations of right and wrong, of the exalted and the damned, had changed the course of Joe's life. As a teenager he'd gone into hiding, and he still hadn't ventured out. Now his father, disabled by dementia, had no access to those crippling thoughts. But Abigail did.

I'm not going to her house, Joe decided. What he needed was to be alone in a hotel room, and to get Bowman, his partner, on the phone. For almost ten years Bowman had been the most direct route to restoring his sanity. He was the one who'd helped him get his life on track, encouraged him to finish his education so that he could teach elementary school, what he'd always wanted to do, even though he was working in sales when they met. And he was the one who told him that he was perfect exactly the way he was.

If he had enough guts, he'd call Abigail and tell her that he had no intention of showing up at her house, but he didn't, so he turned his cell phone off to be unreachable. It was an old trick in a new skin. As a child he'd retreat into the woods until his mother called him home for dinner, and as a teenager he'd lock his bedroom door and crank Metallica or Black Sabbath, music that always worked as big sister repellent. In Washington D.C., where he shared a home with Bowman, he was a man, but in Massachusetts he was a nail biting seven-year-old.

His eyes scanned the beautiful bay in front of him. A boat carrying tourists was making its leisurely way down the canal. With his windows open, Joe could hear a bluesy riff coming from it. Music floating happily through the breeze would feel inappropriate at most funerals, but not at Paige's. It felt like the music was being played specifically for her, and he could imagine her dancing to it with her bare feet hugging the earth and her willowy arms outstretched, wide open to the world, the way she'd always been.

A shiver ran through him. He rolled up the windows, as if the ocean breeze had caused it.

There was still a small group gathered around the gazebo. With his eyes focused on them, he caught Abby in his peripheral vision. She was leaning against a tree near the parking lot and reading from a book. He had no desire to know what the book was, or his sister's multitude of opinions regarding it. His hand reached for the key and turned the ignition.

April 2, 2009: I had the word Ahimsa tattooed on my arm. It means compassion and noninjury toward all living beings, including myself. It is there to remind me of who I am choosing to be and to treat all life with sanctity, a philosophy that comes from the Indian religions. I'm not as good at this as I would like to be, but I'm working on it.

There's a man in my yoga class from India, Faruk, who is an artist and today he showed me some of his work. It is called mehndi, which are henna tattoos, mostly on the hands and feet of women, lacy designs created for wedding ceremonies. Their hands are breathtakingly beautiful. It's enough to make me want to get married in India. Or to be covered in henna ink as an act of love.

April 3, 2009: I'm thinking of writing my thesis on Native American spirituality. The idea was prompted by a fascinating book I happened upon called Gospel of the Red Man, an Indian Bible. Searching the internet, I discovered that in Onset Village, about an hour's drive from Abby and Jim's house in Norwell, there is a wigwam that was erected by a group of Spiritualists in honor of the Wampanoag Natives who used to live there. I need to find out more about these Spiritualists and their connection to Native American spirituality. A trip to Onset could be in order.

April 5, 2009: There is a man frequenting my dreams, a beautiful boy-like man with deep brown eyes and unkempt hair of the same color. He came for the first time two weeks ago. I saw myself asleep in my bed and him hovering before me, curiosity in his eyes and on his lips, watching. Just watching, like he knew me. My awareness of him startled me from sleep. But then he came again, a week later. He was kneeling beside the bed, holding my hand, and we were conversing as if we knew each other. I still remember the last thing I said to him. "I'll kiss your chest and heal your heart." I think it must have been a lucid dream, though I've never had one.

April 8, 2009: It turns out there's tons of stuff on the internet about lucid dreams and astral projection. Some people even practice it deliberately. According to the articles I read, I'm not really dreaming, even though I'm asleep. Supposedly my spirit is leaving my body so that I can be with someone else who's doing the same thing. My brain wants to dismiss it as science fiction, but I keep thinking about how my vision is panoramic during these meetings, a feat my physical eyes could never muster.

Chapter Three

Abigail, *the Catholic*

All that we are arises with our thoughts. With our thoughts, we make the world.
—*Buddha*

Why couldn't Paige get her feet on the ground? Abigail wondered and closed the journal.

Her husband, Jim, was chopping garlic for the marinara sauce he was cooking. He heard the notebook slap as it closed and turned his head toward his wife. He saw her strained expression but knew better than to ask what was wrong. Instead, he tossed the garlic into the olive oil warming in the pot and waited for his favorite aroma to fill the air. It didn't take long, less time in fact than it took his wife to speak her mind.

Maria, Abigail's Italian mother, had taught Jim to cook. Her cooking was famous in the Delaney family. The three siblings— unlike Jim who passionately recreated them—had shown no interest in learning her recipes, but still loved to reminisce about them. Even Joe Senior would occasionally ask for an anisette cookie after dinner. Maria's kitchen had been so well-stocked that Joe still expected to find her goodies tucked away in the pantry. In his dementia, he'd forgotten the passing of time. The family home in Hanson was sold after his wife's death, nearly a decade before. Still, some days he expected not only to find Maria's anisette cookies in the kitchen, but Maria herself.

"Astral projection?" Abigail suddenly threw out. "What's next, crop circles?"

Jim shrugged his oversized shoulders. He looked more like a linebacker than a chef, even with the apron. "What's astral projection?" he asked.

"I think it's like dreaming, but with control."

Controlled was the most accurate word to describe Abby's personality and Jim had noticed that she often used the word. Order and control were the cornerstones of her life. Paige had been a challenge to her carefully planned universe. Even Paige's illness had plagued her because she wasn't able to immobilize it under her thumb. Paige, like her mother before her, had died without her consent, and Abigail was furious about it.

"Paige wrote in her journal that she met someone while she was sleeping," she continued. "She talked to him and thought he was real. Can you believe that?"

Jim mulled it over. "Well, remember after my dad died how I saw him in a dream, and it was so real that I felt sure I'd talked to him? I had control in that dream. I remember thinking about reaching out to touch him before I did it. I could see the veins on his hands and the spots—you know how he had those brown liver spots? Maybe for Paige it was like that."

"It's not the same," his wife argued. "Your brain is full of memories of your father. It's natural that some of those images spill out in your dreams, but Paige didn't know this person, so she didn't have any memories of him."

He stopped chopping onions and met her eyes. "But that's just it," he countered. "I don't think my experience was based on memory, and it wasn't disjointed like a dream. I think there's a space—like a window—that people who've passed over can slip through while we sleep. Maybe other people can, too. Their souls."

"If that were true, it would be a miracle," Abby pronounced.

"But you believe in miracles," he challenged.

She clicked her tongue. "Of course, I believe *Jesus* performed miracles. They don't happen now, and certainly not to people like Paige."

"But why not? How about the guy in Brazil who heals people with his hands?" Jim pressed. "Or mediums who bring messages from people who've passed over?"

"Mediums aren't real," she reeled. "They're con artists. Like Gabriel."

"All of them, Abby? Why is it okay to believe that mediums and healers existed when Jesus walked the Earth, but not now? Maybe miracles are happening, but we aren't paying attention."

Abigail narrowed her eyes. Jim braced himself for the comeback, but her focus shifted to the clock. "Where the Hell is Joey? It's six o'clock."

"Why don't you relax for a while," he suggested, "take a bath or something? He'll turn up. Maybe he ran into an old friend."

"Or a new one," she snapped.

On an ordinary day Abigail was tightly wound, but on this day—that of her sister's unorthodox funeral service—she was like a wind-up toy with the key turned all the way. She was convinced her brother was sitting at a bar picking up women. Since he was a teenager, females had flocked to him like he exhaled the scent of chocolate. He always seemed to ignore them, but she could never decide whether his reaction was real or fabricated. Who wouldn't love that kind of attention from the opposite sex?

"It's heinous, isn't it?"

"What?" Jim asked.

"Joey's behavior on the day of his sister's funeral."

Jim's legal mind wanted to point out the holes in her assertion. Neither of them had knowledge of where Joe was, never mind what he was doing. But another part of his mind, the part that had developed over the course of his marriage, took a wiser route.

"Maybe he brought his vial of ashes somewhere," he suggested as he scraped the onion off the cutting board into the olive oil.

Abigail gasped softly. That possibility hadn't occurred to her. Still, not wanting to be viewed as insensitive or worse, wrong, she asked, "to where, California?"

"I don't know, Ab," Jim conceded.

"It's just like him to disappear and not tell anyone where he is."

"He's always been private," Jim stated calmly. Jim knew his brother-in-law was gay. He'd suspected it the first time they'd met, when Joe was still in junior high school. "Cut him some slack, Abby," he coaxed. "You know how much he loved Paige."

"More than he loves me, you mean?"

Jim sighed. "Of course not. I would never say that."

She was contemplative for a long moment before words seethed from her throat. "It's my parents' fault. What were they thinking putting me in charge of them all the time? It made them love each other more and me less—"

"No, Abby." He placed his hands on her hips. Abigail pushed them off.

"Yes, Jim! You don't understand. They were allies. I wasn't one of them."

"Paige loved you so much," he said softly. "Please don't doubt that."

"Paige adored Joey. She resented me," Abigail grumbled and dropped her head onto Jim's shoulder. There was nothing Abigail hated more than being the odd man out, but that seemed to be her lot in life. All she'd ever wanted was to be included, to feel like part of the pack. When they were kids, on summer nights they used to sleep on the screened porch. Joey always got scared and jumped under the blankets with Paige, never her. She could hear them whispering before they fell asleep. Why didn't they share their secrets with her?

Tears were fighting for release, but she refused to break down in front of anyone, even her husband.

"Why don't I turn off the burner and open a bottle of wine?" Jim suggested. Abigail pulled away. It was a mistake to reveal her envy of her sibling's friendship. The disclosure made her weak, and she hated weakness. Relationships weren't her forte. As a little girl Abigail was so bright and capable that she'd believed she could someday be anything, even the ruler of the free world. When she discovered an interest in numbers and analysis, she turned her attention to the stock market. She was only fifteen when she purchased her first shares, in her father's name, but she was the one who chose the companies to invest in, not because he coached her, but because she had been reading the financial pages. By the time she applied to Wellesley College, she'd collected enough profits to pay tuition for the first year.

As an adult, Abigail made a good living as an investment broker. She had a good feel for the right time to buy and the right time to sell. How much was intellect and how much intuition? She was never sure, but that was a thought contained to the inner workings of her mind, not shared with her family, or God forbid, her clients. To the world, she declared that her success was based on hard work. And it was a fair assertion. She worked harder than anyone she knew. Her job was the safe spot in her life. Stock values were predictable. Human beings were not.

She held up her hand, fingers splayed, signaling Jim to give her space. He backed away, like he always did. He understood her needs and wasn't hesitant to credit his intuition for it.

"I'll make the salad," she offered, and Jim turned back to the marinara sauce, stinging from the slap of her rejection. Just once, he'd like to finish a meaningful conversation with his wife.

It took Abigail an exorbitant amount of time to prepare the salad, most of which was consumed by washing the vegetables. They were organic. Still, she scrubbed thoroughly to make sure everything was clean of contaminants. All the while she cleaned and chopped, she was silent. Her mind, however, was anything but still. She was replaying old childhood tapes. Abby was so familiar with them that she could pause and rewind at exactly the right moments that had caused her to store the memories.

The Delaney children were raised to be well-behaved and polite, particularly in public view and essentially at church.

Every Sunday morning, she sat in the pew, the perfect child her parents expected her to be, with her hands crossed on her lap and her feet completely still. Beside her, Paige and Joey whispered and wriggled like fish caught in a net. They were annoying to people sitting nearby, but more so to Abigail, who was in charge of them. Her parents always sat on the other side of her, closer to the aisle. "Don't make me reach over, Abby," their father warned every week, but he'd never carried out the threat. Until once, when Joey was about six, he was entertaining Paige during communion by making farting sounds with his armpit. Abigail warned him before she gave him a slap across the back of his head. Only then had her father carried out his threat. He'd dragged Abigail out of the church with everyone watching, and once outside had shouted at her so loudly she was sure the entire congregation heard.

It was a betrayal to blame her and not Joey. And she still hadn't forgiven him for it. Too many times she'd been disciplined because of her siblings' bad behavior, like the time she escorted them to the Cumberland Farms convenience store and Joey insisted on walking on the wall in front of the cemetery. Abigail told him to get down, but instead of listening, he fell off and hit his head on a rock. She was scolded while Joey wailed the entire way to the hospital. And Paige was the hero because she held ice on his head, even though the accident wouldn't have happened if not for her clever idea. *I'm Peter Pan and you're one of the lost boys following me across a river on a bridge made from a fallen tree.*

The lost boys. The phrase haunted Abby because that was exactly what she thought of her little brother, even as a grown man. But where Joey was difficult, Paige was impossible. As a child she was mischievous, as a teenager rebellious, and as an adult irreverent. Joey was not any of those things, unless influenced by Paige. Like the time he lit a bonfire and burned down a small patch of trees in the woods behind their house. He never admitted her involvement, but that stunt had Paige written all over it. Still, he was difficult to watch over because of his secrecy. Joey had his own universe that only Paige was allowed to enter. He never told Abigail anything. There were no arguments between them. Only silence.

Paige couldn't have stayed silent if the salvation of the human race depended on it. And her comments were often incendiary. When Abigail scolded her for leaving the newspaper before finding a new job, like all responsible adults, she'd commented that Abigail's expectations were straight out of George Orwell's novel *1984*. Paige reacted like it was a mortal sin to keep stride with humanity. She was looking for something creative that made her feel like she was helping to change the world. "Artists and musicians don't change the world, Paige," Abigail stated. "Lawyers and politicians do."

Paige had snorted loudly before replying, "Artists do change the world, Abby, only they do it without killing anyone. That's why it doesn't make the headlines."

She'd never said it out loud, but Abigail sometimes questioned Paige's mental stability. Mental health issues were sometimes the only explanation she could muster for how she and Paige seemed to have been living in two different worlds, even when residing in the same home. Although she didn't understand her, she loved her, and right to the end she was determined to prevent her from being hurt. That's why she stepped in between Paige and Gabriel. He was wrong for her, and if her little sister couldn't see that, then Abigail would be her eyes.

Right before their mother passed, she had uttered a key phrase to Abigail. *Watch over them.* It was not intended as a disservice to her oldest child, only an expression of trust. But to Abigail it meant that even though they were adults, her mother still counted on her to keep Paige and Joey safe, and she would be what her mother expected her to be, the dam's levy that held back the turbulent waters of her siblings' bad judgments and untamed behaviors.

"Why do I always have to be the strong one?" she asked Jim a little while later, while the marinara sauce was simmering, and he was relaxing in the living room.

Strength, Jim knew, had little in common with protection. One day, when Abby was ready, the real strength would be in letting her siblings go. He glanced up from his book, *Happiness: A Guide to Developing Life's Most Important Skill*, by Matthieu Ricard, a Buddhist monk who donates all the profits from his writing to humanitarian projects.

"You don't," he said quietly, and turned his eyes back to the book.

The sound of Joe's cell phone vibrating against the bedside table interrupted his dream. He'd been back in D.C. teaching his class. The fourth graders were unusually quiet as they stared at the assignment he was writing on the blackboard in the slow motion that dreams evoke. *My Biggest Secret is. . .*

Joe grabbed the phone without looking at it. "Bowman," he breathed into the receiver. He'd meant to call but had fallen asleep—or maybe passed out. The funeral followed by numerous vodka martinis at a bar in Onset had knocked him out. Paige was always saying how much she loved Onset, and now he understood. There was an interesting quality to the place that reminded him of New Orleans. A particular juxtaposition of light and shadow. He was still wearing the clothes he wore to the service, but the sun was seeping through the hotel blinds. Apparently, a new day had begun.

"It's your sister," Abigail sternly replied. Joe sprang into a sitting position. "What happened to you last night? Jim and I were waiting for you."

"Oh hey, I'm sorry. It was just, it was a lot. I'm sorry, Abby. I needed to be alone."

"Well, are you now?"

The question took him off guard. "Of course," he replied, and then laughed when he realized she thought he was with a woman. "I'm not flying out until tonight. Want to meet for lunch?"

"Actually, you're flying out at 4:30—we both are, as long as you have your passport with you. We're going to Rome."

"Rome, Italy?" Joe ran his fingers through his messy curls. His head was pounding from the vodka. Way too much vodka. It felt like his eyes were bleeding.

"Yes, Rome, Italy," Abigail answered, as if he'd asked a foolish question. "I've been thinking about Paige's ashes, and I don't know what to do with them—"

"So, you're flying them to Italy?"

"Joey, would you just listen? I need your help. Last night I couldn't sleep. I kept thinking what a big responsibility this is. I don't want to let Paige down."

He sighed. "Abby, you won't let her down. You know how easy she is—I mean was—to please." *Unlike you* he wanted to add but didn't.

"I'm setting a higher standard for myself than she would have."

"Yeah," he agreed.

"I went to church this morning and prayed about it. While I was there, I thought about the Vatican, and I remembered Paige saying that she wanted to go to Italy. Where are your ashes?"

He looked down at the floor. The vial was sitting in his shoe because he was afraid it would roll off the night table and break, but he didn't want to disclose that.

"Uh, right here. With me."

"You haven't brought them anywhere yet? Why not?"

Because I don't have a fucking clue what to do with them, he thought. "I don't know," he muttered. Bowman might fall into a depression if he brought them home. He was so sensitive that his eyes teared up every time they fell on the picture of Fiona, Bowman's grandmother who'd been dead for three years. The photo had been in the bedroom of their townhouse, but after watching his partner's reaction to it for months, Joe moved it to a bookshelf in the living room, a place that didn't draw his eye as often.

"Maybe we can figure it out together," Abigail said. "Did you take the whole week off?"

He had because he wanted enough time to compose himself before he had to face his fourth-grade class and their relentless questions about his absence. But he wasn't planning on spending that time with Abigail. "Well, yeah but–"

"But what? There's no reason you have to go back to D.C. today, is there?"

"Well, no," he grumbled.

"And you have your passport?"

For a split second he considered lying, but then he'd have to keep up the lie for the rest of his life, and frankly, he'd had enough of that. Bowman always attached his passport to his travel documents. "I've got it," he admitted.

"Great. So, it's done then?" she said brightly.

"Well, I guess." Bowman was going to be bullshit, or worse, hurt. He'd been wanting to go to Europe for years. How was he going to explain all this, let alone pay for it?

"It's a birthday gift," Abigail said, as if she'd read his mind. "I'll book it now and pay for the tickets. Come over after you've showered. Jim's making breakfast. And Joey?"

Now what, a stopover in Paris?

"Thank you. I feel more at peace with this already. I know it's right."

Even if it's not, in your mind it is. And in the end, that's all that matters. He didn't have the nerve to whisper his thoughts out loud. Instead, he said the one thing that would make her stop giving orders and hang up the phone. "See you soon, Abby."

April 12, 2009: I had an argument with Abby over dinner tonight. It started as a discussion about my failure to attend church. She called me a heretic, and I've come to the conclusion that she's probably right. And maybe I'm even okay with that. It's not only required Sunday services that I'm opposed to. The God I believe in would never drop babies into a pit of flames because they haven't partaken in a ritual. It makes me wonder, who would want to worship such a God?

People are so sure that we're made in the image of God, but I think we've got it backwards. I believe we've made God in the image of us.

April 15, 2009: After two days of peace, the argument continues. I should learn to shut my mouth. (How many times in my life have I said that?)

"Have you ever watched Animal Planet?" I ask in the middle of Abby's tirade about how disappointed Mom would be in me for not attending Sunday services, and my dad, too, if he could understand. She didn't get my point, which was that God's presence isn't contained within the walls of a church. I have seen the most remarkable animals on that channel that could only have been created by the hand of God. I mean seriously, monkeys that are two inches tall? It's like something straight out of Alice in Wonderland.

My comments throw me out of Abby's limited grace, but she doesn't threaten to disown me until after our brother calls. It goes something like this:

Abby is disgruntled as she hangs up the phone. She says, "Joey should be in a serious relationship by now. He's thirty-six years old."

"Maybe he is," I reply.

"He's obviously a player," she says, then falters. "I mean, don't you think so?"

(Can you hear the drumroll?) I let go of my undisciplined tongue. "No. I think he's gay and has had the same partner for years, the guy who answers the phone sometimes."

A croak leaps from Abby's throat and her eyes are as round as the full moon outside the window. Picture, if you will, the universe with the earth rotating on its axis, the other planets doing their perfectly ordered dance in space, all working together in unison. That's Abby's world. But now some of those planets have spun off into space and the rest of them are trying to hold on, like a bunch of balls after a juggler muddles the act.

I shouldn't have said it. Now she'll envision both of her siblings burning in Hell. I go to bed crying, feeling like the outcast in my family. Again. Abby is so much like my mother that it sometimes feels like she's still here. And Joe is a quieter version of our dad. They're both sweet and genteel like they were born in a different century. Then there's me. I'm trying to sleep, but all I can think about is how my birth must have been a cosmic mistake.

Dream Journal entry, same date: Suddenly I become conscious—not awake, but nonetheless conscious—of my dream lover lying on top of me, though I understand he didn't just arrive. It's almost like walking into a movie halfway through it. I can see us from an angle both above and to the right of the bed, but at the same time he is so close that I can feel his breath on my skin and his fingers tangled in my hair. His brown irises are so close that I can see specks of black in them.

"Are you okay?" he asks, somehow understanding that I've had a difficult evening. I respond with a question. "Is this real?"

He smiles and my insides feel like I'm plummeting downward on a roller coaster, but it is him that I'm free-falling into. For some reason, my attention is on his left front tooth that is missing its corner. I realize it's this imperfection that makes his smile so perfect. My index finger extends to touch it, and he wraps his lips around it. If it's a dream, how can I feel the warmth of his mouth? But it is. I wake up alone. Loneliness sucks. I fantasize about having one person in my life, not only in my dream states, who is on the same wavelength.

Chapter Four

Jim, *the Agnostic*

He who understands nature walks close with God. In each atom, in each corpuscle, is life. Life is that you worship as God. . . All you may know of heaven or hell is within your own self.
—*Edgar Cayce* (Reading # 1904-2)

Paige's brother-in-law had taken his own vial at the funeral. Jim didn't expect his wife to include him in her own distribution of the ashes. He understood her emotional distance better than she thought he did. After caring for her dying mother for over a year, it was more than she could bear to do the same for Paige. For that reason, during the illness she'd distanced herself from Paige, and thrown herself into work. When she couldn't keep her mind busy enough to push out thoughts of Paige's imminent passing, she'd take a sleeping pill and call it a day.

Now she was in Italy with Joe and their vials of ashes trying to find the perfect place to set them free. It wouldn't have mattered to their sister, Jim knew. Paige would have delighted in being set free anywhere. But to Abby it was a ritual that was helping her deal with the grief, and for that reason, he knew the trip was necessary. Perhaps trekking around Italy would improve her relationship with her little brother and divert her attention away from her resentment for Gabriel.

Although he rarely said so, Jim liked Gabriel. He found him interesting, a free thinker. And when Paige was with him, she reminded Jim of the teenager she was when Jim first met her. She'd been a quirky kid who insisted on beating down her own path rather than following in her big sister's footsteps. She navigated toward misfits, kids who were dropouts or in trouble with the law. She used to drag them home for Sunday dinner with her family, sometimes stoned out of their minds, to "be a good Christian" she always said to her parents, but they all knew it was really to irk them. As the years passed, her family's continuous chiding about her choices eventually wore her down and she became less rebellious. Jim sighed out the open window of his Prius thinking of how they pressured her into conformity. But Paige eventually broke free. During the last year or so of her life, she thrust off their expectations and returned to her true self. And Jim was glad for that. He'd been cheering for her all along, from the sidelines.

To others on the highway, Jim might have looked like a circus clown, squeezed into a car much too small for him. (Conversely his tiny wife drove an SUV. Both cars reflected unspoken truths, Jim's passion for nature and Abigail's fear of death.) His frame had always been bulky, even as a child. "You'll stretch out," his mother used to say, and she'd been partially right. He now stood six feet four inches tall, but Jim was always carrying at least forty extra pounds. His body never turned out the way he'd hoped—slender near the point of frailty, like his father.

Everything about his father had seemed unobtainable. As a child, Jim thought he'd grow up to be a musician because his father was a concert pianist. He'd learned to play, but never with great precision or passion. His fingers were thick and clumsy on the keys and he never felt the connection to the instrument that his father did. As Jim drove across the Sagamore Bridge that linked the mainland to Cape Cod, he tried to recall his father being angry, but couldn't think of a single incident. The man had been eternally composed, until his fingers touched down on the keys. Then emotion exploded from his fingers like it was a living thing being set free.

He'd died of a heart attack. Compared to the illness that killed Abby's mother, it seemed to Jim that even in death his father had maintained control. If, just once, he could have seen his dad vulnerable, he might have regarded him as human.

That's why the dream meant so much to him, and why he'd reminded Abby about it. Jim thought of the dream as a meeting with his dead father. His dad had been sitting on the bed watching him and Jim realized it was pride he was wearing in his expression, although he'd never noticed it there when his dad was alive. It was a split second that cleared and cleansed their history. Jim reached for his hand and his father actually took it. Even now, he could remember the feeling of his father's fingers squeezing his own.

He'd inherited the baby grand, and although the piano looked beautiful in their home, Jim never played it. It was a reminder that he was too big, too awkward, too dense, for such a refined instrument. Not enough like his father. Not enough.

He was on his way to the Sandwich Boardwalk, a place he'd promised Paige he'd take her to someday, but never had. When Paige was still healthy and living with them, they'd shared an experience that led him to tell her about the boardwalk, one of the places he would run to whenever he needed to retreat from the world of appellate briefs and cross examinations. No one knew that he was an escapist, except for Paige.

His cell phone had rung on a Friday afternoon and when he'd answered heard Paige's hysterical voice. An injured bird was in the backyard and a neighborhood cat was on the prowl. "Bring it inside," he'd advised. Jim understood her pause and assured her, "I'll get home before Abby." When he arrived, Paige was crying on the kitchen floor, a shoebox on her lap.

She'd made a nest from toilet tissue and grass for a robin with a broken wing. It looked near death to Jim, but he took it to a wildlife center. The robin died within a few hours, but he never told Paige. Instead, he made up a story about the robin being returned to the woods once it healed. That was the day he told her about the boardwalk in Sandwich and all the birds that lived there. He never told Abby about the robin, or about the boardwalk. His wife, he knew, would never weep over an injured bird.

The only person Jim mentioned the robin to was his father-in-law because Joe Sr. was supposed to forget, and not tell Abigail who would have been furious about the bird (full of bugs and germs!) being in their house. But despite the dementia, he'd remembered the robin. The last time before the funeral that Jim saw him, at Paige and Gabriel's house in Onset, he'd spoken the word "robin" during a lull in conversation and given Jim an exaggerated wink. Jim had stifled a laugh and winked back at him.

Paige was bedridden by then, but the hospital bed was in the living room so she could be part of the daily activities. Her scraggly cat, Crazy Horse, was in its usual spot, nestled against Paige. It was a strange looking creature, with enormous blue eyes and no fur to speak of, but Paige coddled it, and the cat responded like any orphaned baby, with complete devotion.

That day, Evelyn, Joe Senior's wife, had driven him down to visit Paige and took an immediate dislike to the cat. She made the mistake of saying it looked "like a demon."

"What difference does it make what we look like?" Paige snapped.

Evelyn was taken aback that Paige included herself in her outburst, as if she'd accused *her* of looking like a demon. Due to the cancer, Evelyn often thought Paige resembled a skeleton. Still, she would never have said so.

Paige's father moved to the hospital bed where his daughter was crying into the cat's bald neck. "Prettiest Paige I know," he whispered and kissed the top of her head. His words stopped her tears. The comment was something he'd often said when she was a child. No one expected him to make sense anymore, but Joe Senior still had more going on than most people thought, Jim realized. He still knew how to comfort his child. Who cared if the guy couldn't add numbers anymore, or remember names?

That day Jim discovered a spiritual truth. Joe's mind was infiltrated by dementia, yet he was still Joe: *Because we are not our mind.* Paige's body was decimated by cancer, yet she was still Paige: *Because we are not our body.* What is it then, he asked himself, that defines us? *We are consciousness,* he finally concluded, and that is unchangeable.

None of this convinced him to believe in the existence of Abby's God, although he wasn't opposed to the possibility. He was an attorney, after all; he required evidence. What Jim believed in was the invincibility of the spirit. He was certain of that since his father's "visit," but to Jim that principle applied to all life, not only human beings.

As he pulled into the parking lot near the boardwalk, he noticed a woman and child exiting their car with a Boston terrier. The dog looked like it was smiling, its mouth stretched like the Joker's in a Batman comic. It stared at Jim with its bulbous brown eyes until Jim smiled back, and he noticed that the muscles around his mouth felt stiff from not using them enough.

Jim watched the little girl scamper off with her bow-legged dog. It reminded him of Mojo, their dog that was hit by a car when Jim was ten years old. His parents never wanted to get another dog because Mojo, they said, was irreplaceable. Now that Jim was an adult, he understood that everyone is irreplaceable. Still, his heart was open. He would love to rescue a dog, but how could he make such a proposal if he couldn't even approach the subject of having a child?

Jim shed the jacket and tie, shoes and socks and tossed them in the back seat of the car before walking down the boardwalk with his Brooks Brothers pants rolled up. The boardwalk formed a bridge over the marsh from the parking lot to its destination — Town Neck Beach. Each plank in the boardwalk bore the name of the person who paid for it when it was rebuilt after a hurricane destroyed the original boardwalk. He could happily spend an entire day reading the messages, many of which were tributes to family members or pets who had passed away. Each plank represented the story of a family or a love affair. *I love Chris 1992* one person had engraved. *Do you still?* he mused as he sat down and let his legs hang over the edge.

The marsh grass was green already and reaching for the blue Cape Cod sky. The tide was coming in, the water below his bare feet getting deeper by the minute. Every living thing in his vision seemed to vibrate with the arrival of spring. A painted turtle poked its head out of the water, curious about the creature sitting above him. Jim smiled again, this time with more ease, but he didn't reach toward the turtle or make any noise. He understood that all of nature was not laid at his feet to do with as he pleased any more than all of nature was laid at the painted turtle's feet. Jim and the turtle, the black ducks flying overhead and the swans in the distance were all distinctly designed parts of the same whole. He was content just to be one of them.

The sun was beating down on him, raising his body heat. He unbuttoned his shirt and felt the relief of a cool breeze on his neck and torso. Here, in the midst of nature, no one knew he was a prosecutor. No one had expectations of him. With his legs over the side of the wooden boardwalk, he wished the tide was high enough for his toes to graze the frigid salt water. The cold water had a way of reminding him that he was alive.

Life had become like a pattern on a dress, a continuous repetition of the same routine. Every morning looked like the one before it, except that the weather changed with the seasons. His suits varied from navy to black, but he always wore a white shirt and conservatively colored tie. Uniformity was important because he was a representative of the criminal justice system, the face of a massive machine.

He missed the feeling of adrenaline rushing through his bloodstream. The most intoxicating rush he'd ever experienced was during law school when he met Abby. It was a Friday night at a bar in Kenmore Square called the Rathskeller, but everyone called it *The Rat*. She was with a group of girls, all students at Wellesley College. Her thick golden hair reached neatly to the top of her shoulders and her alert eyes curiously scanned the room. The first thing Jim noticed was the contrast between her and the club environment. The Rat smelled like stale beer and vomit. Sweaty bodies bounced off each other in front of a live band. The front man groaned, strutted, and shook the sweat from his hair onto the crowd. And then there was Abby, watching the scene demurely, as clean and pure as a second grader at First Communion.

It was love at first sight. Jim liked to think that their meeting was the greatest thing that ever happened in that dingy bar. Sometimes, though, it was fun to imagine all the couples who might have come together under the same roof. Like the planks on the boardwalk, each meeting told a story. The one-night stands, the short-lived relationships prompted by a shared love of punk and rock music, and the couples who made the venue part of their life story, like Abby and himself.

They'd known each other now for over twenty years and their lives were so integrated that sometimes it was hard to tell where an idea originated, with her or with him. They'd made a life together that met some of their goals. They owned an impressive home in a town known for its school system, mostly because they had planned to have children, but Abby had miscarried twice, and right as they were mentally prepared to try again, her mother's lung cancer diagnosis came crashing down on them. All their energies were consumed by Maria's illness, and afterward, by grief. He'd tried once to approach the subject, but it was too soon after Maria's passing, and Abby had resented it. Since then, he had left it alone.

The week before, when Jim had retrieved Joe from the airport, he'd driven past a little breakfast joint in South Boston that he and Abby had frequented as students. Over $1.99 omelets and decanters of coffee they'd discussed the life they would create. He'd wanted to use his law degree to make the world a better place, to navigate foreigners through the immigration system, and after law school he spent a year at the Legal Aid office in Hyannis doing exactly that. His stomach used to flip flop just because he was sitting next to Abby. He was like a plane on the runway, ready to take to the skies.

Something unidentifiable had been sacrificed during their marriage. *How is it,* he sometimes wondered, *that we know exactly how we want to live, yet end up living differently?*

The water beneath him was now deep enough to jump into. If it were up to him, he would stay longer, daydream for a while on the boardwalk, with the sun overhead in the perfect blue sky, and the turtles and fish under his feet. Or better yet, he'd climb onto the boardwalk railing and leap off it into the green sea water, like a teenager.

But the life of a prosecutor leaves little time for daydreaming or bridge jumping. He envisioned the piles of papers in his briefcase and felt pressured to keep moving. *Keep moving* was the most pervasive mantra of his lifetime, an unfortunate repetition for someone who valued stillness and tranquility over everything else.

He forced his mind back to his purpose for coming here and took the vial of ashes from his shirt pocket. Just then, a robin landed on the railing of the boardwalk, not three feet away from him, and stood still on its skinny yellow legs, watching him. The visual was enough to make his hand freeze in space, and his heart skip a beat. Its appearance in the very moment he was to release Paige's ashes made him think that the robin represented her. She was watching him and making him aware of it.

He took a few breaths to calm his emotions, but he never took his eyes off the bird. "It's still our secret, Paige," he said out loud as he opened the vial and poured her ashes into the marsh water.

April 27, 2009. Jim is the big brother I never had. I hope he finds a way to free himself, not from Abby, but from his own expectations. I don't think he realizes that he's the one who built the fence.

April 29, 2009: Once, when I was little, my mother brought home a vial of mercury from the hospital where she was working. I remember her pouring it onto the kitchen counter and my fascination at the way it moves. When she poured an exact replica of the first blob of silver, I used a pencil eraser to push them together. They instantly merged, with no hint that they had ever been anything other than that. Now that's what I think of when I watch Abby with Jim.

Tonight, I went to a party with them. I guess they're hoping I'll meet someone suitable because they introduced me to lawyers and investment brokers, no one who captured my imagination. The whole time I felt like I was watching the room full of people through a windshield coated with smoke. If I'd accepted every drink that was offered to me, I might have felt like I fit in, but it sometimes strikes me as extreme, having to kill off brain cells to have a good time.

Dream Journal entry, same date: He asks the most intriguing questions: "What do you think colors sound like? Is electric blue a sweet A major and red an E flat minor? If so, purple must be a D with a flat 9 and flat 13, a waterfall of notes."

(I write this down as soon as I awaken while the words are fresh in my memory. I've had no musical training since I was 12, but somehow everything he said made sense. Weird, I know.)

I ask, "What do you think heaven smells like?" and without a pause, he says, "Orange blossoms." God, I hope he's right.

He suggests that in Heaven flowers make music. "Do fruits?" he wonders.

"What would a pomegranate sound like?" I counter, and his eyes light up.

"Like love so deep it cuts you. Like this." There is a flutter of piano keys, light and giddy, as if they are wind blowing over a grassy field. The music suddenly soars—the notes filling the entire room now— and I catch sight of a pomegranate in his hand. He reveals it like a magician. The fruit is split open with the seeds bleeding magenta juice down the ivory skin of his forearm. He brings it to my mouth, and I am startled awake by the tart taste of it on my tongue.

Imagination captured.

May 14, 2009: An extraordinary day. I drive around Onset looking for the wigwam when I arrive at a small bridge I've already crossed, and realize I've been driving in a circle. But the sun is out, and the sky is a flawless indigo, so I find a place to park and get out of the car to walk across the bridge. It's only May, but the moment I am in is pure summer, like the first day school lets out in elementary school. Time stands still in the heat and the promise of more to come. I breathe sunshine deep into my lungs and imagine it exiting through my pores, surrounding me in a globe of golden light. In my visual, I glow like an angel as I step onto the bridge and walk past the window boxes overflowing with red flowers.

I notice someone standing alone, looking down into the water that passes beneath him. He uses his upper body to lift his weight onto the railing and stays crouched momentarily like a monkey on a tree limb. From where I stand, I can see that this is a man, not a teenage boy. A flash of panic as I consider that he might be attempting suicide. But the bridge is not high enough. Although cars are passing, he seems unaware of them, and of me, as he extends his lanky body into a standing position and holds his arms out against the wind. A bird taking flight.

The strange creature bends at the waist, and his body is the shape of a V as his hands get comfortable on the concrete. Then he flips his feet into the air and begins to walk slowly on his hands across the railing. I consider my options. Should I drag him back onto the asphalt before he falls, or run away?

His voice makes the decision for me. "Hey, do me a favor, would you?" he calls. "Check for boats."

"Check for wh-what?" I stammer.

From his upside-down place on the railing, he actually laughs. "Boats," he repeats, "coming from the other side so I can jump." His laughter throws off the balance, his hands stagger on the railing like drunken feet.

Jesus. I race to the other railing and sure enough a small motorboat is nearing. "Don't jump!" I scream. I watch the boat go under the bridge, and a moment later hear the splash. My head spins toward the empty railing the guy was clinging to a moment before. I run like a maniac and peer over. There are only bubbles where his body broke the surface. Then his head bobs up, and he's laughing. That's when I see it, the chip in his front tooth.

Chapter Five

Abigail & Joe Jr., *the Catholic & the Dissident*

All right, then, I'll go to hell.
—Mark Twain

Joe had never seen anything like the airport in Rome with swarms of people racing through it as if a war was breaking out. There were no lines to go through customs, only a mob moving in the same direction. It was a madhouse compared to every other airport he'd passed through, which were all in the United States. What he needed was a tall cup of coffee that he could carry into the taxicab, but apparently "to go" was an American custom. He followed Abigail to a café in the terminal where she ordered two cappuccinos that they slugged down while standing at a tall table.

In the taxicab that carried them from the airport to the hotel near Termini Train Station, Joe was forced to close his eyes or suffer a near-death experience every couple of minutes. "Why's he driving so fast?" he whispered in the back seat.

"Because everyone else is," Abigail replied calmly. She was a big believer in social conformity. In her opinion, the ones who didn't conform were the dangerous ones.

Once they'd checked in at the hotel and left their suitcases in their rooms, they headed for the Vatican. It was only about a half hour walk, which gave them a chance to take a look around the city. The men, Joe noticed, were dressed as fashionably as the women. Only in Beverly Hills had he seen that level of scrutiny with men's appearance. When they happened upon a street vendor selling hats, he stopped to try some on.

"You don't strike me as a hat person," Abigail commented, and he smiled without explanation. The hat was for Bowman, who was undoubtedly a hat person. Joe settled on a Monte Cristi Italiano Panama and Abby counted the euros from his hand.

"Aren't you going to wear it?" Abigail asked.

"Not today," he replied.

Even if he'd bought the hat for himself, he wouldn't wear it to the Vatican. Given the Catholic Church's stance that homosexuality is an "intrinsic moral evil" he wasn't entirely comfortable visiting the Vatican, but on some level, he still carried the respect for the church that was bred in him as a child. For the same reason, he was wearing the shirt and slacks that he'd worn to Paige's funeral.

Joe bought them each a glass bottle of ice-cold Coke from a shop near the entrance to the pavilion, then followed Abigail through security and into the Vatican. She knew exactly where she was going—to visit the tombs of the popes, specifically that of Pope John Paul II who had died since her last visit to Rome. Gregorian chants playing through speakers and the underground chill pervaded Joe's skin as he followed Abigail downward, past the dead popes in their ornate sarcophagi. When they arrived at Pope John Paul II's resting place, he noticed that, unlike most of the popes, his body was contained in an underground crypt with a stone slab bearing his name.

Abigail fell to her knees, and Joe followed suit. They weren't the only people kneeling. A small crowd was gathered. Some wept, others prayed audibly. Flowers were piled on the floor near the tomb, which made it smell like a funeral home and reminded Joe of Paige's death. He scrambled to his feet and walked away. Abigail looked up from her prayer to find him, and for the first time in his life, he noticed a bewildered look in her eyes.

And that lost gaze in his big sister's eyes shifted his perception. For all his life he'd been following her because she'd insisted on leading, but maybe, he suddenly realized, she didn't know the way. Abigail was praying to a dead priest about their dead sister who did not consider herself Catholic. If this was

Abby's way of finding truth, then so be it—and he wished her well on that journey—but as for him, he was done following.

Two days later they were walking on Viale Marco Polo headed toward Trastevere when Abby said, "There are a million beautiful places in this city, but I don't feel right leaving Paige's ashes at any of them. I don't feel her here, do you?"

Joe had begun to think of the trip as an elaborate wild goose chase. "We don't have to," he suggested. "We can bring them home."

"How'd you feel about going to Venice for a day or two?" she asked, and he laughed.

"As long as we're back in Boston on Friday," he said, thinking of Bowman waiting for him.

They took a flight and then a boat taxi called a vaporetto to get to Venice. The green water looked as mysterious as the buildings they approached. And when the water taxi pulled up at the dock, they seemed to be in another world. The city was like a fairytale land from a childhood story. They stepped off the boat into a stream of human beings, and within minutes were in San Marco Square with the great cathedral standing guard, and hundreds of pigeons diving toward the children, who were feeding them from their hands.

"Bowman would love it here," he murmured. Lack of sleep and caffeine had made his mind a fuzzy instrument he had less control over than usual.

"Who's Bowman?" Abigail asked, and Joe jumped to hear the name come from her mouth.

"Oh, a friend. This way?" he asked to end the conversation and stepped into the pedestrian traffic. Abigail was studying a map that illustrated the direction to their hotel. The streets were so narrow that they had to walk single file with their suitcases rolling behind them in order to allow people to walk in the opposite direction. The city was like a maze of meandering paths through brightly colored stucco buildings.

"Know what the Italians call Venice?" Abigail asked as they rounded a corner and were nearly plowed down by a pair of statuesque women.

"Mi scusi! Mi Scusi!" the women ordered.

"What?" Joe asked as the women walked away like models on a runway.

"Serenissima. It means 'the most serene.'"

"Serenissima," he repeated. The word melted like marzipan on his tongue. The small shops they passed displayed their goods in lavish assortments: pastries, flamboyant masks, and Venetian glass. Venice was an artist's paradise overflowing with a palette of colors. *Serenissima, serenissima* his brain chanted.

They were nearing a cobblestone courtyard when Abigail stopped short. "This is it!" she exclaimed, and Joe's gaze turned to the hotel. Two young men, barely beyond their teenage years, were conversing in front of the entrance. Joe didn't need to speak Italian to understand that they were lovers. One man's hand cradled the other's jaw and held it as if it were framing a magnificent work of art while he spoke beautiful incomprehensible words. His lover dropped the briefest of kisses on his lips before they walked off with their fingers entwined.

It was only at their departure that Joe realized Abigail was watching, too. His eyes met hers briefly before he turned them down to the cobblestones under his Converse sneakers, sure that she could not comprehend the coil of knots in his stomach. Bowman loved to hold hands, but Joe very rarely allowed it. There was a wall he'd carefully crafted when he was a teenager to prevent the world from viewing his interior. Complete freedom, like the Italian lovers displayed, was an ideal beyond his grasp.

"What a great place to be in love," Abigail commented, her gaze still firmly on Joe.

"What?" he mumbled and raised his eyes to meet hers.

"I said 'what a great place to be in love,'" she repeated. "Don't you agree?"

He wasn't sure what she was asking. Was her question directed at him, or was he being paranoid? "Yeah, I guess," he softly acknowledged.

She hand-motioned toward the hotel and they started walking again. After they checked into their rooms, they found a small restaurant that served truffles in cream sauce with freshly made angel hair pasta and frizzante described by the waiter as "water with gas," a phrase they agreed would have prompted endless jokes by Paige. When they finished, they walked along the canal bridges until they found what Abigail thought was the right place to drop the ashes.

"Did you know Paige met Gabriel while he was jumping off a bridge?" she asked as they looked down at the waterway and the occasional gondola that passed underneath.

"No," Joe laughed, "But that sounds like her life."

"She never followed the rules," she stated quietly.

"What rules?" Joe threw out.

"What do you mean?"

"That's what Paige would say—*what rules?*"

Abigail's eyes blinked as she processed the comment. It never occurred to her to question the guidelines set out for her as a child, never mind completely disregard them, the way Paige so often had. She thought it was what made her a good person, what her parents expected her to be.

"I've started reading her journal," she disclosed. "Gabriel let me borrow it. This morning I read the part where she talks about meeting Gabriel on a bridge in Onset. There were planters with red flowers, like this bridge has. That's why I think this is the right place. Maybe the red flowers are a sign."

Her brother chuckled. "You don't follow signs. That's Paige. You follow rules."

Abigail twisted her lips into a pout. "That doesn't seem fair to me anymore. I mean, who decided that? Why is it that I got Rome and Paige got Venice?"

A laugh burst out of Joe. It was a perfect metaphor for his sisters, Abigail the staunchly religious rule follower and Paige the reckless bohemian. "Paige decided it for herself," he replied. "I don't know who decided it for you, or for me. Us, I guess."

"Are you going to drop your ashes here, too?" she asked.

"No. I don't know where I'm bringing them yet, but I think it will come to me."

"I'm sure it will," Abigail agreed. "Hey, Joey." She waited for him to look over at her before she continued. "Paige and I have always adored you. You know that, right?"

"Of course," he answered, but he couldn't maintain eye contact. Would they have adored him if they'd known the truth?

"Because now that Paige is gone, we only have each other."

"I love you, Abby, and I know you love me," he said dismissively.

"Well, yes, but I'd like it if we were closer," she pressed.

He was searching for the right way to tell her that he'd purposefully distanced himself because he felt like a nonentity in their family. He couldn't be who he really was because they wouldn't accept that, and he was worn out by the charade. "Maybe when people grow up, they grow apart," he asserted.

His statement startled her. "It doesn't have to be that way," she argued.

With his elbows on the railing, Joe's head was cradled in his hands. His golden curls begged Abigail to stroke them like when they were kids, but she resisted. He wasn't a boy anymore, and it finally occurred to her that she had to stop treating him like one.

"I'm sorry, Joe," she offered, consciously using his adult's name for the first time in her life. It was enough to make him turn in her direction. "I'm sorry I bossed you around so much when we were kids. I thought I was supposed to. I hope that's not why you left."

His tongue stroked his lip, his eyebrows tugged together, but he remained silent.

"Paige said something once," she continued. "I don't even know if it's true. I'm not sure how to say this, but whatever your life is like, I want to know about it. If you want to tell me."

When he didn't reply, she took the vial of ashes from her bag and popped off the rubber top. She knew that if she pushed her brother he would retreat. She brought the vial to her nose. "Oh, God," she suddenly sobbed. "I must be losing my mind."

"What is it?" he asked cautiously.

"I could have sworn I smelled Paige's perfume, the one I bought for her fortieth birthday. I thought it might be coming from the vial. Where could it have come from?"

Joe's eyes swept the bridge. There was no one approaching or departing who might have left a scent. Although he didn't say so, he had also caught a brief hint of citrus. "Want me to do it?" he offered, but Abigail shook her head and pulled in a breath.

"Arrivederci, Paige," she muttered with the exhale, her voice muffled by emotion.

"Goodbye?"

"No, not goodbye," she said. "Until we meet again."

Joe moved to the other side of the bridge to make sure no gondolas were approaching, and Abigail let the ashes fall into the soft breeze that carried them to the water. Afterward, she cried into her hands while Joe stroked her back. Her cheek came to rest on the bridge railing, and her brother watched the tears stream down her pretty face. He'd never seen her vulnerable, crying in public like an ordinary person. Before that moment, Joe would have compared her to one of the statues scattered around Rome—standing erect and strong—not to one of the human beings who stopped to envy such godlike invincibility.

They walked wordlessly to the hotel, arm in arm. After they climbed the narrow stairway to their rooms, Joe said, "You know what you said earlier about rules and who decides them? What if it's all an illusion? What if we're living according to whatever rules we were told as kids and none of them are real?"

"Then we've all wasted a lot of time," Abigail replied with a sad smile.

Joe had no intention of wasting any more time. As soon as he was alone in his room, he called Bowman. There were a thousand things to tell him, a list he'd been creating of everything he wanted him to know about the city of Venice and the unexpected words his sister had spoken. But mostly he wanted to hear his voice so that he could feel like he was whole again.

"Are you bringing your ashes to the tree?" Bowman asked.

"What tree?" he asked absently.

"*The* tree," Bowman replied. "The slanted tree in the woods, behind your house in Hanson." Joe gasped almost silently, but not silently enough to miss his partner's attention. The slanted tree was a landmark of his childhood, the place where he'd finally been accepted by the neighborhood kids, because of Paige. If there was one thing Paige wouldn't tolerate, it was a group of people banding together against the weakest link.

"See how much you need me?" Bowman teased.

"You have no idea how true that is," Joe admitted.

It was no secret how devoted Bowman was to Joe, but Joe rarely admitted his own attachment, and that distance, that lack of commitment, had given birth to insecurity in his partner. *You make me safe* Bowman had told him once, and the phrase lived on uncomfortably in Joe's mind. He understood that Bowman meant his presence made him feel safe from the outside world, and although he didn't say it out loud, he couldn't help thinking about how ironic it was that Bowman could live free of fear of being hurt by anyone else except for the person most important to him, except for himself.

"Want to come with me?" found its way out of his mouth.

"To the tree?"

Joe had never brought Bowman to Massachusetts, not for any visits home, not even when tragedy struck. When they'd received the news that Paige had died, Bowman packed Joe's bags like he always did, and cried the whole time. "Poor Gabriel," he kept repeating. "How is he going to live without her?" Bowman was the only person he knew who would weep for someone he'd never met, a person who didn't even know he existed. It was that empathy that had drawn Joe to him in the first place.

In his mind's eye, Joe could see his face beaming in response to the invitation. Bowman had childlike features, a small nose and mouth that was shaped in clean lines like a doll's lips, and round eyes that lit up when he was excited, all of which made him resemble a teenager, even though he was three years older than Joe. There were countless things he could do or say on a daily basis to make Bowman's face light up like a meteor shower. So, why didn't he?

"Yeah, to the tree," he said. "Book a flight for Saturday—I'll pick you up in Boston. And Bow?" he added as an afterthought. "I can't wait to see you."

April 18, 2009: The Universe is talking to us. If you listen closely, you just might hear it. We are part of a web that breathes the answers to our questions, paints pictures to reassure us, and gives us guidance when we need it most. But there's a catch. We can't see anything that we're not tuned into. In other words, the more conscious we become, the more conscious we become.

April 22, 2009: The sun is shining in Norwell today and it's warm outside, which feels surreal after the mountain of snow we've been buried beneath in this relentless Massachusetts winter. It's time to venture out and start a new life. "April is the cruelest month," T.S. Eliot said. I get that. I'm scared to start over, to break through the frozen, but familiar ground. I feel like a child on the first day of kindergarten when I have to let go of my mother's hand.

Adult bodies are an illusion. They conceal the truth, that on the inside we are still little kids with the same fears and curiosities hiding underneath aging skin and thinning hair. Look closely and you'll see it lingering there in anyone's eyes, the inquisitiveness of a three-year-old. Even in old age life is flickering there, reminding anyone who cares to notice that a powerful spirit resides within.

We construct our own cages with the fears we cling to as dearly as our mother's hands. What would happen if we just let go?

Chapter Six

Bowman, *the Baptist*

Love is my religion—I could die for that.
—John Keats

Bowman Todd was born in North Carolina, the only child of a Baptist minister. Although his parents had planned to have a houseful, it hadn't happened that way. For whatever reason—God's will (as they believed) or physiological limitation—Bowman was the only child his mother bore. He was named after his grandfather, who'd also been a minister, as well as an avid hunter. Hence the name "Bow man" was passed down in the hopes that he, too, would be a great hunter. But never was there a greater misnomer than in the case of Bowman Todd. Although he gravitated toward the church, he couldn't resolve the discrepancy over praying for God's creatures and then purposefully shooting an arrow through one of them. It was a profound disappointment to his father that he didn't find joy in bringing death to anything.

In his neighborhood everyone got along, adults and children alike. They all attended the church where Bowman's dad presided. On Sunday mornings when his father boomed, "We are children of God!" Bowman absorbed the words, tucked them away in his heart, so that he could take them out later and marvel over them. *A child of God*, he concluded, must have unlimited potential, but also a great responsibility.

It was the adults, not the kids, who commented that Bowman "walked like a girl" or "talked like a girl." Either the kids didn't notice, or they noticed, but didn't care. He was athletic enough to play kickball, and he could climb a tree if he had to recover a foul ball caught in its branches, but he'd rather practice cartwheels with the girls on the sidelines.

It was a happy childhood. The high school years were the ones that nearly destroyed him. The same kids who had embraced him as a child, tormented him as a teenager. News of his first boyfriend, a cashier he worked with at the Food Lion, spread like a virus through his school. Billy Joe Warren was the boy's name, and, like Bowman, he was intelligent and kind. Also, like Bowman, he was inexperienced and naïve. They knew enough to keep the relationship private, but they had no concept of what the consequence might be of being discovered. It only took one misstep to find out.

Billy Joe's hand was resting on Bowman's leg in the back row of the local movie theater when two girls from school happened to walk by. That Friday night after the football game, a group of boys dragged them into the woods, where they tied ropes around their hands and bandanas around their eyes. Once they were immobilized and blinded, their classmates took turns sodomizing them before they spray painted the word *fag* across their bare chests.

Afterward, Bowman couldn't see because of the blindfold, but he could hear the river moving underneath them and Billy Joe crying as the boys carried them onto the Highlands Bridge. *They're going to kill us* he thought and was hyperventilating when one of them spoke out. He recognized the voice of his next-door neighbor, Jackson, a boy he'd known his entire life.

"You can't throw 'em off!" he shouted at the other boys. "They'll drown."

"Good riddance," another boy taunted, and the rest of them laughed like a pack of hyenas.

"We're bringing them home," Jackson commanded, and the boys dragged them to a car. Minutes later Bowman was on his front lawn, still blindfolded and bound.

That was the event that illuminated Bowman to the true character, not only of his classmates, but his parents. The porch light came on at the sound of tires squealing down the street and his parents ran from the house to find him face down on the grass, a pile of blood and tears.

"What the—" his father spewed when he first caught sight of him. After he yanked the bandana off his son's eyes, he noticed the word emblazoned on his chest in red paint, like a scarlet letter. For the first time in Bowman's life, he caught a glimpse of the demons he'd never imagined resided inside his father. Ignorance, bigotry, vindictiveness. Hate.

"What have you done?" his father growled as his mother untied the rope that had ripped into Bowman's wrists. To his son, Pastor Todd looked like a mad man, with a strand of spit clinging to his whiskers, as he raised his fist again and again, his state championship football ring breaking Bowman's skin. He was trying to stutter out an answer when his father walked away.

Next door, he heard a car pull into the driveway, and then the voices of the boys who had raped him yelling to Jackson, his childhood friend, as he walked toward his house. They had returned, Bowman conjectured, after dumping Billy Joe at his house. A moment later, his father was standing over him again, holding a tin can filled with turpentine. Bowman could hear sloshing inside the container, and he could smell it even before his father flung it onto his bare skin. For a horrific moment he believed his father was about to burn him alive.

"Get it off!" he ordered through clenched teeth and tossed an old rag at Bowman's face before he turned his back and walked briskly away.

He couldn't breathe. No matter how much he inhaled, he couldn't get the air to go down. His bare feet were bloodied and sore from being dragged through the woods. And his face was throbbing from his father's beating. What had happened to his shoes? He managed to get a little bit of air into his nostrils and sucked it all the way down into his lungs. His shaky hands grasped the rag and scrubbed at the foul word on his chest until his skin was raw. The turpentine bit into the open flesh like it had teeth.

Bowman's eyes caught a glimpse of his fingers and the dirt packed under his nails. Chest heaving, he marched to the garage and found a brush his father used to clean the cement garage floor. His fingers bled from the sharp bristles, but still he cleaned the nails with force. It was the birth of something uncontrollable inside of him. The boys had dirtied him, invaded his body, and he had to get them out. Every trace of them.

All the while, his mother silently watched her son ravage his hands as he tried to scrub the incident out of his history. From that day onward, every time Bowman felt invaded or vulnerable, he would bathe his body for hours and scour his hands and nails until they bled.

"Forgive your father, Bow. He doesn't understand," his mother sobbed.

"But I don't either," he replied. His father the preacher, his father the merciful, was an illusion, a garb he threw on like a costume and discarded at will.

That night his mother gave him a painkiller before he went to bed, something his father had been given after knee surgery for an old football wound. The best thing about it was the way it made him fall asleep. In the morning it was all waiting for him as soon as his eyes opened—the savagery of his classmates, who'd acted toward Billy Joe and himself in a manner he had never imagined human beings were capable of, particularly ones that he knew.

Bowman lay in his bed thinking about what his father had said, and about how his mother had defended him. They'd both betrayed him, and none of it was fixable. Home was no longer a safe place. Maybe there was not a single safe place in the entire world.

It was then, in a flash of inspiration, that he thought of his grandmother. Fiona was her name and that was what Bowman had called her from the time he could talk, which irritated his mother, Fiona's daughter. Fiona wasn't like his parents. She used to joke that she didn't believe Bowman's father was the supreme ruler of the universe, and for that reason, she wasn't invited to visit very often. But she'd often send Bowman letters praising him for his talent and intelligence. He was good with numbers, something that served him well later in life when he became an investment broker. Fiona would look over his standardized test scores that he'd send her in the mail and call him to croon over how brilliant he was. *The next Albert Einstein,* she'd joke. His grandmother had a way of making him feel like he was unique, and like that was a good thing.

When Bowman got out of bed that morning, he packed a gym bag with a few changes of clothes and the three hundred and eighty-five dollars he had saved from his job at the Food Lion. It was more than enough to buy a train ticket, and he knew that was all he'd need. He slid flip flops on his feet because they wouldn't irritate the wounds, even though he knew his father wouldn't approve if he saw him wearing them. He called them *fairy shoes.* But it didn't matter anymore what his father thought. Bowman left while his parents were still asleep and without leaving them a note to inform them of where he was headed. He knew they'd figure out soon enough that he was off to live with the radical Fiona, who lived right outside of Washington D.C. And from that day on, she was his only family. Until he met Joe Delaney.

Once, years later, he was on the subway on route to his job at the brokerage firm when he felt someone watching him and looked up from his Wall Street Journal to see the mature face of Jackson turned toward his own. Dressed in a suit and tie, he was only feet away, holding a briefcase. His hair was military short, and his face still handsome. One corner of his mouth was curling into a familiar smile when Bowman abruptly stood up and walked away, his heart pounding in his chest. Fiona, who maintained contact with Bowman's mother, later told him that Jackson worked at the Pentagon.

Go figure, he thought. *Why is it always the brutes that have the power?*

But he hadn't let the brutes win. Bowman continued to live his life in accordance with his own perspective, which was that all living creatures, including the children of God who didn't always behave as such, were born with the right to be treated with kindness and dignity. Another person's refusal to behave in accordance with his or her own nature, he understood, didn't alleviate his own responsibility. If a hand was needed, he extended his. If a kind word was in order, he offered it. If a person was being persecuted, he came to their defense.

"Why don't they ever show two men as soul mates?" he once asked Fiona while they were watching a romantic movie on television, and Fiona had laughed. He was only seventeen when the thought occurred to him.

"Because they haven't figured it out yet," she'd replied.

Her words had comforted him, but the question lived on in his mind. Hollywood set the standard for relationships, and he couldn't figure out why everyone accepted it. The only reason he could muster was that most people don't like to think too much, and they'd rather hand the job off to someone else.

Sexual orientation aside, according to Hollywood, women could be close friends—even very close friends, like Thelma & Louise. But if a movie showed two heterosexual men partnered together, they were either blowing up other men or seducing women, as if violence and random sex were required to balance out any emotion between them. With the subject of homosexual men, the focus was always on the sexual act, as if that was the only part of the relationship. And worse, the sex was rarely portrayed as an expression of love. Did the world actually believe that all gay men were only interested in one-night stands?

For Bowman, that would never be enough. He wanted the same thing most of his heterosexual friends wanted—a lifetime lover, a soul mate; one person with whom he could always feel safe.

He was standing in front of the cash register at Starbucks, waiting to pay for his latte, when Joe walked in. For some reason that he couldn't figure out later, he turned around when he heard the door open behind him. It was 1:22 on a Saturday afternoon. Bowman looked down at his watch to note the time. Rain was making music against the windowpanes when he first glimpsed Joe. His clothes were soaked through because he wasn't wearing a coat, and he was using his fingers to shake water out of his thick, blonde curls. Bowman didn't realize he was staring at him until the cashier cleared her throat to get his attention, and both he and Joe looked up.

In the awkwardness of the moment, Bowman's affinity for numbers vanished, making it a feat to pay for his coffee. He was embarrassed as he walked away without another glance in Joe's direction. Then Joe surprised him (and himself, he would later say) by claiming the stool next to Bowman's that looked onto the sidewalk where people were scampering through the rain. By the time they parted, the sun had broken through the rain clouds, and it was 5:15.

It was the most significant meeting of Bowman's life.

May 14, 2009 (cont.) His name is Gabriel, he tells me once he's walked across the bridge to meet me at its center. "Like the angel?" I ask.

He makes a scoffing sound.

I think my initial silence surprises him, as if he's expecting me to scold him for leaping off the bridge like a lunatic, but I am too confused by the fact that I seem to be meeting the man who's been visiting my dreams. It can't be real; I tell myself repeatedly. So, what if his front left tooth is missing a piece in the very same spot? And, so what if his eyes and hair are the same deep brown? We don't meet dream lovers in real life, not even on perfect days, like this one. Still, there's this feeling—a persistent fluttering in my chest.

He reaches for the T-shirt that is on the ground where he left it and, in that millisecond, I am sure he will walk away without a goodbye. "Why'd you do that?" I ask to prevent it from happening.

"Do what?" he shoots back.

"Jump off the bridge."

Gabriel doesn't look at me. He leans on the bridge railing with his elbows and his head falls back on his shoulders. His eyes are on a group of three seagulls flying fifteen feet above us. I navigate my own eyes down his long slender torso before he tugs the shirt over his head. I swear I know that belly. I remember it.

"Do you like seagulls?" he asks.

I love them, always have and tell him so.

"Some people don't," he remarks. "They call them flying rats. I think they're the living embodiment of freedom." He smiles completely unguarded, and my heart swells so fast that my breath catches in my throat. I nod and remind myself that I'm supposed to be finding the wigwam to collect data for my thesis, but there's no place I'd rather be than on this bridge wondering what comes next. Do we walk away and never meet again? Or do we jump?

"I've been bridge jumping on the first day of summer for ten years," he says.

"It's only May," I stupidly say.

Gabriel doesn't note my stupidity and I'm grateful for it. Instead, he explains that when he was eighteen, he started the ritual with his best friend. He says they used to challenge each other by doing cartwheels, handstands, flips and such off the railing (which explains the hand-walking). His friend died four years ago and he's continued the ritual without him, except for one year that he missed.

He's twenty-eight, I calculate, more than a decade younger than me. Still, I can't seem to turn my attention away. "I'm sorry about your friend," I offer.

He smiles again, revealing the broken tooth that is as inexplicably appealing to me in person as it is in the dreams, and says something unexpected. "Don't be sorry. He's doing okay."

Postscript: Today, as I was walking to my car, Gabriel chased after me and asked for my phone number, which I wrote on the palm of his hand with a sharpie I dug out of the glove box. And tonight, when he called, I took a risk by revealing a feeling I had when we met.

During rare moments in my life, I have noticed a curious light in a fellow human's eyes that ignites something inside me, reminds me that I am alive and perhaps more importantly, actually AWAKE.

Today I had one of those moments. There was this indefinable, but completely beautiful thing going on in Gabriel's expression while he gazed at the water below him, the seagulls overhead, the clouds, the blue sky, everything! Just by being there with him on the bridge I felt like I was part of a piece of art, a creation while it was occurring.

During that brief clarity, I had the understanding that life and art are the same thing, and before we said good night, I told him so.

He didn't quickly hang up on me, the woman brazen enough to tell him that he had ignited something inside me, turned my black & white vision into color. He simply replied, "I'll see you tomorrow, Paige," but he was smiling. I could feel it.

May 15, 2009: I look at Gabriel and feel like I've watched the way his mouth moves when he talks forever, though I only met him yesterday. And his thumb stroking the rim of his coffee cup is so familiar. He has a serious brow and lashes that quiver when he's searching for a word.

"Have you heard of Silver Birch?" he asks and meets my eyes, making my pulse quicken. We are sitting together at a small coffee shop in Onset Village across from the octagonal gazebo that looks out over the harbor. Soon we will be on route to the wigwam because last night during our three-hour telephone conversation, ranging from Sphynx cats to the Dalai Lama, I explained to him the research for my thesis. He not only knows where the wigwam is but has been there many times for what he calls "message circles," and has offered to take me. He tells me that Spiritualists, like Native Americans, believe in the continuity of life after physical death and the ability to maintain communication with those who have passed over. Silver Birch is no longer on the physical plane but is known for channeling his wisdom through a medium.

Gabriel tells me that he is clairvoyant, but he plays it down saying he is "only average," as if he is talking about bowling or chess. He can see spirits, but not hear them or feel their touch like some can. We all have the divine spirit within us, he says, and once we discover that, we can tap into all kinds of hidden abilities.

In other words, we're all sacred. Most of us just don't know it.

"Do you like poetry?" I ask him.

He hesitates. "I used to like song lyrics," he replies. "Does that count?"

Used to? I think, but intuition tells me not to say out loud.

You know the expression "Music soothes the savage beast?" That's me. And I have always loved the sound of words. I give Gabriel a nod without revealing all this.

I have driven my own car because I know it's the safest way to meet a man for coffee whom I don't know. But I am not remotely afraid of him. At his invitation, I walk beside him up the grassy hill to the gazebo. Instead of taking a seat inside of it, we sit on a stone bench with these words engraved on its side: Live, Love, Laugh, Dance, Fish. Life is Short. I smile up at the sky and see a crane fly over us, its long legs hanging behind its slender body. It is a good sign, I tell him, the crane flying over right as we sit down together.

A little while later I jump into his beat-up pickup truck that he uses for work without a second thought, and something catches my attention. The radio knobs are covered with tape, and I can't help but think there is a connection between this and his earlier comment about song lyrics.

Abby would be furious at me for getting in his truck. "Where did you learn such bad judgment?" she often scolds. She said it when I left Chris, and again when I quit my job. When I told her the topic of my thesis, she said something even more insulting, "Hm," but quickly like it's only half a syllable. To me, it's absolutely fascinating. And look where it has led me.

May 17, 2009: I am beside Gabriel in a church of all places. But this is no typical church. It is a small room filled with rows of fold-up chairs, almost all of them taken, and angels painted on the ceiling. At the front of the church two more angels in the form of stone statues hold onto flickering candles in front of the pastor, who is wearing a pale pink suit. She is a pretty lady and when she greets the crowd with a smile, she reminds me of one of the angels on the ceiling.

Gabriel reaches for my hand, and everything goes electric. The little hairs on my arms are standing on end and I have to focus to breathe normally. For three days, since we met, I've been telling myself that because of our age difference, he sees me as a friend. Now my brain is doing cartwheels because I was wrong.

The pastor flips the light switch off and instructs us to close the window blinds before she leads us in a guided meditation. In the candlelight it's even harder than usual to turn my eyes away from Gabriel. His cheeks are flushed, and his hair looks adorably mussed. He opens his eyes and catches me looking at him.

"Are you okay?" he asks, and I'm reminded of the dream.

"Yes," I answer, and nod my head reassuringly. I am so very okay.

After the meditation, there's a short lecture by a woman who introduces herself as a medium and says that mediumship is a form of healing.

My companion is sizing me up with his intelligent eyes, wondering, I am sure, if I'm enjoying the experience or if I'm freaked out.

The truth is, I haven't decided yet, but everything the woman says makes sense. The gist of her message is that we're all healers. Some people, like her, heal others by bringing messages from those who've passed out of the physical world. Others offer healing by taking time to listen to a friend, or to prepare food for a family grieving a loss. There are countless ways to heal, she says. Sometimes we provide healing just by smiling at a person who needs it. I think about Gabriel's hand holding mine and get her point. Every dormant cell inside me has sprung to life.

When my mom died, my family fell apart. The hub tore off the wheel and bounced off the tarmac into the weeds. How do you hold something together without its center? When I was seven, I used to make burlap dolls in Brownies. The felt lips and eyes never stayed on the faces the way they were supposed to, but my despair was only momentary. My mother could fix anything. And that's what she was, my mother, throughout my life, the fixer of all things great and small. What happens when the person who is the glue itself is no longer here? It's obvious that no one can fill the role, so for a while no one tries. In our family, my dad became the one thing he had never been. Hopeless. My brother closed up like a clam. And I bounced off the walls of my narrow life, drinking and smoking way too much. It was Abby who took the lead. She called and told us she was having Thanksgiving at her house (even though it had always been at our parents' house in Hanson), and that she expected us to be there. "We're still a family," she breathed into the phone, and even though I resented her at the time, now I respect her for it.

She got us back on track. In the face of a devastating loss, all you can see are the pieces on the ground, and you're filled with the thought that the damage done can never be corrected. But that's the grief talking. The recovery comes from tiny steps, like picking up the telephone.

I'm still thinking about this when the medium starts to work. She picks up the energy of a woman's dead husband, comments that she is wearing his favorite dress and says he wants to wish her a happy anniversary. The woman breaks down in tears and I, too, have to struggle not to cry. What would it be like, I wonder, to be in spirit form and still wanting to be with your lover on Earth? Then she turns to an old couple in the front row and tells them that their son, who died in a car accident, is standing behind them. Grief melts from the mother's face like butter in a pan. She looks a decade younger in an instant, and I understand how mediumship is healing.

Later, I giggle for no obvious reason and Gabriel faces me. His fingertips graze across my palm, and still thinking of the woman's husband who can't celebrate their anniversary with her, I offer silent thanks for my physical body so that I can feel him touching me.

"My father would hate it here," I whisper in explanation.

"Mine too," he says. The picture of my father in this church is absurd, like seeing a devout Hindu meditating cross-legged in the aisle of Saint Paul's, where my father attends services. It would call into question his entire belief system.

Chapter Seven

Joe Senior & Evelyn, *the Old-School Catholics*

Brother, you say that you are sent to instruct us how to worship the Great Spirit agreeably to His mind, and if we do not take hold of the religion which you white people teach, we shall be unhappy hereafter; you say that you are right and we are lost. We understand that your religion is written in a book; if it was intended for us as well as you, why has not the Great Spirit given it to us? *Red Jacket, Reply to Missionary Cram*

Paige's father was a tired old man, still handsome, but the dementia had stripped away the dignified, intelligent demeanor he'd carried most of his life. Now, mostly, he looked like a confused boy in an old man's body. His second wife, Evelyn, was his life preserver. She kept him afloat when his mind was drifting and unable to find its way back. He'd spent his life as an internal auditor for a research hospital in Boston, a "numbers man" he'd say, but now his brain could no longer compute.

Joe carried a small pad of paper and a pencil in his shirt pocket, which was a force of habit from his earlier days before computers took over the business. Every night Evelyn found his shirt folded neatly on the bed and would take the notebook out and place it on his dresser where he'd look for it the next day. She always opened it, hoping to find a clue to the mystery that was her husband's brain. Instead, she'd find random words, such as "robin" or "quarters." Sometimes he'd list the names of his family members, but instead of writing her name, he would write the name of his deceased wife, and she would be left to wonder whether he understood that he was married to her.

On days when it seemed worth the effort, she would go to great lengths to make that point clear. She'd carry a picture of them on their wedding day to the kitchen table where he was methodically eating his shredded wheat. His alert gray eyes would glance over at it, but he never commented, and Evelyn would be left alone with the photograph of the man she'd married.

They'd known each other for over thirty years. Evelyn had been a secretary at the same hospital where Joe had worked. They attended the same company Christmas parties and weddings and had known each other's first spouses. After Maria, Joe's wife, died from lung cancer, the very same disease that had taken Evelyn's husband's life, they started meeting for coffee on their work breaks. Now they'd been married for seven years. It was at the end of the fourth year that Evelyn began to suspect there was something medically wrong with her husband. From the start he'd been absent minded, but in a harmless way. It began with missing keys and wallets and progressed to forgetting names of people with whom he had regular contact.

Then one day when they were driving back from Shaw's Supermarket in Hanson with their weekly groceries, Joe took a wrong turn. Instead of driving toward the condominium they shared in Pembroke, he drove to the house where he'd lived with his first wife. No matter what Evelyn said, she could not redirect him. He pulled into the driveway and was intent on entering the home until the current owner stepped out the front door. The visual of an unfamiliar female exiting the house was a shock. Evelyn quickly moved into the driver's seat. Joe didn't say a word about the incident, but they both knew something was terribly wrong.

As children they'd been introduced to Catholicism and, having never questioned that course as adults, were active at their local church. Every Christmas Joe collected toys for children whose parents couldn't afford them and dressed as Santa Claus for the annual Christmas party. Evelyn ran clothing drives. They perceived themselves as well blessed and took pleasure from sharing those blessings with others. When his kids were small, Joe had provided them with his finest words of wisdom *be the best Abigail (or Paige or Joey) you can be.* Throughout his life he had strived to meet that bar. He knew, like all good parents, that he had to walk the talk if he wanted his children to follow suit. Early in his children's lives he'd noticed that—good, bad or indifferent—they imitated his actions.

His children were a curious blend of his own physical characteristics and personality traits, and those of Maria. Abigail's fair eyes and hair and milky complexion could not hide how much she was like her mother on the inside. Life was harder for her than for anyone her father had ever known because she lacked the ability to take anything lightly. It was nearly as challenging to get her to laugh as it was to get Paige to stop. As a toddler, she had been sweet and trusting. When her siblings were born, she'd received them as if they were dolls placed under the Christmas tree. It had started innocently, Abigail's protection and care of Paige and Joseph Junior, but with time it grew into something her parents had not anticipated. She saw them as her own.

But Paige could not be owned by anyone. Her nature was akin to their family cat, Bosco, who lived in the woods behind their house before Paige found it while climbing trees. Paige looked like her mother, but acted like her father. And Joe Junior looked just like Joe Senior, but he was neither rigid and self-sacrificing like his mother and Abigail, nor carefree and wildly imaginative like his father and Paige. He was quiet and thoughtful. As a child, because he was shy, he spent more time with Bosco, the wild cat, than he did with other children.

Evelyn's belief system was more tightly spun than her husband's. She believed in Purgatory and was sure that Paige had taken up residence there. In some respects, her perspective was like a Monopoly game — if you don't pass GO, you don't collect two hundred dollars. The rules were laid out and you either followed them or you didn't and bore the consequences.

A week or so prior to Paige's death, when it was obvious that her passing was imminent, Evelyn had made a point of telling Gabriel that a priest should be called in to perform Last Rites. It was her duty, she believed, to insist upon it. To her chagrin, Gabriel had shown his true colors by refusing. "I won't have anyone frightening her," he'd stated flatly, as if he'd had a right to, even though he wasn't married to Paige. To Evelyn's surprise, Joe had agreed — or at least pretended to — she never really knew what his vigorous head nods meant. It was the dementia, she believed, that had caused him to acquiesce. And God, she felt sure, would forgive that.

Now Joe and Evelyn were driving to the cemetery in Hanson to dispose of Paige's ashes in the way she thought most suitable, which was to make it as close to a burial as possible. Although she belonged to a religion that professed to believe in life after death, Evelyn decided that the best way for Paige to be with her dead mother was to drop her remains on the grave. Joe didn't decide anything, not the clothes he was wearing or the food he ate for breakfast. He'd awakened that morning as lost as he'd been when he'd fallen asleep the night before.

"Want a coffee, Joe?" Evelyn asked as they approached the Dunkin' Donuts in Hanson. When he didn't respond, she suggested, "We'll stop on the way back."

She turned onto High Street, where the Fern Hill Cemetery was located. It was founded in 1750 and had a stone arch at its entrance that cars had to carefully navigate through due to its narrowness. When they were children, Paige, Abigail and Joe used to walk along the stone wall that ran the length of the cemetery on route to the Cumberland Farms store for candy or ice cream. As far as cemeteries go, it was a beautiful place with dirt paths that resembled old country roads twisting through trees that turned orange, yellow and red in autumn. Mourning doves arose like the dust from the dirt roads in response to vehicles carrying early morning visitors.

The gravestones were nestled up against Wampatuck Pond, which Hanson residents called the Town Hall Pond because the Town Hall was located on the other side of it, and that was the way most people accessed it for boating or feeding the ducks. In the summer, back when the water was clean, the kids fished in it, and in the winter, ice skated on it. Every spring there were hydroplane races so loud they could be heard from the Delaney's neighborhood, a mile away.

Paige would bolt inside to tell her parents she was riding her bike to the races and her father would repeat the same ritual as every other time she ran off with her friends. He'd dig his hand into the pocket of his trousers and pull out a handful of quarters. Her big brown eyes would get bigger before they turned to the cool gray eyes of her father.

"Take as many as you think you'll need," he'd say. Paige would have to find the balance between taking what she wanted, without taking advantage of him. Five quarters was standard. Four wasn't enough to get an ice cream cone, and six left extra for bubble gum, but she could never buy ice cream *and* bubble gum without feeling guilty. Five was right. When she thanked him, his reply was always the same, "When I'm an old man you can buy me ice cream."

"No," Joe suddenly said as Evelyn turned the steering wheel sharply to the right to venture up one of the dirt roads between the rows of graves.

"It's okay, I know the way," Evelyn assured him.

"Go back," he insisted.

Joe pointed over Evelyn's shoulder at the pond that was visible through the rear window. There was a small parking area there for people who wanted to sit and look out at the water.

She disregarded his suggestion as nonsensical. The car crept onward past headstone after headstone, many of which marked the graves of people Joe used to know, other parents he met on the pond while skating with his children, or at school events. Some had been neighbors, other people he knew from their jobs at local businesses—the drug store, supermarket, post office, gas station and liquor store. More than a handful of gravestones marked the short lives of people who had been his children's contemporaries, kids who had delivered their newspapers, bagged their groceries at Shaw's, or sold Girl Scout cookies at their door. Joe's eyes appeared to be reading the names as he gazed out the open window.

In 2010, Hanson, situated about halfway between Boston and Cape Cod, was still a small town, with a population of roughly eight thousand people. But it used to be much smaller. When the Delaney children were growing up, Joe knew every person in town by name. Like many small towns, it held a certain charm born from an interesting combination of the mundane and the strange, its residents like characters in a book collaboration by Norman Rockwell and Timothy Leary. By the time Paige was a teenager, the drug culture era had ended, and rock had prevailed over disco. Nonetheless, she picked up the torch and ran with it. Led Zeppelin and rebellion pulsed through her veins as steadily as it had through the bloodstreams of the teenagers a decade ahead of hers. To Paige and her friends, Fern Hill Cemetery was less about death than it was, like the woods behind her house, a place to get stoned in peace.

When the car stopped in front of Maria's grave, Joe asked, "Is this the place?" The vial of ashes was in a paper bag to conceal it from Joe during the drive. It was gripped in her hand now as she exited the car. Joe got out, too, without her having to prompt him. The day was hot for May in Massachusetts and Joe was dressed in a navy suit and tie because that's what Evelyn had laid out for him, as if they were attending a funeral—a real one, not like the one planned by Paige's irreligious boyfriend. Now Joe's fingers were fidgeting with the tie's knot, and his face was flushed.

"We can loosen it if it's too warm," Evelyn suggested.

"It's not the place," he complained.

She took his hands in hers. "I wouldn't take you here if it wasn't," she said, and meant it. For over three years, since the diagnosis, she'd dedicated her life to steering him through his, and she had done so selflessly by always putting him first. "Joe, Paige's ashes are in this bag," she said softly, and he nodded, but Evelyn knew that Joe's head nod was usually a response to anything and everything that he no longer understood. It was sometimes the only way he could participate or pretend to participate in a conversation.

For no reason, it seemed, Joe's feet started to turn in a circle, slowly, his eyes like the lens of a camera panning the landscape around him, first the rolling green hills spattered with gravestones, then the pond behind it all, and finally the cerulean sky over head with its clouds adrift like white cotton candy. Through Joe's strange dance, Evelyn waited patiently. When he'd completed the circle, he stepped assertively toward the car and grasped the door handle. In that brief moment, he resembled the man he used to be—strong, thoughtful and decisive.

"Not yet," Evelyn intervened. She took his hand and led him closer to the grave. Once they were standing next to the stone that read MARIA COSTANZO DELANEY, she withdrew the vial from the brown paper bag and tried to hand it to Joe, but he pulled his hand away. "Remember we decided this would be the right thing to do?"

Joe was smiling at a robin perched on a nearby branch. Evelyn ignored his fascination with the bird, got down on her knees and removed the plug from the glass vial, the spongy earth leaving dirt stains on her pantyhose. Carefully, she spread

Paige's ashes on her mother's grave as if she were fertilizing a garden, and then called Joe to join her. He knelt while she recited the *Our Father*, and made the sign of the cross, but his eyes were on a strand of sunlight bouncing off an object near his wife's knee.

It took some time for Evelyn to get back on her feet. Her knees were arthritic and painful. All the while, Joe's hand was rummaging through the grass in front of the headstone. When his wife questioned him, he opened it to reveal a handful of quarters.

His recent fascination with coins was an annoyance. He seemed to find them everywhere, even once or twice— inexplicably—in his shoe. As she led him to the car and strapped on his seatbelt, Joe smiled with the money clenched in his fist and Evelyn shook her head in frustration. He never remembered that money was dirty, and not to touch it, no matter how many times she repeated it. For all she knew, he might not remember that his daughter had died. He could recall a baseball game he pitched in 1952 with photographic recollection and could give a detailed account of a family trip to Disney World in 1977, but he could not recall what a calculator was, or how to use it. Even if he realized their reason for visiting the cemetery, he would forget momentarily.

What really mattered, she thought, was that they'd properly disposed of Paige's ashes. It baffled her that anyone would wish for their body to be cremated, but in her eyes, Paige had been an odd person. Secretly, Evelyn had labeled her "the beatnik." She never spoke the word out loud anymore, however, because she didn't believe in speaking ill of the dead. And after all, Paige had been a nice girl. She hadn't been mature and responsible like Abigail, or sweet and respectful like Joe Junior, but she had been good to her father. She used to bring him anisette cookies from an Italian bakery, and that always made him smile. Now her remains were where they should be, and Evelyn could add her name to the list of people she prayed for so that God would consider releasing her from the confines of Purgatory.

"Now we'll get you that coffee," she told Joe.

"Ice cream," he countered, and opened his hands to reveal all five quarters.

Nonsense, Evelyn thought. *Who ever heard of eating ice cream at ten o'clock in the morning?* Joe paid no attention to her disapproving sighs. His fingers curled lovingly around the quarters as the car passed under the stone arch and pulled onto High Street.

May 23, 2009: Why do we believe the things we believe? Is it because we have some substantial reason to accept them as truth, or is it because someone told us they were true when our minds were impressionable?

When I was six, I stole a pack of gum and got away with it, except for the fact that I very quickly became convinced I was going to Hell. I'd wake up at night and swear I saw demons hovering near the end of my bed. I prayed for forgiveness so the demons would go away. But there were never any there to begin with.

We're powerful beings—we humans—capable of vast creations. With such potential, why don't we create paradise? Why do we so often go the route of fear? I worry about my brother and how he's shutting himself away because my parents branded their beliefs into his brain. What made them think they have any greater right to God than he does?

I believe Heaven and Hell exist concurrently while we are on Earth and afterward, too. They are states of being, not physical places, unless we choose to create them that way. That means we get to choose. We're responsible for how we feel, for our own state of being. Selfishness or love, anger or understanding, darkness or light. Hell or Heaven. I choose Heaven.

Chapter Eight

Joe Jr. & Bowman, *the Dissident & the Baptist*

The kingdom of Heaven is within you.
—Jesus of Nazareth

"This is trespassing," Joe breathed after he turned off the car's ignition. The night was silent except for a sound from his childhood. The persistent chirping made by crickets rubbing their forewings against each other. *Or maybe frogs*, he considered, but didn't voice it because of Bowman's irrational fear of them. He'd nearly had a nervous breakdown once when he'd awakened to find a tree frog staring at him from the top of the coffee maker.

"We could be arrested!" Bowman gleefully replied.

Joe grunted at the thought.

Bowman laughed. "Come on," he nudged. "Where's your sense of adventure? Paige would love that you're doing this, wouldn't she?"

The truth was that Paige would have loved Bowman. They shared a common flair for life that couldn't be suppressed no matter how hard or unfair it became. What Bowman had said was true, Paige would love the fact that they were creeping into the woods at night behind a stranger's house that used to be their family home so they could climb a tree and fling her ashes from it. When they were kids, Paige was always sneaking out the window to go somewhere.

"I wish you could have known her," he said. It was dark in the car, and he couldn't see Bowman's face. "I was wrong, Bow, not to bring you here before."

Joe heard him sigh and then felt his hand close on his own. "I'm not angry," he replied.

"I know," Joe conceded, "but you should be. You let me get away with too much."

"Let's go find the tree," Bowman suggested.

Joe acquiesced, but he was still thinking about it. Even the phrase he just used, *You let me get away with too much*, put the blame on Bowman, not himself. No matter how badly he behaved, Bowman, he knew, would never leave, but it was wrong to take advantage of that. More than wrong, *egregious*, his father would have said back when he was still capable of complex thought.

Joe leaned toward the passenger seat. "Thank you for coming with me," he said, reached over Bowman's lap and opened his door for him. Maybe in the end, being brave wasn't really about strength, he considered as they exited the car. Maybe it was about being honest regardless of the consequences. The most precious thing in Joe's life was his relationship with Bowman. It was pure because Bowman was pure. His intentions and his actions came from love, not self-interest, and if other people couldn't see that, then it had to be because the lenses they were seeing him through were dirty, not the other way around. Even the sun looks filthy when looking at it through a window smudged with dirt. It all came down to perception.

As they got out of the car, a dog barked in the distance causing Bowman to draw his breath in.

"It's far away," Joe assured him as he held a tree branch back for him to pass. "So, did you miss me when I was in Europe?"

"You know I hate being home alone," Bowman said.

"Right, but I mean, did you miss me?"

"Obviously. What's on your mind, Joe? Just say it."

Joe sighed. There was no sense in ducking the issue. Bowman could see through his bullshit. "I missed you," he disclosed. "I wanted you to be with me the whole time, especially in Venice."

"I know that even when you don't say it," Bowman replied, and Joe laughed.

"Next time we go together, all right?"

"If you say so," Bowman agreed. "Hey, know what these woods remind me of?"

"What?" Joe asked hesitantly. He was leading the way by flashlight and waiting for Bowman to say *the place those boys dragged me off to. The place I was raped.* "A Midsummer Night's Dream," he said instead. "All the green leaves and the pine needles under our feet. I can practically hear them whispering to each other."

While Joe was thinking of traumatic childhood events, Bowman was imagining fairies in the trees. Joe was sweeping the flashlight left to right, trying to get his bearings. He stopped walking abruptly and laughed. "That's the alligator pit!" he exclaimed with the flashlight focused on a wide, round dip in the ground.

"The what?" Bowman screamed and nearly jumped out of his skin.

"No, no, not really," Joe quickly said. He'd momentarily forgotten that his partner was raised in a state that had alligators. "It was just something my dad made up to tease us."

"Oh," Bowman said with relief and let go of Joe's arm.

After several minutes of walking in silence, and after Bowman's breathing returned to normal, Joe threw out, "Gabriel is a cool guy."

"Oh yeah?" Bowman asked and Joe recognized the question inside the question. No matter how often Joe reassured him, Bowman carried the fear underneath his skin that at any moment his world could be swept away by a stranger's glance in Joe's direction.

He was annoyed at the question, but less by Bowman's insecurity than by his own ambivalence that he knew had created it. "He's Paige's boyfriend," Joe muttered.

"I know. Is he cute?"

"He's very good looking."

"What color eyes?" Bowman inquired.

"I didn't notice." When Bowman was conspicuously quiet, he added, "brown."

"You always like brown eyes."

"For Christ's sake, Bow," Joe snapped. "He's my dead sister's boyfriend."

"You're right. I'm sorry."

Joe was quiet, reconsidering the harshness in his tone. There were scars on Bowman's fingertips from scrubbing them. His fears and insecurities had driven him to it. Even though there were manicure brushes with soft bristles (bought by Joe to replace the ones with wire bristles) lined up next to the bathroom sink in their townhouse, it had been a few years since Bowman had felt the compulsion to use them.

"What's he like?" he asked.

"Well, he's. . . interesting," Joe gently offered. "He told me that he saw Paige after she left her body. He said he was asleep in a chair by her bed when something woke him, and he saw her standing there smiling at him. My mother was behind her and two other people, but he couldn't see their faces, only their outlines. Spirit guides, he thinks."

Bowman gasped. "That sounds just like *Ghost Whisperer*! What else did he say?"

"He said—where the fuck is the tree?"

"What?" Following a confused pause, Bowman burst out laughing. "I thought you meant that's what Gabriel said!" he exclaimed.

"I could have sworn it was right here." Joe said, ignoring his outburst, even though his partner was bent over laughing with his hands on his knees—cracking himself up, something that happened daily. Joe rotated with the flashlight in his hand, looking for it. "Let's try this way," he suggested and stepped to the right.

"I think this way," Bowman countered and pointed toward Joe's childhood home.

Bowman was always telling him he should follow his intuition. Joe wasn't even sure he had intuition, but he was willing to follow Bowman's. "All right," he agreed and stepped behind him before he picked up the conversation again. "Gabriel said Paige's hair was long, and she was wearing an emerald-green dress. Maybe that was her way of reminding him to tell everyone to wear bright colors to the funeral?"

"Did you wear the pink shirt I packed you?" Bowman asked.

"I couldn't," Joe admitted. It wasn't pale preppy pink. It was more like fuchsia. There was no way Joe could justify wearing it, not even for Paige.

"*I* would have," Bowman proclaimed.

"Of course, you would have. You're braver than I am."

"Except when it comes to big dogs. And alligators," Bowman laughed.

"And tree frogs. But I meant big things, *real* things. Okay, how did you know?"

"Know what?"

"Where the tree was. It's right there." In the flashlight they could make out a tree that had fallen and crashed into another one. "The slanted tree," Joe laughed. "It's way smaller than I remember, and I swear it wasn't this close to my house."

"That's because you were smaller and your legs were shorter," Bowman suggested.

"Hand me the ashes. Here, you hold the flashlight." The ashes were tucked snugly in Bowman's shirt pocket. Joe took them from him and took a long moment to consider what he was holding in his hand. He took a deep breath for strength before putting one foot and then the other on the trunk and started climbing it like a monkey.

"Slow down or you'll fall," Bowman scolded.

"No, I won't." On some cellular level, his body remembered how to climb trees. "I might puke, but I won't fall," he added.

Joe sat down and held onto a branch for balance. There were certain smells that always transported him back to childhood. Asphalt during a summer rainstorm brought to mind images of heat lightning and kids running home in their wet cut offs. Marinara sauce simmering was his mother singing in the kitchen. The sticky sweet smell of cotton candy made his stomach flip like he was on a Tilt-a-Whirl at the Brockton Fair. And leaves rotting on a forest floor recalled a picture of himself afraid and hiding in the woods. It was that memory that made him feel sick.

"The last time I was here I was about to get my ass kicked," he revealed. "And I would have if Paige didn't jump out of the tree on top of the asshole."

Kevin Carlsbad, the biggest kid in the neighborhood, had been tormenting Joe for weeks. On that day, he followed him into the woods with a couple of friends. Joe was headed to the fort the neighborhood kids had built just beyond the slanted tree and found Paige in the tree smoking a cigarette—she was twelve or thirteen then—climbed it and sat beside her. And when Paige jumped, Joe followed. He landed on top of the smallest boy, who burst into tears and ran away. He didn't even have to throw a punch. And after that day, no kid—not even Kevin Carlsbad—bothered Joe again.

"Why didn't I ever fight for her?" he sputtered and his voice broke. "I didn't come to see her, Bow. I didn't even come home when she was sick."

Bowman had tried to convince him to return to Massachusetts, but the idea of visiting Paige while she was dying, Joe believed, was beyond his ability. When he first received word of the diagnosis, he convinced himself that somehow, she would miraculously triumph over cancer. But instead, as time passed, she grew sicker, and the idea of visiting her was more difficult. In the end, he put it off until it was too late.

"Come back down," Bowman urged. "We can put the ashes under the tree."

"Can you come up?" Joe pleaded. His voice was raspy, on the verge of tears.

"You know I'm scared of heights."

"It's not that high. Even if you fall, you won't get hurt. You'll land in the moss."

Joe could hear Bowman muttering as he pulled himself onto the tree trunk. He had a habit of carrying on conversations with himself. Right now, he was complaining about the possibility of falling out of the tree and landing in the moss. Joe held out his hand and he took it. Seconds later, Bowman was sitting next to him on the tree limb with his legs hanging over the side and grinning proudly. "I'm not scared," he whispered, then repeated it like he was coaching himself.

His newfound bravery made Joe smile. "Time's a weird thing, isn't it?" he said. "Sitting here in the slanted tree, I feel like I'm ten again, like I never grew up and moved away. And there's such comfort in that." A moment later he added, "Not that it was easy when I was ten either, but it was different. I felt protected. What was your life like when you were ten?"

"Perfect, believe it or not. I wasn't gay yet. Well, I was, but I didn't know it."

"Did you have a lot of friends?" Joe asked.

"Tons. Jackson was my best friend. He taught me how to throw a baseball—"

"Jackson? Isn't he the one—?"

Bowman cut him off. "I know, I know, but he was my friend once. That's why I still pray for him. Fiona taught me that if I pray for people, it's easier to forgive them."

What Bowman didn't say out loud, but thought for the millionth time, was that if he had never been raped, he wouldn't have moved to D.C. and he wouldn't have been in Starbucks waiting for Joe when he scuttled in out of the rain. It was a hard thing to get his arms around, the fact that the worst thing that ever happened to him had precipitated the best.

Joe was silent before he softly asked, "Who else did you play with?"

"All the kids in the neighborhood were friends. We used to play kick the can and softball in the cul de sac. When the girls started cheerleading, I learned the cheers with them, and no one thought there was anything wrong with it."

Joe wiped his nose on his shirt sleeve as a scratchy chuckle escaped him. "The kids in my neighborhood would have kicked my ass for that, but I bet you were good at it."

"Well. You know. I've always been a perfectionist."

Joe laughed again. He could imagine his life partner as a little boy, how adorable he must have been with his big, inquisitive eyes and small, tidy lips. He was diminutive for such an enormous soul and moved with the agility of a ballet dancer. He could have been one of Shakespeare's tree fairies that he'd just been imagining. No one could have made a better Puck.

"Back then," Bowman continued, "when we were kids, the only thing that mattered was having other kids to play with."

Joe nodded. He remembered. "Let's drop the ashes and go home," he suggested.

"You won't let me fall in the moss?"

"I won't let you fall, Bow. Not ever," Joe promised. "I have a couple of things I want to say to Paige first, in case she can hear me. Okay, so mostly it's this—I'm sorry, Paige, that I left all the hard stuff to you. I should have come to see you." He caught his breath that was hiccupping with emotion. "I couldn't bear the thought of a world without you in it. But going forward, I'll try to be brave. I'd really like you to be proud of me."

He pressed his forehead against Bowman's shoulder and gave himself a moment to cry before he pulled the stopper out of the vial and poured the ashes out of it onto the tree trunk and next to the tree. Then he held onto Bowman to ensure his safety until they were on the ground again. The first sweep of the flashlight on the forest floor caught something that made Joe's body immobilize as if he were eight years old and playing freeze tag in the woods. One single pink flower, shaped like a tiny balloon.

"It's a lady slipper," he sputtered, breaking the silence.

Bowman stooped down to get a better look. "I've never seen a flower like this."

"That's because there aren't a lot of them," Joe explained. "When we were kids, everyone used to say it was against the law to pick them because they were endangered. Paige loved them. I have a memory of her sitting out here in the woods surrounded by them with streaks of sun coming through the trees all around her, making the pine needles look like they were about to burst into flames. I remember thinking she looked like she was in a fairy tale. Once, I picked a bunch of lady slippers and left them on her pillow. I didn't want anyone to know I did it because I thought I'd get in trouble, but I guess she knew it was me because that night she came in to kiss me good night and told me she was proud of me for not believing everything I hear. It turned out it wasn't illegal to pick lady slippers, only to rip the roots from the ground."

"Maybe you were supposed to see the lady slipper to remind you that you were a good brother. Maybe that's Paige's way of helping you remember," Bowman suggested.

Joe threw his head back and smiled up at the stars twinkling like frolicking fairies in the inky black sky. Beyond those stars another galaxy existed, then another and another. It was all too immense to absorb with his merely human brain. Who was he to say that Paige hadn't played a role in placing the lady slipper at his feet? Who was he to place limitations on the power of love?

When he was ready to move forward again, he reached for Bowman's hand.

"You never hold hands," Bowman remarked.

"I do now."

"Because it's dark?"

"No. Not because it's dark, Bow."

They walked the rest of the way to the car without speaking. When Joe turned the ignition and the radio sprang to life, he turned it off. With Bowman, silence was better.

They were half a mile down High Street, in front of the cemetery's stone wall when he pulled over near a streetlight, not ten feet away from the place he fell off the wall and gashed his head when he was a boy. *Life moves in the oddest circles,* he thought.

"I need to make a quick call," he explained.

Joe found the person he was looking for in his contact list and pressed the button. It was hard to pull his breath into his lungs as he heard it ring. The fear was present, but this time he wouldn't let it be an obstacle.

"What's the matter?" his perceptive boyfriend asked.

Joe looked over at him sitting beside him in the passenger's seat, wearing the hat he'd brought back from Italy. Bowman had worn it because he was afraid that bats would dive at him in the woods and get tangled in his hair. He was the only person Joe had ever met who had the ability to live courageously despite his fear. Even though he was terrified of people consumed with hate and prejudice, he never let them decide who he was or how he should live his life. And for that reason, above all else, Joe admired him. In that regard, he now realized Bowman was just like Paige.

"Nothing's the matter," he responded confidently and squeezed Bowman's hand. Then Abigail's voice was on the receiver. "It's Joe," he said quietly. "I know it's late, but—" He bit his lip. "There's something I need to tell you. And more importantly, there's someone I want you to meet."

May 28, 2009: We all become healers when we choose to be. We can wait for someone else to lead us into the light, or we can become the light.

June 18, 2009: At Gabriel's cottage it feels like the sun is ever-present. We sit on his deck, sipping something concocted in his blender, and watch the people at Sandy Beach. He is quick-witted and makes amusing comments about people that I half-believe are true.

"The woman with big hair whose eyes search the beach is looking for the soul mate she lost at a Poison concert in 1989. The little boy building sandcastles is a future famous architect who will one day reconstruct the entire village of Onset. Someday," Gabriel asserts, "Onset will be governed by the little girl with pigtails who's bossing the other children around."

I sip and giggle. "Keep going," I say quite often in his presence.

"The old man with the metal detector is a former FBI agent who is rumored to have been involved in the Kennedy assassinations."

"Shhh!" I scold, as if the guy can hear, and Gabriel laughs. It's my new favorite thing—Gabriel with his head thrown back and laughter erupting like musical notes from his throat.

He lives on Love Street, like the Doors song. Well, not really—it's Cove Street, but someone crossed off the word on the sign and wrote "Love" in its place, and we like it better that way. Gabriel does a spot-on Jim Morrison imitation, not only the vocals, but the swagger. They are built similarly with a long torso and legs, and narrow hips that move gracefully with each step.

"Were you always like that?" I asked him once.

He followed my eyes down his belly and legs, as usual clad in faded jeans, as if he was born in them, to his bare feet. "You mean thin?" he innocently asked.

It's such an understatement. Does he see what I see in him when he looks in a mirror? I doubt it.

His steps are confident, but his eyes tell a different story. Like me, he doubts himself. He wonders if he's good enough.

Even on rainy days the house on Love Street is full of light. One of the great advantages of living in a cottage is that the elements feel close. This morning in bed, while the rain pelted the roof and the wind lashed at the windows, Gabriel asked me to move in with him. He's been hinting at it for a week, but I was waiting for the actual invitation. I say yes without hesitation and try to remember the last time I felt this much happiness. Have I ever?

June 23, 2009: "Elated" is the word of the day. Gabriel has opened my heart and now the universe is flowing through it. I feel like a cloud with the breeze pushing it gently this way and that and hitting no blockages, only finding more and more expansion. There's no way life could be better than this, but I thought that yesterday, too, and then today arrived adorned like an ancient king in golden robes. (Hands in prayer position): thank you, thank you, thank you.

June 25, 2009: Abby doesn't understand what could motivate me to move in with a man "I barely know" and who "could be a criminal." Instead of arguing, I tell her I love her and thank her for her concern. (Maybe Gabriel's spiritual approach to life is rubbing off on me?)

She looks confused, but then she hugs me and says she only wants me to be happy. "I am happy," I say. "Besides, it's not your job to keep me safe."

"I don't know how to stop," she confesses. I know she feels responsible for Joe and me. It's hard enough to navigate one person through this tumultuous world, let alone three. I ask her to come visit me in Onset and to meet Gabriel. She agrees.

Gabriel says what we send out always bounces back. The conversation with my sister today might be an example of that. I've been judging her for our entire lives. Maybe that's why she feels the need to judge me. On my way home with my car full of stuff, I make a list of everything I admire about Abby. It surprises me that the list continues all the way from Norwell to Onset.

July 5, 2009: I just met our neighbors, an interesting pair. The first thing I notice about Ben is the smell of weed clinging to his clothes, his red eyes and apprehensive smile. This is a guy who is laid back not by nature, but with a little help. He acts like he doesn't care, but I think he does, probably very deeply, hence the weed. Ben is dressed in Patagonia-style clothes that look like they were picked out by someone else, suggesting a girlfriend at home, one with sizable influence.

She steps out the front door and I immediately get it. Her name is Arica, she says, not with an "E" but an "A". Arica. She looks like she just walked off the cover of Ebony Magazine. Talk about gorgeous. But despite the astounding natural beauty (she has no makeup on and is wearing a guy's white beater with hacked off denim shorts), it's not what hits you first. It's her self-confidence that demands attention.

With Arica and me it's like at first sight.

July 3, 2009: I've been thinking about Gabriel's comments and have come to an, albeit tenuous, conclusion. Fear of death gives birth to religion. A glimpse of the Universe and our place in it gives birth to spirituality. It's a fall to your knees moment when you realize you are so much more than you ever imagined and at the same time are only a speck in the whole Magnificence.

July 13, 2009: It turns out Gabriel plays piano, something he's never mentioned, and that he even studied at Berklee College of Music. According to Ben Cohen who lives next door, he plays astoundingly well. We've become friends with Ben and Arica, who is a counselor in a women's shelter on Cape Cod. (I love her—she's so BADASS. And Ben is so NOT, which I love, too.)

The other day Gabriel helped Ben move some furniture out of his family home in Chatham and they have a grand piano in their living room that Gabriel was eyeing. Mrs. Cohen invited him to try it out, and according to Ben, Gabriel's playing silenced her, which I gather is an extraordinary thing. Since then, I've noticed him practicing finger movements, and I wonder if he is hearing the notes. I ask why he stopped playing and his response scares me at first because he says it reminds him too much of someone he loves. It's not an ex-girlfriend, though. It's Billy, his best friend who died in a car accident. His bridge jumping friend.

Last night we went on a Cape Cod Canal blues cruise with Ben and Arica and had a blast. Gabriel was lit up by the music and his energy was contagious. There's much to be said for being barefoot on a boat under the moon, laughing until your gut hurts, dancing to songs you've never even heard, and then afterward going home with the one person you adore more than anyone.

July 24, 2009: Ben and I have been spending a lot of time together lately because Arica is in Nigeria, visiting her mother, and he's like a lost puppy in her absence. He gets stoned more, too. I can smell it coming from his house every time I step onto the back deck. He looks thinner than usual and his mouth, that's always pouty and wet like a child's, has the slightest trace of fur above it, like he's trying unsuccessfully to grow a mustache. When I ask if he's okay, Ben informs me that he's been arguing with his mother because he's living with a "shiksa" (non-Jewish woman), and he doesn't know how to resolve it.

I don't have an answer for him because, even though my first thought was "talk about not seeing the forest for the trees," it would be unfair of me to pass this judgment. First, I don't know Mrs. Cohen. In fact, the only thing I know about her is that she loves music, and I can certainly relate to that. Second, I don't know what it's like to be Jewish. So, instead of trying to advise him, I just listen to his feelings while we both watch the various birds visit the feeder Gabriel attached outside our kitchen window for my amusement. I like the Native American belief that birds are messengers from the Spirit World. They communicate a sense of peace. I said this out loud to Ben, and he laughed, but I noticed that after watching the birds hop around on the feeder, their shiny black eyes taking us in cautiously, he did seem to feel better.

"Maybe she'll change her mind when she gets to know her," he murmurs

"Yeah," I say, like I'm confident, though I'm not.

Mrs. Cohen grew up in Israel. Her parents narrowly escaped death during the holocaust. If I were her, I'd be suspicious of everyone, especially those who ventured close to my only child. Still, I wish she could see the way her son's entire body smiles every time Arica's around, and how he slumps in his chair and talks a little slower when she's not.

Ben and Gabriel could pass as brothers. They're both tall and lanky with eyes and hair like unsweetened chocolate. But Gabriel's features are finer than Ben's, as if someone chiseled him out of clay. When they're together, I catch glimpses of Gabriel's childhood. They're always skipping stones at the beach, walking on their hands or showing off in some other manner. I'm waiting for them to land in a wrestling match on our living room floor. Their playfulness is a nice diversion from Gabriel's sullen side, the part that creeps in on silent feet when we're not looking.

"You need to delve into this and discover why it's controlling you," I said to him once about his mood shift. One quick flicker of his eyes revealed the truth. There's no need to dig. He knows but is choosing not to tell me. I think he's grieving Billy, but I'm not sure.

For this reason, more than any other, I believe it's necessary for Gabriel to indulge the playful side of his personality. I am convinced it is as important for adults to play as it is for children.

"You can't lose this," I tell him today as he walks me to the coffee pot on his feet like I'm four. He laughs, perhaps thinking that I'm out of my mind to imagine a part of you can ever be lost.

But it can be. I saw it happen to my ex-husband, Chris. He chose the college we both attended because they had a good baseball team. Picture, if you will, the universe as a huge buffet table displaying thousands of options for our choosing. Can you see it? Okay then, here's Christopher in a nutshell: as a teenager/young adult he repeatedly loaded his plate with baseball, baseball, baseball and nothing else but baseball because nothing else came close. I think he loved baseball even more than he loved me. Years passed; he gave up his job as a sports reporter then started missing games in his league. After a while, he became a staff writer and somehow forgot that part of him, ignored it for so long that it disintegrated into something that used to be, but no longer is. There are bases he used in his league, discarded under the back deck of our old house, and covered in spiderwebs now. I wish he'd take them out again. I wish he'd remember how to play.

Chapter Nine

Christopher, *the Episcopalian*

Earth's crammed with heaven and every common bush
afire with God: But only he who sees takes off his shoes.
—*Elizabeth Barrett Browning*

When Christopher met Paige during their sophomore year of college, she was known on campus for her ability to drink more beer than any other student, and voicing her opinions loudly, whether she was drunk, stoned or completely sober. Her hair was cropped like a guy's and dyed a deep shade of red, which was in alluring contrast to her long slender body.

Not that Paige was beautiful in the traditional sense, like her sister, Abigail—the poster child for beauty. Paige's nose was more prominent than Abigail's, her eyes more intense and her skin not remarkably fair or perfect. But her small mouth always seemed to be curled into a grin, as if she were enjoying a private joke. Paige was compelling.

No matter how he tried, Christopher couldn't break the inexplicable attraction he felt for her. She was the kind of girl he'd always steered clear of, the sort that could get him into trouble before he even saw it coming. During freshman year she'd been seen around campus with a guy from the drama club that he'd assumed was gay—until he saw him lying on top of Paige on the lawn in front of the administration building. Even now, two decades later, he had photographic recollection of Paige's hands on the guy's back, her fingers pulling him against her, as if they were making love. Those hands still haunted him. He never felt like Paige held onto him as tightly as she had the drama guy.

Maybe he should have taken it as a sign from God the first time he spoke to her that she disagreed with almost every value he'd held close since childhood. Christopher was old fashioned. He listened to his parents and followed their advice. Church attendance was important to him, even while living in a dormitory. The God he believed in needed to be shown that he was in His camp, something Paige never understood. "It's God," she'd say. "She knows everything, whether you go to church or not." The "She" he disregarded but prayed Paige wouldn't repeat to his family.

Paige was anti-church, anti-establishment, anti-everything it seemed to Christopher, and he wasn't anti-anything. He didn't take rules personally, the way Paige did, or feel the need to change them. On a deep, intuitive level, she scared him. Why then couldn't he stop staring at her and doing everything in his power to be in her proximity? He never did figure it out, but there it was, the strongest attraction he'd ever felt for another human being. Sometimes he thought God had placed her in his path to test him. If, ultimately, he was condemned to Hell, he figured Paige would be traipsing along beside him. And that was the fine point that made it worth the risk.

"You don't want to go out with me," she replied, when he finally asked.

"Yes, I do," he insisted.

"Why?" she wanted to know.

"I don't know," he admitted, and she laughed.

"If you want to go to a movie or something, okay, but if you're looking for a girlfriend, you're asking out the wrong girl. Are you?"

He swallowed the lump in his throat and nodded slightly.

"Christopher," Paige crooned and touched his face with her cool fingertips. "You're adorable and sweet and smart, but I would drive you crazy."

"I know," he groaned and that won her over. She liked his honesty. That night over a pizza she told him she was tired of the typical male mentality. Men would say anything, she asserted, if they thought it would get them laid. And just because she was unorthodox that didn't mean she was promiscuous. She went on a rant about how that was a female stereotype, and people never made those assumptions about men.

He listened and wondered if asking her out had been the biggest mistake of his life. Twenty years later, he still couldn't answer that question. It didn't matter, though. He'd been like a fish on a hook since the first time he'd noticed her, and the only way he could have wriggled free would have been to tear out a piece of himself.

Once, during the months leading up to filing for divorce, she told him she felt like they were two fireflies trapped under a glass. Christopher wasn't offended by the metaphor. He'd have been content to stay in one place for his entire life. But Paige wanted freedom, and she'd have done anything for that, even smashed the glass if necessary. If she hurt herself or someone else in the process, then so be it. She'd hurt Christopher deeply in her desperation to disentangle herself from their relationship. In his mind, she was like an animal willing to chew off its own leg to get out of a trap.

"You're supposed to feel like that," he responded to her firefly comment without thinking it through. "You're an adult. Why do you expect to feel like a teenager?"

"What do you mean?" she inquired, her eyes narrowing.

"Freedom's a fairy tale," he rashly replied. "You should have outgrown it by now."

She heaved the word *fuuuuuck* out of her lungs with such venom that he was scared to say another word. And tears were spilling down her face.

"I can't breathe," she'd complain after that, and Christopher would stare with uncomprehending eyes. What was so wrong with the life they'd created? They lived in a nice house in a nice town and had nice little jobs that brought in a nice income. How much more could a person want?

Paige wanted to travel through Europe by train. She wanted to spend time in an artists' colony in Provincetown. She wanted to buy a pottery wheel and kiln. "Let's use this year's tax return to take a cruise," he threw out one day, but she turned her back and walked away, unsatisfied.

The things she desired seemed unattainable to Christopher, and foolish. He thought that surely with time she would come around to reason, but instead she rebelled. And for the life of him, he couldn't figure out how to get her back under the glass.

He was in his recliner in the living room of the home they'd once shared, holding the vial of ashes. The chair she used to sit in was still in the same place it was the day she walked out for the last time. Everything was the same, except for the few small items she took with her for sentimental reasons. There was no battle during the divorce over who would get the house. Paige didn't want it. She only wanted *out* of the house. She called it an albatross that she had no intention of wearing around her neck.

It was a Sunday, Christopher's day off, and he'd been sitting in the chair since breakfast, holding Paige's ashes and contemplating where to bring them. The question was, *Am I doing this for Paige or for me?* he realized.

He could easily think of places that would satisfy Paige. The beach, the woods, a meadow down the street where she used to watch for butterflies. But if up to him alone, he'd carry her around in his pocket for the rest of his life. He would take satisfaction from the fact that one small piece of her was in his grasp and couldn't escape.

"You're all I ever wanted, Paige," he said out loud, and let the thought saturate him. He'd always expected to go to college, meet a nice girl—someone like his mother—find a good job, get married and buy a house. *Steady* was the word to describe the life he had envisioned. There'd been nothing steady about Paige. In Christopher's eyes, she was a gypsy. He'd realized what he was up against the first time he took her home to meet his parents.

His mother hadn't understood the unnatural shade of Paige's hair, the feather earrings or the crystal necklace falling between her breasts. She'd dragged him to the living room, where his father was watching the Patriots.

"This is your girlfriend?" she'd demanded. "The smart one you've been telling us about?"

"She is smart," Christopher had replied.

And that was only the reaction to her exterior. Paige's interior was much more provocative. It took Chris months to explain that she didn't eat the flesh of living creatures, or take the life of anything, even insects, and her refusal to attend church services. Inappropriate words frequently slipped from her mouth, causing her to gasp with embarrassment, but then burst into laughter. That was one side of Paige. On the other side, the one they eventually decided counted the most, she was a straight "A" student, a writer for the school magazine, and volunteered her services as his little sister's English tutor. Eventually, she won over Christopher's entire family. Paige became the touch of exotic that turns a family gathering into a party, the color purple against the white backdrop of their lives. Before long, they loved her as much as Chris did, which was saying a lot. He loved her more than baseball.

By the time they married, Paige had transformed in some ways, and her husband imagined that the changes were a result of maturity. She gave up the weed and the bohemian clothes and appeared to have found an appropriate way to channel her strong opinions, through a job working as an editor for a local newspaper. She was quieter, more refined—even polite, for the most part. They could dine with other couples without outlandish comments escaping her mouth. She was easier to be in a relationship with, although Christopher would be the first to admit that she didn't seem as happy. Her light had dimmed.

"You're all I ever wanted," he said again. "Did I ever tell you that?" In the silence that followed he could hear the clock on the mantel ticking rhythmically, steadily. "Probably not," he replied to his own question. Expressing emotion was not his forte. It was what he resented most about the drama guy, Paige's former boyfriend, and about her last boyfriend. An actor and a musician, how was he supposed to compete with that?

The day he found out about Gabriel, from Kim, Paige's friend and former dorm mate, he got so drunk that he threw a quartz bookend (that used to hold Paige's poetry books) through the bay window, the place she used to sit with her coffee and watch the birds and squirrels. He didn't realize until he saw blood on a windowpane that he'd hit a small bird with the stone in the process of destroying Paige's favorite nook.

Even as he carried the dead sparrow into the woods, he had to fight the urge to call her and scream, "What the fuck are you thinking? A fucking house painter?" But Gabriel was more than a house painter; he was a pianist and that was the part, he assumed, that attracted Paige. She would have described him as a man with the soul of a poet if he gave her the opportunity, but he didn't. Christopher never spoke to her again, not even after he found out about the cancer. He never allowed himself the chance to tell her how important she was to him or how much pain he was in due to her suffering because he knew if he called her, she'd want to tell him about her new lover, and he'd have to carry her words around for the rest of his life. Retrospectively, he wished he had told her that she was the love of his life. Even if he wasn't hers.

It was at the funeral that he first learned of the age difference between Paige and Gabriel, but it wasn't his age that bothered him as much as his build. Like the drama guy, Gabriel was tall and slender, not stocky like himself. And with his dark hair and eyes, he struck Christopher as almost a male version of Paige. It was easy to picture them walking side by side, and when his defenses were not in place, his imagination gave him glimpses of them making love, his latest means of self-torture. At the funeral he heard Abigail's comment that Gabriel claimed to be a psychic. Leave it to Paige, he thought, to finally give her heart away to a clown from a freak show. To Christopher, that's all Gabriel was and all he would ever be, even if he could play the piano. He replayed that tape in his brain relentlessly and every time he re-lived the resentment that came with it because Paige was *his* wife, not some freak's who she'd met at the very end of her life, some random guy who never understood her or tried to give her a good life, like he had. If only she'd appreciated it, everything would have been different.

The clock ticking in the silent room caught his attention. It was nearly noon and still he hadn't decided on the right place to scatter the ashes. Today was their wedding anniversary, which was the reason he chose this date. His eyes scanned the empty bookshelves that he'd never restocked and the wood floor that could be seen properly without the wildly colorful Moroccan rug Paige had chosen to cover it. Now the room was understated, like the living room of the house he grew up in. It read like a study in neutrals, the walls ivory and the furniture a muted gray. In his gray J. Crew shirt, Christopher blended right into it, as if he were part of the room.

The garden, he suddenly thought, and got to his feet. The garden still whispered Paige's name every time he walked past it. Although Christopher had ignored them, the perennials she planted had come back for the second summer that she was not here to care for them. It was unfair that they were still here, and Paige was not. Even though he had purposefully not watered them, they'd survived.

If he put the ashes in the garden, he could visit them whenever he wanted. It crossed his mind that he could bury the vial near the perennials with a stone on top of it so he would know where it was whenever he wanted to dig it up. But he was only angry, not cruel. He could never do that to a piece of Paige—confine her in the earth under a rock.

He stepped out the front door into the blinding sunlight, the vial of ashes in hand, and immediately noticed a small plant growing next to the front steps. Every spring, during the years they lived together, Paige had planted seeds to grow giant sunflowers, and every August the garden had burst into a field of bright yellow faces. The enormous stalks would sway in the wind in a festive manner, like they were dancing. Paige always made a special meal and insisted that they eat outside, in view of the sunflowers.

The season before, when Paige was living with Gabriel, was Christopher's first summer without them. They were annuals that needed to be replanted every year. When August came around and no golden giants had taken over the garden, it felt like they'd packed up and moved away, too.

But now, inexplicably, one was growing at his feet. From the steps he examined the plant. It was only about eighteen inches high, but undoubtedly it was a sunflower. It struck him as odd that it would reseed after two years, and so close to the front steps, almost as if it were trying to get his attention. It seemed poignant because he'd ordered two bouquets of giant sunflowers for Paige's funeral. It was the best gesture he could think of to show her how he still felt about her.

Every morning Christopher had trudged down his front steps and every evening he'd trudged back up them without noticing the sunflower that was now beckoning to him. He couldn't help but wonder if it was because the ashes were in his hand.

Just beyond it there was a white peony blossom that was still as tight as a golf ball but nonetheless reaching toward the sun, with purple salvia gathered at its feet. The stark contrast of color reminded him of something his wife had once said to him. *Gardening is like painting, but with flowers.* "No, it isn't," he'd argued at the time. "Why do you always try to turn things into something more than what they are?"

"So, what if I find beauty in places you don't?" she'd countered.

His words had hurt her feelings. His heart ached to think of it. He blinked back tears and noticed that the colors from the flowers ran together. Like paint. He emptied the ashes into a circle around the infant sunflower, all the while wishing that somehow Paige could come back beyond all odds like the sunflower had, so that he could tell her he now understood what she meant. But Christopher knew better than to believe in miracles or magic. His reality, the one he had created, was steadfast and predictable. The constant beat of a drum, not the excited shrill of a flute.

He made it all the way into the house before he walked back outside to take one more look at the diminutive plant that he knew would someday be as tall as him. The ashes were too vulnerable lying there in the open. He got down on his knees and gathered some old wood chips, remnants of the mulch Paige spread two years prior, and used them to cover the ashes. That way he didn't have to worry that the wind might pick up and carry them away.

August 1, 2009: I called Chris today because I've been thinking about the mean things I said as our marriage was crumbling. With some distance, I can now see how the problem began. When we started dating, I was trying to be the person my parents expected me to be. I felt like my life was predestined and I had little free will. I fell into a robotic mode and signed up for journalism and business classes (instead of creative writing and art) to please my family even though I was bored out of my skull. Chris was on the same track. He was well-matched with the person I was trying to be, not the person I was. And here's the most important thing that I realized: that was my fault, not his.

Weirdly, my voice is still on Chris' answering machine. I left a long, rambling, nonsensical message, but I did say "I'm sorry," and I guess that was the point. I might never get to say this directly to Chris because he won't return my call, but I'd like to send a few of those thoughts out into the Universe, anyway.

So, here they are. I love you, Chris, and always will as a once in a lifetime friend. I wish only good things for you. Peace, joy and contentment. But even more, sweet, exhilarating, make-your-spine-tingle and your-heart-pound freedom. Just push the glass off, Chris, and step out from underneath it. Who gives a shit if it breaks??? You don't need that kind of security, anyway. It's an illusion.

Oh, and there's one more thing I would manifest for you if it were in my hands. Love and enough humility to recognize it when it walks in your front door.

August 3, 2009: Dream Journal Entry, 3:10 a.m.

I've just awakened from a lucid dream. I was flying on the back of an enormous eagle, high above a raging river, and I wasn't scared of falling. There were mountains all around and below me sparkling water and small pebbles on the shore. Then I was on the shore, the eagle was gone, and I was alone in this place of complete tranquility. It is the most peace I have ever felt, but even in my serenity I missed Gabriel. I woke up lonely and scared.

He's asleep beside me, but I'm not convinced we haven't been separated. I kiss his back until he rolls over to face me, eyes half open. "What's wrong?" he asks.

"*I miss you,*" I sob.

He pulls me against him, and I am safe in his arms, but I know I won't sleep. I've carried his absence from the dream. It feels like some invisible barrier has come between us and I can't reach him. Is it premonitory? I can't help but feel that it is.

"*I'm not going anywhere, Paige,*" he says. But what if it's me that's leaving? What if there's a massive eagle waiting to fly me away? The fear sits like a boulder on my chest, preventing me from breathing properly. Until the sun rises, I can do nothing but lay here and try to get oxygen into my lungs.

August 4, 2009: I've made myself a promise to never again think of that dream or its implications. It was only a fantastical tale my imagination crafted while I slept. But the eagle, the eagle was so real. I still remember its eyes. Yellow, mystical.

August 5, 2009: To me spiritual growth is about breaking through the illusions I have accepted as truth, opening my mind and heart to understandings that might not have occurred to me based on my childhood teachings. Consider this concept, for example: the world is a mirror. What I see in you, whether I like it or not, is myself. When I get annoyed that Abby is controlling, I don't like it because it shows me that I'm too controlling. When Joe angers me for not speaking out, it's because there have been many times when I should have spoken but didn't. The flip side of the coin feels better. When Gabriel makes me laugh, it's my own sense of humor that recognizes it. Arica's strength is my own shining back at me, every bit as much as Ben's sensitivity mirrors mine.

Great fodder for thought, right? Here's another one: My friend Julia was raised Catholic like me but has strayed from her childhood beliefs. Julia says she's suspicious of religion but prays and meditates every day. She believes strongly in a benevolent life force. When I asked her why she's so sure our Creator is entirely benevolent, check out what she said: "Because I've never seen an ugly flower."

August 7, 2009: Last night I met my college roommates, Kim and Julia, at a bar in Quincy. Kim was already drunk when I arrived, and because she is going through a divorce, she was venting angrily and loudly.

"You don't really hate him. You just think you do," I say to her about Baker, her soon to be ex-husband, the same guy who proposed to her on bended knee in front of all of us and is now fighting her for custody of their two daughters.

I learned something from my own divorce from the person who used to be my best friend, the guy who loved me so much he kept his mouth shut when everyone was criticizing me behind my back, even though he agreed with them. It's this: Being hurt by someone you love is hard to fess up to. So, the hurt wraps itself in the guise of anger, and anger disguises its ugly face as hate.

Kim's shoulders slump over the bar and it is a frightful image, like she's melting into her empty martini glass. My tongue has a mind of its own and spits out, "Why don't you get together with Christopher sometime? You've always gotten along."

It's an odd thing, no doubt, trying to hook up one of your closest friends with your ex-husband, but I'm aware of Kim's attraction to Chris and always have been. Whenever they're in the same room, I swear I can smell the pheromones.

"I need another drink," she says.

I glance down at the Tanqueray and tonic in my hand and realize I have no use for it. I used to drink and get stoned a lot. I thought it was part of the "living like a rock star" lifestyle I wanted. But I think I've successfully pierced that illusion. Now I know there's no freedom in self destruction, not even for rock stars.

Chapter Ten

Kim & Julia, *the Atheist & the New Ager*

We are all in the gutter, but some of us are looking at the stars.
-Oscar Wilde

"How handsome is Paige's little brother?" Kim gushed from the driver's seat. Her hair was recently cut and colored even blonder than usual. It was pulled back in a tiny ponytail for the adventure awaiting them. A lit cigarette dangled from her lips.

"Oh my God, I know," Julia crooned. "I've been trying to figure out how old he is."

"Old enough."

"Seriously, though. He's in his thirties, right?"

"Yeah, definitely," Kim agreed. "He was in high school when we met him. What's his name?"

"Joe." Julia rolled the window down to let out the smoke and glanced down at her other hand that was holding the vial of ashes. "We shouldn't be doing this."

"What?"

"Lusting over Paige's baby brother with her dead body in the car."

A scratchy laugh crept out of Kim's throat. "Oh please, if he wasn't her brother she'd have been lusting after him, too. Did you see his eyes? I mean Jesus fucking Christ."

Julia drew in a sharp breath as if the comment had physically hurt her and glanced at the ashes again. "Sorry, Paige," she whispered.

"She can't hear you," Kim said and steered her Solstice, with the convertible top down, into a Burger King parking lot. They had already covered this topic a dozen times. Julia was 100%

convinced that Paige's spirit would accompany them on their mission to scatter her ashes. Kim was 100% sure she was wrong.

"Are you feeling God yet?" Kim teased.

"I will once we get there," Julia replied. "Being in nature makes me feel connected."

"Look in the bag on the floor," Kim suggested. "It'll get you there quicker."

Julia opened the paper bag and discovered countless nips of Smirnoff blue label and Kahlua. "Why didn't you buy big bottles?" she asked. "It would have been cheaper."

"Sentimental reasons," Kim replied. Given her recent financial situation, she probably should have bought quart bottles, but she didn't voice that to her friend. "Two milks and two cups with ice," she said into the microphone. It had been nearly twenty years since they'd blown off their responsibilities to drink Burger King White Russians.

They were on route to the Kancamagus Highway in New Hampshire, where together with Paige and other friends they used to wander into the surrounding woods to camp. Now they had to enter the location into the GPS. It was one of their favorite places on Earth. How was it possible to forget how to get there?

The teenage boy at the window handed them their order, and Kim pulled over to mix the drinks—two shots of both vodka and Kahlua followed by a splash of milk.

"You know, we could get arrested for drinking and driving," Julia noted.

"And wouldn't Paige love that?" Kim replied. "Remember the time we got pulled over in Hanson after we left JJ's pub? I thought for sure we were getting arrested that night. The cops made Paige walk a straight line, and you puked out the window right in the middle of it."

Julia groaned. "Ohhh fuck, yes. It was St. Patrick's Day—we were drinking green beer. There was green vomit all over the side of Mr. Delaney's white car."

"Paige told the cops that you were having an allergic reaction. They followed us home and watched us walk in the house. The next day we were all shitting green, and Paige joked that it was karma for lying to the cops."

Julia laughed so abruptly that White Russian shot out her nostrils. "I completely forgot about that!" she snorted. "The boys we'd been drinking with at JJ's came to Paige's bedroom window 'cause we were supposed to meet them and didn't show."

"We climbed out her window into like two feet of snow and were soaked when we got to their van. They had a beer ball in the back with a tap on it."

Julia was still giggling about the green shit. The beer ball comment made her laugh harder. "Paige was sitting on that guy's lap while he was driving—what was his name? He visited us at school a couple of times."

"He came to New Hampshire, too," Kim answered, "I can't remember his name, but beer balls? I mean, seriously, when's the last time you drank from a beer ball?"

"Probably that night. We should do it again sometime," Julia suggested.

"Scratch that onto the bucket list—*drink from a beer ball while riding in the back of a van*. What would we tell the cops this time without Paige here to bullshit our way out of it?"

Julia sighed. "That we're taking our friend's ashes to the Kancamagus Highway, and we had to drink White Russians to do it because that was our tradition?"

"That sounds good. You do the talking. Make sure you show them the ashes."

"Before we get shitfaced," Julia threw out, "I want to say one thing and get it out of the way—but wait, do people still say *shitfaced*?"

"Who the fuck knows? I don't even know if they make beer balls anymore."

"Well, what I wanted to say is that I'm going to ask out Joe."

"I've got a three-drink maximum until we get to the hotel, so we don't die on the highway," Kim asserted. "Wait—" She turned to Julia. "Who's Joe?"

Julia was staring at herself in the rear-view mirror. "Paige's brother! We just talked about him, like five minutes ago. He was checking us out at the funeral."

"I wish I had a dollar for every time I caught you looking at your teeth in a mirror," Kim said. The space between Julia's two front teeth was so wide that she could fit the tip of her tongue in it. "He was, though, checking us out?"

"I'm thinking about getting braces. Yeah, didn't you notice him watching us when we walked past him in the parking lot?"

"I don't even remember seeing Joe in the parking lot, but I do remember him sitting in front of us during the service. Broad shoulders, great hair."

"Well, *yeah*. You know what I like?" Julia asked. "The beauty mark on his face."

"I don't think men call them beauty marks," Kim said.

"Whatever it is—I like it."

"I didn't look away from his eyes long enough to notice," Kim admitted. "But tell you what, if you call him today, you get the first shot. If you don't then I can, fair?" Kim wasn't really interested in Joe. She was just trying to light a fire under Julia.

Julia narrowed her eyes. She hated bargaining with Kim. Academically, she was the brighter one, but when it came to street sense, Kim's IQ was significantly higher.

"Think of all the White Russians you'll have drunk by tonight," Kim pointed out. "You can tell him about Paige's ashes. If you're ever going to call him, today's the day."

"You're right," Julia agreed and drained her cup.

The Kancamagus Highway in New Hampshire starts in North Conway and twists through the White Mountains to Lincoln. The Swift River runs alongside it and provides rocky swimming holes for those not dissuaded by the cold-water run-off.

It was the first week in June, a perfect time for a visit to the lush granite state. Trees along the river and on the mountains in the distance were bursting with fresh green life. Even the river moved in celebratory fashion. Because kids weren't out of school for the summer, the area wasn't crawling with tourists like it would be in a few weeks.

Kim and Julia were quiet as the Solstice maneuvered the curvy stretch of road. They had already left their bags at the small inn where they would be spending the night and were moments away from Sabbaday Falls, where they would release Paige's ashes.

"Crazy on You" by Heart came on the radio, and Kim turned her head to meet Julia's eyes. Silently, they shared a memory.

The song had been the impetus for their friendship with Paige. During freshman year of college, she'd written an essay about it for their English Composition class. The professor, a stern tiny woman from Wales, had assigned an interpretation of a twentieth-century poem. Most students talked about the poetry of Anne Sexton, Robert Frost or Emily Dickinson; poets suggested by the professor. Paige was the only student who chose to write about a lyricist. She was in front of the class explaining that to her the song spoke of the healing power of an intimate relationship when the professor began preparing to leave the classroom. She was snapping the strap of her fur trapper hat under her chin when Paige quietly stated, "I'm sorry, but I wasn't finished."

"I don't allow the discussion of pornography in my classroom, Ms. Delaney," the professor said. "I suggest you choose a real poem and draft an interpretation over the weekend. If I deem it appropriate, I'll allow an opportunity to present it to your peers."

Paige's face turned as red as her hair. "Not all sex is pornographic," she argued.

"Wicked girl!" the professor exclaimed in perfect Queen's English which, paired with the trapper hat strapped to her head, prompted a roar of laughter from Kim and Julia.

Paige marched out of the classroom and into the Dean of Academic Affairs' office, where she complained that her teacher was treating her unjustly based on her own narrow view of sexuality. The dean carried the torch for Paige, which kept her from failing the assignment, though she had to struggle against the professor for the rest of the semester. It was worth it, though. She made two new friends that day, Kim and Julia, who were rooming together already and looking for a third roommate. Paige proved to be a perfect fit.

Kim pulled the car over. It was only a short trek from where they were parked through the woods to Sabbaday Falls. They listened wordlessly as Anne Wilson concluded the song. It seemed a strange coincidence that the song was playing right as they pulled into the place where they were planning to scatter Paige's ashes. The haunting lyrics made the hair rise on Kim's arms. They were a reminder of Paige's obvious absence from a trip she never would have missed.

"Let's go," she said, and slapped on her Wayfarer wannabes before stepping out of the car into the warm New Hampshire sun.

"Does the song make you feel like Paige is here?" Julia quietly asked.

"No," her friend replied. "It makes me feel like she's not."

They were silent after that until Kim started grumbling about Julia walking too fast. Her new Pumas she bought for the trip were covered in mud and her sweatshirt was soaked with water from tree branches. Small twigs and leaves were tangled in her hair. Finally, she came to a complete stop and bent over with her hands on her knees.

"You should toss your cigarettes into the falls," Julia advised. She was annoyed that her clothes smelled like smoke from the car trip. The fact that they had to stop for Kim to catch her breath, even though the waterfalls were only a short walk, was worrisome.

"Tell me again why we're doing this," Kim griped, and willed her feet to move again.

"Because Paige thought it was the most beautiful place on Earth," Julia replied. She handed the flask to Kim as they stepped onto the footbridge that looked down over the first two waterfalls.

"Oh God, she was right," Kim surrendered. "I forgot that. How could I forget that?" From the footbridge they could see the two highest waterfalls crashing below them. The roar of the moving water caused them to raise their voices to be heard.

"The last time we came here we were tripping on microdot!" Julia shouted.

Kim jerked her head to see if anyone else heard the comment. There were only a few people in sight. "I'd lose my job if anyone found out about that," she snapped.

"I doubt any of those people are from your office," Julia pointed out. "Besides, the people we work with probably tripped on acid when they were kids, too. Everyone used to do it, but now no one remembers."

"I remember," Kim replied. "It's not something I want everyone to know, but I remember. Our friends back then were different. We could stay stupid shit or fall down drunk, and it wouldn't matter. They'd still be there the next day. The relationships I have now would never survive a trek through the woods tripping on microdot—"

"It was during peak foliage," Julia interrupted with a grin. "We were all flipped out about the colors of the leaves. What you said before, though, about adult relationships, that's really sad and true. I wish we still had a group of friends like we had back then."

Kim shot more liquid into her mouth from the flask and then into Julia's before she threw out a Paige quote, "What would the world look like if the sky was orange?"

"Would it bleed into the mountains and turn them red the way the blue sky turns them purple?" Julia replied, playing along, and then added, "Hey, remember the moose?" The moose—that appeared out of nowhere—had scared Kim so much that she slid off the rocks and into the falls. A couple of hikers had jumped in to drag her out.

"Who knew they were so big?" Kim spewed. "I thought it was a fuckin' dinosaur."

"Of course, that had nothing to do with the acid," Julia joked.

"My bones were stronger then," Kim mused. "I'd never survive that fall now."

"Yeah, we should stay off the rocks. They're wet and I bet they're slippery."

"Trust me, they're slippery. Let's sit," Kim suggested, "and drop the ashes from the bridge."

Julia sat beside her friend on the footbridge and allowed her legs to dangle over the side. The last time she was here, all three friends sat together, never guessing that one of them would be gone before the next visit. What would happen in the next twenty years? Would both she and Kim still be around? "Another thing," she said, "we should come here more than once every two decades. This place makes me feel cleaner, like the air is purging me from the inside out."

"Ah, to be clean again," Kim mused. "Hey, remember Paige started that debate with the hiker guys that pulled me out of the water?" Julia shook her head. "One of them was a Physics major, I think," Kim continued. "The argument was about Einstein's theory that energy can't be destroyed. I guess he said that when we die, the energy has to go somewhere—and that was Paige's point. That was her scientific proof of life after death. She was into some way-out shit, wasn't she?"

"Paige *was* way out—that's what made her Paige." Julia replied. "Pop the top off the vial, and we'll hold it together. Anything you want to say to her first?"

Kim lit a cigarette and drew the smoke into her body with vacuum cleaner strength, and then heaved it out of her lungs. "Just this. You were the life of this party, Paige. You were the trip. Even more than the microdot, you were the trip."

August 8, 2009: "Do you think I'm a wicked girl?" I ask Gabriel. We've been wrestling and otherwise playing so he takes the comment lightly. His tongue is on my forearm trying to trace all the letters on my tattoo in one movement.

He laughs and breaks the sweep. "That's why I love you," he answers. He's curled behind me on the couch. When I don't laugh, he moves so he can see my face, his belly against my hip.

"Someone said that to me once," I reveal, "that I'm wicked. It just popped into my head. Probably because you were French kissing my tattoo."

Gabriel sighs. He knows how I internalize people's comments. "Someone who didn't know you must have said that," he asserts.

"I don't remember who said it, only the hate I felt directed at me."

"No one could hate you. You're the most innocent person I know," he says.

I can't imagine why he would think that. I've never been well-behaved and lots of people probably hate me, my ex-husband, for example. "You're the one who's innocent," I reply because he is the gentlest person I've ever met. Just then the light in the living room blinks off and then on again. It happens a lot, though only when Gabriel is home. I like to tease him that it's his magnetism affecting the electricity, but this time when the light blinks, his body stiffens in my arms.

"I'm not innocent," he says gruffly and pushes his body over mine onto the floor. "There are people in this world entitled to hate me." His back is to me as he slides on his shirt, covering his tattoos.

On one arm musical notes float from the tree of life as if the tree is breathing them. A small black snake makes its way up the trunk, though it is closer to the roots than the branches, and at the top an eagle is perched. They represent wisdom and vision respectively. On the other forearm a yogi sits cross-legged with hands wide open. Golden light radiates from his palms, head and shoulders, not from above, though that is where his eyes are turned.

"No one is entitled to hate anyone," I say, but he holds his silence and I'm left to wonder what could have put such a thought in his head.

Chapter Eleven

Kim & Julia; Joe Jr. & Bowman, *the Atheist, the New Ager, the Dissident & the Baptist*

Welcome to planet Earth. There is nothing that you cannot be, or do, or have. You are a magnificent creator.
—Abraham

"Why do you think Paige left Chris?" Kim asked.

Both she and Julia were prostrate on the hotel beds, drunk, and deep in conversation. Their quick jaunt to New Hampshire had proven to be unexpectedly exhausting. It hadn't occurred to them that drinking while tending to Paige's ashes was mixing a depressant into an already emotionally difficult task. They'd been using alcohol for so long that it rarely occurred to them not to. For Kim it had caused damage, sucked the love right out of her marriage. It accomplished what alcohol often does when it's overused. Twisted the relationship into something ugly.

"Because she wasn't in love with him," Julia replied. "Why?"

"I called him the other day," Kim slurred. "He sounded like shit. Like a flat tire, you know, or a deflated balloon? He's not like he used to be."

Julia belched as she sat up and pulled her legs into lotus pose. With the vodka in her bloodstream, she wasn't able to keep her balance. Luckily, the wall kept her from landing headfirst on the floor. "You called Christopher? Why would you call Christopher?" she asked.

Kim shrugged. "Because I was thinking about him. And we used to be friends."

"Yeah, but even back then, you liked him."

"So what? That was twenty years ago, before any of us knew Paige," Kim argued.

"Baker would drop dead of an aneurysm if you dated Christopher."

"I never said anything about dating him," Kim asserted, but grinned at the thought of it. "Besides, like I'd give a shit if Baker dropped dead." The words pushed a sigh from her lips. "If he wasn't such a dick, I wouldn't hate him so much."

"Paige was never right for Christopher—she'd be the first one to admit that," Julia replied. "And he did like you once before we met her. She wouldn't care, you know—"

Kim groaned, cutting off Julia's comments. It was too much to think about, her old college crush and how his attention was diverted from her when Paige emerged on the scene like a leading lady in a Broadway play. It was still painful to think about. Baker had been her second choice. She'd loved him once, but he was never the one who made her adrenal rush by merely speaking into a telephone receiver. She'd since given up on that kind of love, resigned her life to being driven by some sort of internal autopilot, not by passion or desire. Her heart felt as empty as oil drum in the basement of her home.

"Want to call Joe now?" Julia asked, tugging on the tiny Buddha pendant attached to her neck that she'd bought recently at a craft fair in Hyannis. She'd be astonished to know that it was made by Paige's friend Yara. Like a page out of Paige's own playbook, the transaction supported her spiderweb theory. Some of the people in her life were connected in ways that they never suspected.

"Hm?" Kim responded. "Oh yeah, Paige's brother. You know I didn't mean what I said about Baker, right? I don't really want him to die. I just want him to go away."

"I know," Julia acknowledged, "but I don't think he's going anywhere."

"That's what I thought about Paige."

Paige had been one of her best friends, but she'd also been her scapegoat. Everything seemed to magically drop onto her lap, like Christopher. From her viewpoint, life seemed effortless for Paige, and she'd resented her for that. She had cursed her good fortune and then, as if to illuminate her own silent betrayal, her friend had been diagnosed with a terminal illness.

"You might try to fix it then," Julia suggested.

Kim looked up from her broken fingernails. She'd spent fifty dollars for that manicure three days prior and now it was ruined by the hike through the woods. The money could have been spent more wisely—like on food, she thought now that Baker had decided to stop paying child support with no notice or explanation.

"Fix what?" she asked acerbically. She was thinking about how she hadn't fixed things with Paige. She'd never come clean about her feelings for Christopher, or that he'd once been interested in her. It was a well-preserved secret, like a love letter locked in a time capsule.

"Your relationship with Baker," Julia responded, and Kim snorted anger through her nose. "I'm not saying you should reunite. I just think you should make peace."

"I'm what, supposed to forget that Baker's screwing someone else?"

"Who cares who Baker's screwing?" Julia said. She had her cell phone in her hand to call Joe. "What town does he live in?" she muttered, more to herself than to Kim.

"I don't know—wherever the whore lives."

"I meant Joe. . . Delaney."

"Who knows? There could be dozens of Joe Delaneys in Massachusetts. Try Abigail."

Julia scrolled down to the number already programmed in her phone. During Paige's illness she'd called Abigail periodically to check in. This time it only took a quick conversation to get the information she needed. She jotted the number down on a pamphlet lying on the end table. "I'm doing this right now before I lose the nerve," she said, and quickly pushed the numbers on her cell phone. The telephone was already ringing when she panicked and threw it to Kim.

"I knew you wouldn't do it," Kim said with satisfaction. She was resenting Julia's careless remarks about Baker and was about to give her a dig about the fact that she'd never been married and could not possibly understand what it feels like to go through a divorce, when a male voice answered the phone. "Is this Joe?" she asked.

"This is Bowman," the voice answered.

"Oh. Are you Joe's—roommate?"

Four hundred miles away Bowman smiled, sitting on the sofa beside Joe watching *Ghost Whisperer*, his favorite show. "Um, sure," he said. "May I ask who's calling?"

"This is Kim. I'm Paige's friend."

"Oh. He's right here." *Paige's friend Kim,* he whispered, and handed the phone to Joe.

From Joe's side of the conversation, it was apparent to Bowman that they were talking about Paige's illness and death. Joe's shoulders were slumped forward, and his spine was rounded as if the subject was adding weight to his back. But then he suddenly sat up straight, his clear gray irises looking straight into Bowman's.

"What?" Bowman asked softly.

"Hold on a sec," Joe muttered and covered the receiver with his hand. His mouth was posed in a smirk, as if he was about to burst out laughing. "It's Paige's college friends. They're drunk, and they want us to go out with them."

"No!" Bowman roared.

"Shhh, yes," Joe answered, and let the laughter escape before his head fell back on the sofa. He was always telling Bowman not to answer the phone if he didn't recognize the number. The telephone held the potential for drama, which Bowman loved, and tonight he'd hit the jackpot.

"Oh my God!" Bowman exclaimed. He found the remote control and hit mute. "This is even better than *Ghost Whisperer*. Maybe you should tell them my favorite line."

"What? No, I'm not saying that," Joe argued. "I don't even like when you say it." His favorite line was: *If he's prettier than you, chances are he's gay.* There was nothing Joe hated more than being called "pretty," which happened with some frequency.

Bowman laughed, completely entertained. "But they're not in town, are they?"

Joe shrugged his shoulders. "Where are you?" he breathed into the phone.

"You sound sexy," Bowman reprimanded. "Tone it down!"

"They're in New Hampshire," Joe stated calmly.

"New Hampshire? That's like a zillion miles away. Tell them not tonight," he tittered.

"Do you know that we live in D.C.?" Joe asked Kim. He shook his head to convey to Bowman that they did not know and pointed his index finger and thumb toward his temple like he was shooting himself in the head. "Uh. . . once in a while," he stammered, his elusive response to her question regarding how often he visited Massachusetts. *Should I tell them the truth?* he mouthed.

"No," Bowman sighed.

"Hang on. I'm sorry," Joe said so that he could consult with Bowman privately.

"They probably saw you at the funeral and fell in love with you, just like I did the first time I saw you. Remember that day?"

"Of course," Joe said patiently.

"It took me two days, four hours and thirteen minutes to get the nerve to call you. If you said you were already with someone, it would have killed me."

Joe grinned at him. "What do you want me to say, Bow?"

"Tell them thanks for calling, and that we'll look them up if we're ever in town."

"Kim?" Joe said and quoted him word for word.

"I told you he noticed us," Julia said once Kim hung up and conveyed the message.

Kim tossed the phone back to Julia then went to the bathroom to relieve her bladder for at least the twentieth time that day. What were the odds, she wondered, of landing a guy like Joe Delaney? Not very high she decided but looking like a Greek God wasn't high on her priority list, anyway. All she wanted was someone who would be nice.

She stepped out of the bathroom and revealed her thoughts to Julia, who was now under the covers, and hit the light switch before she got in her own bed.

Julia heard her out and then offered, "The other night I watched a movie called *The Secret*, which is supposedly a formula for how lots of people got to be successful. From what I gathered, the big secret is that if you focus on something it comes into your life, whether you want it or not. The idea is that our thoughts are creating our reality. That's what the Buddha said, too. Since then, I've been trying to focus only on good things."

Kim was slowly being drawn into the New Age movement through the concepts Julia discovered and put a fascinating spin on. She could relate to the self-help information, even if she couldn't swallow the idea that there was a Higher Power somewhere in the Universe who gave a shit about her. It suddenly dawned on her that Julia was talking about her. "Are you saying I focus on bad things?"

There was silence while Julia thought it over. "I'm saying that if you keep thinking about Baker's faults, you're only going to magnify them and keep bringing them into your life, either through him or someone else."

"Why would that happen? He doesn't even know what I'm thinking."

"That doesn't matter. Thoughts have a vibration like objects do. Remember in Physics the professor taught us that nothing is solid, even human bodies? It's an illusion. We're a bunch of atoms with space in between them, but they're moving quickly like a swarm of bees, which makes us appear solid. That's the vibration."

"Okay," Kim threw out, her voice hoarse from smoking too much and dripping with sarcasm, "so, our bodies are like bugs flying super-fast, and so are our thoughts?"

"Maybe the bees aren't a good analogy. The atoms are moving. This bed for instance. The slower something moves — or vibrates — the more solid the object appears. Our thoughts vibrate at a faster rate because they aren't dense like a body, or a bed."

Kim sighed. "I forget everything about Physics class except Chris sitting in front of me in his baseball uniform."

Julia smiled at her. "It's kind of cute that you still have a crush on him. What I kept thinking when I was watching the movie is how guys always show up in clusters. No one's around for months until someone asks you out, and then the next day someone else does, then out of the blue a guy calls that you haven't heard from in years." "Feast or famine," Kim commented.

"Exactly. The same thing happens with money. I think it's because you're thinking about the fact that money is coming in that attracts more to come in. You *feel* rich so you are rich. When you vibrate the fact that you're broke, you get more of that."

"*More* brokeness?"

"Stop thinking that," Julia chastised, and Kim groaned. "Do you get it, though?"

"I don't know," Kim admitted. "Kind of."

"Maybe try imagining the kind of guy you'd like to have in your life."

"You mean someone like Christopher?" Kim asked.

"Maybe. Forget Baker. He's making his new life. You need to create yours."

The idea of creating her own life was a new concept. Kim always lived defensively, ducking the slivers of shit that had already been obliterated by the fan blades.

Her imagination began concocting the ideal mate—a nice guy who could be trusted. Someone who was soft-spoken and good with kids. Every characteristic brought her back to Chris. *What else do I want?* she asked herself. The list came sluggishly, slowed down by her alcohol infiltrated brain, but before she fell asleep, she'd gotten this far: a job that doesn't suck, a good relationship with her daughters, and a body that doesn't feel like it's falling apart. She glanced at the cigarette pack on the bedside table and recalled how easy it had been for Julia to trek through the woods. Tomorrow, she thought, tomorrow I'll think more about that. *Or not think about it,* she corrected.

Having only positive thoughts might be hard. She decided to make a new list of things already in her life. There was Miranda, her oldest and most precocious daughter, who at nine years old had already read every one of the Harry Potter books, Kristen her six-year-old "baby" who had an infallible ability to make people feel good. And she had Julia, who knew absolutely everything about her, and loved her all the same.

"Hey, Julia," she said. "There's nothing wrong with your teeth, you know."

"You wouldn't think that if they were yours," her friend replied.

Julia had once told her that in high school she was chosen as a candidate for "best smile" in her senior class. Her feelings had been hurt because she believed she was the brunt of a joke. But it wasn't a joke at all, Kim only now realized. Her classmates had simply seen something in her that she couldn't see in herself. In her mind, the space between her teeth was the one thing that kept her from accepting herself the way she was.

"But that's just it—they're not mine, they're yours," Kim pointed out. "That space between your teeth is part of what makes you *you*. Do whatever you want, but I wouldn't change it. I think it's the one thing, you know, the unique thing about you that makes you beautiful."

August 10, 2009: Laugh lines are the opposite of scars, permanent keepsakes from all the good times we've had. But the scars are important, too. They add to our character and our beauty, like Gabriel's broken tooth. Isn't it fascinating how nothing's perfect, yet at the same time everything is?

August 12, 2009: I am in sav asana (corpse pose) on the deck watching fireflies dip and weave through the air when Gabriel comes looking for me. The scent of citronella wafts in the air between us. Candles are lined up like tiny soldiers on the railing to ward off mosquitoes and are doing a fine job of it. "Join me," I suggest.

"Doesn't look very comfortable," he replies.

The boards dig into my shoulder blades and tailbone. I'm thinner than I used to be, though I'm not sure why. "My ass is fatter than yours," I say anyway, and he laughs.

A minute or two later he's at the door with our mattress, grinning. It's enough to make me break my pose. Being the adult that I am, clearly, I should object, but maybe I haven't changed since I was ten and convinced the neighborhood kids to drag my little brother's mattress—spiderman comforter and all—into the backyard so we could jump on it. It was a memorable day doing gymnastics on Joey's bed until my mom returned from her shift at the hospital. To this day I can get nauseous just by remembering the "Paige!!! What have you done now???" look in her eyes.

But I can get away with it this time. I jump out of the way as Gabriel tosses the mattress onto the hard boards, and then curl up with him on it. "Want to sleep here tonight?" he asks. "We could use the mosquito netting from our bed."

"Yesss!" I exclaim. I am ten again, living out a fantasy. This small space we are occupying quickly becomes my entire world. The soft breeze touching down on my skin as gently as moth wings and making the candles blink, moonlight trickling like raindrops through the trees, and Gabriel's raspy laugh. All pieces of my heaven.

"Take off our clothes?" he throws out playfully.

"Subtle," I reply.

"I want to feel your skin," he claims.

I've heard this line before. It works every time. I love the feel of his skin, too, but there are houses close by, and it's only 10:30. "Get a blanket," I suggest.

"That would ruin it," he says and rolls on top of me. It's over. As if there was ever a battle. His shirt is off. I lift my arms and seconds later it is just skin against skin, the perfect wrapping for these bodies. I look around to assure myself that no one is watching. We are such shy creatures in magnificent packages.

August 13, 2009: Last week we took a ride over the Bourne Bridge to check out an Ashtanga yoga class, which totally kicked my ass. Honestly, I thought all I took from it was how attractive my boyfriend looks in yoga pants.

But once I'd recovered from the humiliation, I decided to give it another try. The class meets every morning and I've decided to attend three times per week. Gabriel can't always join me because he has houses to paint, but he's promised to participate on Fridays, which are slow days for him because families often take long weekends at their Cape Cod vacation homes and don't want workers around.

Instead of finding a job, I've fallen into the habit of helping Gabriel with his house painting and find it satisfying. We always pack a lunch and spread a blanket on the homeowners' lawn to share it. It's kind of like trying on someone else's life, but at the end of the day, it's our home that I want to return to. No architectural masterpiece could be more alluring to me than our little cottage by the sea.

After yoga today, I stuck around to meet people from class in the tearoom where everyone congregates. I made a new friend, Yara, who is my age, but has the spine of a six-year-old. She makes jewelry, and even though we just met, she promised to make me a tiny Buddha pendant like the one she wears.

Yara's boyfriend, Davi, is also in our class. He's as beautiful as her, with black curls, latte-colored skin and an infectious grin. It came out over tea that Davi heard Gabriel play piano at the Berklee Performance Center when Gabriel was a student there. Davi called him a "player" and laughed when I thought he meant with women. He raised his hand above his head while he searched for the English words. (Portuguese is his native tongue.) "A high level, you know? A player."

I mentioned it to Gabriel when I returned home. "That part of me died in a car accident four years ago," he snapped and laced his sneakers before running toward Sandy Beach. Through the window I saw him stop at the end of the driveway. He was bent over with his hands on his knees like he was trying to catch the breath that the conversation had knocked out of him.

August 15, 2009: Today I met Yara for lunch at the Common Ground Cafe in Hyannis, where she lives. The restaurant creates the illusion of being in a tree house. To enhance the experience, I ordered a peanut butter and banana sandwich drizzled with honey from the kids' menu.

Yara is Brazilian and she tells me that her name means "small butterfly," to which I reveal that mine means "young servant." She laughs and asks me why my parents named me that. I can't ask my father because it would confuse him. I wish it meant "small butterfly," although it is a fitting description of Yara.

Later I called Abby to ask her if she knows why our parents chose the name. "I named you after a doll I saw on television," she replied.

Abby was three when I was born. You know the pictures in magazines of the perfect toddler that looks strikingly like a cherub? That was Abby at three years old. Her hair was not yellow, but gold. Her eyes were round and crystal clear, the whiteness of her skin interrupted only by the perfect pink flush on her cheeks. Most of my baby pictures were taken with me on her lap, something I've always thought was unfair. There I am—untamed curls, bottom lip protruding, my arms pushing her away—and Abigail smiling sweetly at me all the while.

She named me. "Why?" I ask in the silence that follows her statement.

"Because I thought you were mine," she says. That explains so much.

Chapter Twelve

Yara & Davi, *the Buddhists*

When life becomes conscious and takes human—and even, in its lower stage, animal form—it should be entitled to be treated with sacredness. Life should not be held cheaply, for life is the Great Spirit in expression.
—*Silver Birch*

When Yara was a little girl, she played with all ten of her cousins, but Davi was her favorite. He lived in Brazil and visited every summer with his mother, Leilah. When Yara was six, Davi was almost eight and knew lots of important things, like how to climb trees and swing a baseball bat. He could catch fish with a net and frogs with his hands. Davi taught her how to play Queimada, and how to swear in Portuguese. He danced for the adults, which always drew enthusiastic applause. Sometimes he'd claim to be an expert at Capoiera, a Brazilian hybrid of martial arts and dance, and demonstrate the movements. The adults advised her not to believe him, but he had big brown eyes and always smelled like something her mother had baked, laden with nutmeg or cinnamon. Yara believed everything the boy said.

During the school year while Davi was in Brazil, Yara played with other children, mostly her brothers, sisters, and cousins who also lived in Hyannis on Cape Cod, but once June returned—and with it Davi—no one else existed. The other children teased and prodded, laughed and scolded, but none of it kept them apart, until their tearful parting at the end of August. Yara refused to look at the calendar for the entire summer. She had no desire to see their time together melting like the popsicles they shared by breaking them in two. Only on the day he departed would she return to it, marking the days with an X until their next reunion.

They had a secret club and were its only members. There was only one rule—whatever one did, the other had to follow. If Davi jumped off the dock at the pond, Yara jumped, even though her swimming skills weren't as strong as his. Once she had to be dragged out of the pond by the lifeguard. Their mothers were furious and didn't allow them to play together for three days.

Usually, the club rules did not play out as dramatically. They would dance and sing and imitate each other or try out new foods and force the other to do the same. Sometimes Davi would play a trick on his mother, like slipping salt in the sugar jar. Then Yara would have to find a way to fool her own mother, and that was the scariest part of being in the club. She wasn't a born rascal like Davi. As a child, he was an elfin character, slight of build and full of pranks. Where he was playful and mischievous, Yara was quiet and cautious.

One steaming August afternoon they were catching bugs in the backyard and holding them captive in coffee cans. Davi became fascinated with a ladybug, but when it urinated on his hand, he smashed it with a rock. Yara watched with a sick feeling in her belly. "Why'd you kill it?" she asked.

"It's only a bug," he claimed with a shrug. "It doesn't matter." Something inside her rebelled against what he said and what he had done, so recklessly it seemed to her. He spotted a silver insect crawling out of the dirt, then he picked up a rusty nail and handed it to Yara. "Kill it," he instructed. "You have to. I did."

She used the nail to flip the insect onto its back. Its legs were moving furiously trying to turn itself over until she pushed the point of the nail through the bug. The sickness in her stomach overwhelmed her when the legs stopped moving. She ran to her bedroom and locked the door to keep Davi out. Yara was angry at him for making her kill the bug, but also at herself, for listening to him instead of her own conscience. For the first time in her life, she had intentionally caused something to stop being alive and it made her heart ache.

"You need to make peace," her mother said through the door. The aroma of spices cooking spilled into her room when her mother insisted she allow Davi to enter. He didn't talk about it, only knelt beside the bed and sang her favorite Portuguese lullaby.

"I don't want to play that game anymore," Yara told him. Their secret club ended at that moment and never resurfaced. She brushed off her tears and followed him to the table where they ate spare ribs her mother had prepared for dinner, without question.

Later she would question it, though, the killing of any living creature for any purpose, and became a vegetarian at a young age, and later, a Buddhist. Like other Buddhists, Hindus, Jains and even the earliest Christians—the ones who knew Jesus— Yara was a vegetarian not for the health benefits, but because she believed that all life was sacred. The killing of the bug was the impetus for her life of noninjury to all sentient beings. It had defined her spiritual path.

Although they stayed in contact through their teenage years, Davi did not travel to the United States every summer like he did as a child. He worked full time during the summer to help his mother pay the bills. It was not until Yara was seventeen, and Davi was making plans to study Biology at a Boston university, that her mother revealed a family secret. Davi and his mother were not related to them. Leilah had been adopted after being abandoned as a toddler in the streets of Rio de Janeiro.

"Why tell me now?" Yara asked, "After all these years of keeping it a secret?"

"Why do you think?" her mother said. "Because of your relationship with Davi. It's now more important to say it than to not say it."

The flow of air in Yara's body stopped. But her blood was coursing like turbulent river water through her hyper-stimulated brain. *Davi was not her cousin.* "What is he to

136

me then?" she asked. If not her family, then what was the deep connection she felt?

"One day you'll have to make your own decision about that," her mother replied.

A few months later he walked in their door, bearing his familiar grin, and Yara was a butterfly caught in his net. No longer the lanky boy, he stood six feet tall and walked like a man, with his chest out and his head held high. And in a quiet place inside her that understood unspoken words, she knew he would never return to Brazil. He would stay with Yara and their life paths would intertwine.

Once he finished college and his student Visa expired, the possibility of deportation weighed heavily on their minds. Two years after graduation, in 1990, at Yara's insistence, Davi sought assistance with his illegal immigration status at the Legal Services office in Hyannis, where he met Jim, Paige's brother-in-law. Davi knick-named him "Joe Montana" because he looked like an American football player. If not for that nickname, Jim would not have known Davi when they met again at the funeral service. Until that day, they had not made the connection. Jim heard the words *Joe Montana* in a Portuguese accent and it brought him back twenty years.

Jim's advice was for Davi to return to Brazil, and then to marry Yara. It would be easier that way to obtain United States citizenship, he explained, than marrying her without leaving because then he would have to admit his illegal status. They refused his advice, frightened that Davi would be barred from returning. Marriage ceremony or not, Yara knew that she would spend her life by his side, and the next life, and the next life. They had traveled together before, in other lifetimes. She was sure of it.

Davi had his own unique approach to life. He never liked to stay in any one place for long. He'd catch wind of a fishing expedition in Maine or an avocado farm in California that needed workers, and off he would go. But he always returned to Hyannis where he lived with Yara. In the middle of the night, she'd feel him slip into the bed beside her and she'd dig her fingers into his curls and exhale the worry from her chest. Finally, she could absorb the comforting sensation of home. Without him, it was only a house.

Davi was a free spirit, but he was also in the peculiar situation of being unable to procure legal work in his field because he was not a United States citizen or a permanent resident. He traveled wherever he could find work. Even though he'd come to the United States to develop his mind, he wasn't opposed to using his body for labor if it was necessary to remain with Yara. She would find an envelope in the mailbox with money enclosed, usually just in time to pay the rent on their small home in Hyannis.

Their life together was laden with challenges, but Davi floated above them on the musical notes that were an integral part of his life. He loved to sing and played several instruments and could sing beautifully. As soon as his bare feet touched the wooden planks of their bedroom floor each morning, lyrics danced off his lips.

They were driving in their old beat-up pickup truck, on their way to the campground in Bourne, to meet the yoga class, when she told him she was sure Paige would find a way to let her know she was present. "I feel her sometimes," she disclosed.

Davi nodded. He trusted her finely tuned intuition.

The Bourne Bridge was visible from their campsite. It was the same spot where the group had camped out with Paige and Gabriel the prior autumn, before Paige's diagnosis. That night had been colder than they'd expected, but they'd dressed in layers and huddled around the fire with their blankets wrapped around them. This time, the group was gathered to release Paige's ashes. They built a campfire, each one of the friends from yoga class collecting wood. Yara made a small circle out of flat stones in the center, where it would be ignited, and slowly laid the ashes on top of the stones.

"This is a Zen circle," she said to the group. "The starting point represents Paige's birth, the end her physical death. The small break between where the ashes begin and where they end is a symbol of the transition between life and death. But notice that the design is a circle—it begins again—because there is always rebirth."

Davi ignited the fire with a torch. No one spoke, yet they all did the same thing without communicating it. They sat in a circle around the bonfire, with—like the ashes—only a small break between them, the spot where Paige had sat the year before, and silently watched her ashes become one with the flames. When they were no longer visible, Davi began singing softly in Portuguese, although only Yara understood the words. The lullaby he had sung to her as a child was now wishing Paige a peaceful slumber.

She closed her eyes to listen, to absorb the sound more than the words. Musical notes rose and fell as they were sent by way of his breath into the world, like smoke from the fire. There was something divine inside this man who was irrelevant to most of the world, yet extraordinarily precious to her. His voice reminded her of the transformative power of music. In that moment, it wasn't sorrow she felt over her friend's death, but a sense of release and freedom. She was sure Paige's journey hadn't ended any more than hers had. It had only moved to a new location.

Davi had the restless nature of a child. He often danced while he sang, allowing the essence of the music to move him like a spirit he was channeling. But on this night, he remained still, by Yara's side.

A single winged creature, however, did its own dance around the campfire and captured Yara's vision. It rose from the golden flames as if it had arisen from the ashes and appeared to be moving in time to the music that escaped through her partner's mouth. Soon the entire group was watching it drop and rise, flying in circles in the magical light emitted by the fire that had merged with the ashes of their friend.

One of the women eventually broke the silence. "The moth is moving with such intention," she remarked, "almost like it's entertaining us." Several in the circle murmured their agreement.

Yara met Davi's eyes.

He understood and stated out loud what he knew she was thinking. "It's not a moth," he said. "It is a small butterfly."

August 19, 2009: Onset is a different universe from Norwell. In Norwell, most homes are kept freshly painted and sit perfectly situated on manicured lawns, like architectural sentries. Almost every house is beautiful and dignified. In Onset the beauty is unpredictable, and rougher around the edges. Gorgeous Victorian homes line up beside dilapidated cottages, and the paint peeling off historical homes really doesn't detract from them. They remind me of those lovely old ladies who wear lavender voile dresses with gloves, and hats with wide brims and satin bows, the kind of ladies who are elegant to the end, despite their deteriorating bodies.

*"When I'm old I want to be like that,"
I tell Gabriel.*

"It's hard to imagine you in a frilly dress and hat," he says.

*"Let's dress up and go to an expensive restaurant,"
I suggest. We're floating on a small rowboat in the harbor that is tied to a dock and admiring the stars.*

"I'd rather have dinner out here," he counters.

"We'll do both," I tell him, and his fingers squeeze mine in assent. There's plenty of time to do all the things that bubble up from our imaginations. With Gabriel I could travel the world on foot and be perfectly content.

But it's in Onset that I'm at home. That was true even before I moved in with him. I think it happened that first day on the bridge.

That was the day I jumped.

September 12, 2009: The Great Spirit breaks the darkness. Sunlight radiates through the windowpanes. It's Sunday morning, we're still in bed and the church bells are ringing. I love the sound they make. It always makes me feel simultaneously happy and sad, I think because of John Donne's poem. I was nineteen the first time I read it, in an English Literature class taught by an enlightened professor whom most people labeled "eccentric."

I don't recall the entire poem, but the end is instilled in my mind. I quote it out loud for Gabriel's benefit: "Each man's death diminishes me/For I am involved in mankind/Therefore, send not to know/For whom the bell tolls/It tolls for thee."

His eyes linger on my face, communicating silently that he understands.

The awareness of our mortality sits deftly on the surface like a water bug on a pond, even after our bodies have begun their dance, trying against all odds to achieve oneness, to bleed his energy into mine and mine into his. It's beautiful and sad all at once. Like the church bells.

October 4, 2009: When I wake up this morning, Gabriel is looking at my face, but not the way he usually does. I immediately see the concern in his eyes.

"What?" I ask, but he brushes it off.

Today we're going to The King Richard's Renaissance Faire in Carver with Arica, Ben and his two kids. I'm going to wear a wreath of flowers in my hair and ride an elephant! And there are tigers! Did you catch that? Tigers!

We've been excited about this for weeks, but now suddenly and inexplicably Gabriel is not.

Then during breakfast, he voices it softly. "There's something going on with your skin." He lifts my arm to study it. "Can't you see it?"

"It's the way the light's hitting it," I answer and shovel a spoonful of raisin bran and almond milk into my mouth. Admittedly, my skin has a yellowish hue.

He shakes his head. "I noticed it last night and thought the same thing. But look." He holds his arm next to mine and the difference is ridiculous. "You need to get checked out. Call your doctor and I'll go next door to cancel," he says sternly and makes it halfway to the door before he comes back to kiss me. And that's what scares me the most. It's the moment I know something is wrong.

October 7, 2009: Terrified. Waiting for test results.

October 10, 2009: Liver cancer beyond surgical intervention. How could this be real?

We are too silent. Someone has dropped a shroud over our sunny home, and all I can see is shadows.

Chapter Thirteen

Christopher & Kim, *the Episcopalian & the Ex-Atheist*

Do you know what you are?
You are a manuscript of a divine letter.
You are a mirror reflecting a noble face.
This universe is not outside of you.
Look inside yourself;
everything that you want,
you are already that.
—*Rumi*

The curtains were closed tightly, preventing any light from eking in with the exception of a sliver of daylight. Outside the bay window, a group of squirrels was rustling around on Paige's bird feeder. Christopher was consciously ignoring them. To Paige, they had been "darling babies." To him, they were bushy-tailed rats.

His own elongated shadow appeared to face off against him like an outlaw in a gun slinging match. He was vacuuming the living room. The shadow made the appliance look like part of his body, a magnanimous robot with a flat base instead of feet. It wasn't often that he had visitors. The smell of dust, despite the neat arrangement of furniture, knickknacks and prescription bottles on the kitchen counter, spoke of an old person's house. Christopher could imagine himself aging with the speed of Dorian Gray's picture, locked away in his living room.

Kim, Paige's friend, had called the night before and invited him out for breakfast. He wasn't sure what to make of that. They hadn't spent time together without Paige since they were eighteen or nineteen years old. But she was bringing her two daughters along, so it didn't feel like a date. Had she asked him to go out with her alone, he would have declined, not because he was dating anyone else, and not even because he didn't like Kim, but because he was too emotionally exhausted to deal with a potential romance. Life was easier sealed up in his own space. Still, the palms of his hands were sweaty, and he could feel anxiety creeping in beneath his skin. His mind might not have acknowledged that it was a date, but his body did.

The second he responded to the doorbell, two giggling girls, who looked like miniature versions of Kim, pushed past him into the house. Their energy drew his attention away from the fact that Kim kissed his cheek and was still holding his hand. She only let go when she heard the small voice of her daughter's yell "Look, look!" Kristen had found the squirrels and were peeking excitedly at them from behind the curtain.

"Sorry," she offered and raced toward them.

"They're okay," Christopher quickly replied. He didn't find their exuberance disarming. All the noise they made reminded him of the house he grew up in, the home that, despite his efforts to recreate it, still eluded him.

"Do you have any peanuts?" the littlest one, Kristen, asked him. She was six and about to start first grade, which was the main topic of her conversations unless something fascinating, like the squirrels, lured her mind somewhere else.

"I don't think so," Christopher replied. "But we're on our way to breakfast."

Kristen blew air impatiently out of her lungs. "Not for *me*. For *the squirrels*."

"You're being rude," her big sister scolded. She was nine and liked to practice sounding like their mother. She offered her hand to her mother's friend. "I'm Miranda," she said cordially.

"We shouldn't feed the squirrels, Kristen," Kim intervened. "They can be aggressive."

Christopher grinned. That was exactly what he used to say to Paige—who used to give granola to the damned things. No wonder they still hung around, and no wonder he couldn't stand them. Like him, they were foolishly waiting for Paige to return. Once the group got past the obstacle of deciding which restaurant to patronize, the morning went well. Kristen had her mind set on an Egg McMuffin and threw a fit in the back seat when Miranda calmly stated, "We're not going to McDonalds. No one likes McDonalds but you."

"I like McDonalds," Christopher offered amiably. "Next time let's go there." His statement calmed the tantrum and brightened Kim's face. The guy was good with kids, like she'd always imagined, and he'd spoken the magic words: *next time.*

The topics of conversation over breakfast at a nearby Friendly's Restaurant ranged from how omelets are made, to why ice cream sundaes are not served after waffles, to how many fireflies had been captured the night before (Kristen), to the difference between a witch and a warlock (Miranda). When not talking about magical beings, Miranda was mostly silent, whereas Kristen talked the entire time. Chris smiled a lot and laughed at all the pre-first grade jokes Kristen had been concocting for her soon to be classmates. While driving back to his house, listening to a Jonas Brothers CD that Kim carried in her handbag, he could see Kristen in the rear-view mirror, rocking back and forth in her booster seat and singing along.

"Wait here," Kim told the girls when they were in his driveway. "I'll be right back."

Christopher didn't question why she wanted to enter the house with him. They walked together wordlessly down the path that ran parallel to the garden toward the front door. Kim's eyes fell on the three-foot sunflower growing next to the front steps. It was tied to a stake for support with a piece of string. Its center was like a green star closed up tightly to shield the Creator's unique work of art, not to be revealed for another month. She turned her gaze to Chris' face and realized he was staring at the sunflower, too. "Come on," she nudged and clutched his arm that was clad in a long-sleeved shirt, even though it was summer.

"This has got to stop," Kim announced the moment she crossed the threshold.

"What?" he asked and closed the door behind them.

"You're living in a tomb," she said and marched into the house. "Look at this place."

He was too shocked to reply. He'd spent the entire morning cleaning, and this was her response? Kim tugged open the curtains that covered the bay window. Sunlight infiltrated the room and his hand, vampire-like, moved to shade his eyes.

"Don't you get it?" she pressed. "You're still alive."

She continued her path to the kitchen and opened the windows. Her gaze fell on the backyard where old deck chairs and flowerpots were stacked, abandoned. She was trying to regain the emotional balance she'd lost while calling him out on his self-destructive path. During breakfast he had been fun, like the guy she remembered from college, but watching him so animated with the girls had made her feel worse about how he was living.

"Kim—" Christopher started but was struck dumb. He shook his head like he was trying to joggle the words out. It was confusion getting in the way of his ability to communicate. He'd returned home feeling uncharacteristically light of heart, not expecting a battle.

"When exactly was it that your life ended, when Paige died, or when she walked out?" Kim asked as she turned to confront him.

"What do you, what do you want me to do?" he stammered.

"Live," she said softly. "I want you to live, Chris."

He folded his arms across his chest, closed to the possibility she was flinging recklessly at him as if it were a possibility. "What, start over?" he spit out. "It's too late for that."

"Too late? You're forty-one years old, probably only half-way through your life, and you think it's over already? You've forgotten who you are. You've forgotten yourself. But the thing is, Chris, I remember you. I remember you in Technicolor detail." Her index finger swept through the dust on the countertop leaving a clean line of slate blue Corian, chosen by her best friend a decade earlier.

"You remember me the way I used to be. I'm not like that now. The divorce and Paige dying. You couldn't understand."

"Oh, couldn't I?" Kim countered. "I've been through a divorce. And Paige was one of my best friends. Her death has made me feel many things. Sad, scared, lonely, even guilty. But you know what, Christopher? It hasn't made me feel dead—"

"Why guilty?"

It would have been the perfect moment to light a cigarette. It'd been her favorite way to fill those fat, awkward pauses. But she'd stopped smoking after the trip to New Hampshire. And she'd cut back on her alcohol intake, too. If she was going to create a new life, she might as well get it right this time. She stuffed a piece of Nicorette gum in her mouth and ambled over to the seat in front of the bay window. Paige's seat.

"Why?" Christopher asked again. "Why would you feel guilty?"

"Because of my feelings for you," she finally admitted.

One side of his mouth curled into a grin. "That was a long time ago, Kim."

She twisted her legs into a cross-legged pose and looked over her shoulder through the bay window at the bird feeder that was empty except for some acorns the squirrels must have stashed there. The house and yard had the feel of a ghost town.

"Actually," she said without turning to face him, "it wasn't."

It took a minute for the meaning of her words to penetrate. Christopher had known Kim for over twenty years, but he still thought of her as a *nice girl*, the kind of girl he always used to think he'd marry. If Paige hadn't ended it with the drama guy and given him a chance, he probably would have pursued a relationship with Kim. But now he wasn't sure he could meet anyone's expectations.

"You know, when Paige came along. . ." he began.

"I know, I know," Kim huffed. "She was everything you ever wanted."

"No," Christopher laughed. "She was everything I *never* wanted."

Kim finally turned to face him. "What do you mean?"

"I mean I never planned on being with someone like Paige. She was so. . . so difficult. I didn't know how to make her happy. It was harder than I thought it would be, impossible, maybe. But if it was so impossible, how did that other guy—Gabriel—manage it?"

"He didn't. She did." That much was clear to Kim—based on Julia's comments while they were in New Hampshire, the ones that had inspired her to recognize her own fingerprints on the snow globe of her life. "It wasn't your job to make her happy," she pointed out. "It was Paige's job. It just took her a while to figure that out."

"Maybe I'm not good at relationships," he mumbled.

"Maybe none of us are," Kim countered. "Maybe we're not supposed to be great at them. Paige used to say the only way we learn is by really sucking at something."

The remark got a laugh out of him. Paige would say that. He took a moment to weigh out the possibilities. "All right," he drew out slowly, like he was still thinking it over. "Even though I might really suck at this, want to have dinner with me next weekend?"

Okay, she thought as Christopher's unexpected words resonated in her brain, *maybe there is a Higher Power who gives a shit about me.* Someone or something, it seemed, had heard her request. She could at least consider the possibility of its existence. Kim smiled as a reply, but then to seal the deal added, "Even though I probably suck at it, too, sure—I'd love to."

The sunflower was in full bloom next to the front steps when Kim passed by it on her way into the house, its bright yellow and brown face turned in her direction. She didn't knock or ring the doorbell. Christopher was expecting her and the girls, and they had frequented his house enough times by then to be more than typical guests.

"Chris?" she shouted out as she pushed the front door open.

"Come on in!" he yelled from the kitchen.

The house smelled like maple syrup. His back was to her as she entered the kitchen. He was flipping pancakes on the stove. She stopped to watch him and to take in the atmosphere. Sunlight was shining through the windows and through it she could see the picnic table in the backyard adorned with a floral tablecloth and a vase full of perennials from the garden.

Chris turned and offered her a crooked grin, enough to reveal his smile lines. She loved those smile lines. Kim slid her arms around his shoulders. "Hey, you know that sunflower by the front steps. It's taller than me now."

Christopher laughed. "I'm starting to think there's something magical about that flower."

"Did you just use the word *magical*?" Kim teased. "Miranda's rubbing off on you!"

"Maybe she is," he conceded and touched his lips on hers. "Where are the girls?"

"They're bringing stuff from the car. I bought some geraniums for the pots out back and the girls are hoping you'll play wiffleball with them while I plant them."

"Sure," he quickly agreed. "I think I have some old bases out back."

"From your glory days," Kim commented, and he smiled proudly. "I told them you were quite a baseball player in college."

He was wearing that white uniform with the navy pinstripes the first time she saw him. *Glory days.* What an odd expression, she thought, as she stood there with her arms around his shoulders and his hair in the back touching her fingertips. Why do we always assume our past is better than our future? she wondered. Her future looked promising, and the present moment was perfect. She was just about to tell him so when the girls' laughter interrupted her thoughts.

"Here they are," Chris announced majestically as they entered, as if they were Miss America contestants on the runway. "Who's up for pancakes and wiffleball?"

Both girls eagerly raised their hands like they were answering a question in school and hopped on their feet like baby birds. And just like that, Christopher's house came to life. He couldn't ignore the shift in energy that came from two little girls dancing joyfully in his kitchen because he was willing to play with them. What a simple solution it turned out to be after all, turning his house into a home.

His eyes surveyed the small living room beyond them. The bookshelves were no longer empty and collecting dust. Now they were filled with children's books. Chris had purchased all of Shel Silverstein's poetry for Kristen and the entire *Cirque du Freak* series for Miranda. There were dog-eared books on the end tables, too. The gray squirrels were still there, scratching around outside the bay window, but they didn't bother him anymore. They no longer spoke of Paige's absence. Now they reminded him of Kristen and Miranda.

In the kitchen, taped on the refrigerator with masking tape, was a small poster he and Kim had found at a yard sale. It bore the cartoon image of Smurfette from the 1980s Smurfs television show. Underneath, in bold letters, were the words: GIRLS CAN DO ANYTHING. Christopher smiled every time he noticed it. Paige, he knew, would have approved.

Starting the relationship with Kim and her two daughters was the biggest leap of his life. It was that one little *yes* he allowed himself against a history of a thousand *no's*.

The experience reminded him of a feeling he'd had when he was twelve and swimming with the town team at the Bridgewater State College pool. There was a diving board, three meters high, that after all the races were complete, the kids were allowed to use. One of the boys on his team, Michael Gunther, goaded him into climbing the ladder that led to the high dive, even though he feared heights. A crooked row of dripping wet kids snaked down the ladder and across the pool deck behind him. He'd never been as terrified in his entire life as he'd walked across the diving board to the very end, where it extended over the pool. Shivering in their wet bathing suits the crowd of kids had started to shout, "Go! Go!" Had it not been for Michael Gunther, who eventually shoved him off the edge, Christopher might still be standing there, trying to figure out how else to get down.

But damn, the fall was memorable. The exhilaration was worth every second of the fear that led him toward it. It was his skydive, his bungee jump, even if he needed the shove.

October 17, 2009: Life is a leap of faith, a jump from a bridge railing. No one can see the future, yet moment after moment and day after day, we forge ahead. We take it on faith that we're headed in the right direction, and that we'll be safe.

This is what I remind myself of in the face of the relentless fear crawling up my spine, echoing Dr. Schuller's words: "Chances of survival are minimal at best." I'm still here. I'm still alive, and for as long as I'm alive, I need to breathe and feel and love and be myself wholly. That's my new mantra.

And I've come to another realization. Maybe it's okay to continue journaling just because it makes me feel good. Maybe the most important part was never to keep my life on track, but to write for the sheer joy of it. Just for the joy of it, what a concept! Why not pursue other things, too, just for the joy of it?

I couldn't have figured this out on my own. Gabriel said the most profound thing last night, that the word "regret" should never be used by the living. It's still premature, he says, for me to have regrets. I always thought I'd learn how to surf and paint and a thousand other things, I argued, but now, if the cancer has its way, like Dr. Schuller says it will, those things will never happen. I'll never be anything more than what I am right now.

Today, while I was napping, he booked us a trip to California—to celebrate my fortieth birthday, he says, even though it was two months ago, and we already celebrated. We leave Monday. I'm terrified to get on a surfboard, and it makes me wonder how many things I say I want only because they sound good, or because I like the image created in my mind, not because I actually want them.

October 18, 2009: A magical day. I awaken to music. Through the veil of sleep, notes seep in, dancing through my brain like the Snow Queen in the Nutcracker, until it begins to make sense. It's jazz, "Kind of Blue," I think—so I venture out of bed and into the living room to investigate.

And there is Gabriel sitting in front of an old upright piano that he must have dragged up the stairs with Ben, whose voice I remember hearing while I slept, and making music pour out of it that is completely breathtaking. The notes leap and bounce off the cottage walls, and as I watch in stunned silence it occurs to me that some kind of pain is exiting through his fingertips. I don't know where it came from, but I can almost see it going. And in that moment, I realize it's a privileged glimpse I'm receiving, like watching his soul ascend.

His transformation affects me, too. For the first time since the diagnosis, this disease is no longer the only thing in the universe. Gabriel has disempowered it with his spellbinding chords, even if only for this magnificent moment. You can make music out of anything, I think, recalling the dream of the pomegranate and the fluttering of piano keys. Even sickness. Even cancer. The melody is so close to the music from the dream that I half expect there to be magenta juice streaking his forearm when he turns to face me.

"I'm taking it back," he declares, and I nod enthusiastically. Yes, I think, take the music back from whomever or whatever has taken it from you. There's a message in his self-empowerment. No matter our circumstances, we get to choose how we respond to them. And I need to hear that.

October 20, 2009: California. Today I learned that I don't have to be good at something to enjoy it. I was too scared to get on the surfboard by myself, so Gabriel got on it with me. When I expressed my sudden onset of fear, he laughed.

"What's the worst thing that could happen?" he asks.

"We could be eaten by sharks," I say earnestly.

"Then we'll pass to spirit together," he says, and it takes a minute for me to absorb it. If life is a never-ending circle, what is there really to be afraid of? He reaches for my hands to help me stand. He's on his knees facing me.

"Wait," I urge, but this time not because I'm scared. It's because I want to freeze-frame the moment. If I leave this world, I'm carrying this image in my pocket: Gabriel with his dark hair wet and slicked back, his eyebrows lifted in anticipation, one side of his mouth grinning, and the surfer necklace I just bought him dangling from his neck. I love this man with my entire being and I am convinced that nothing could take it from me. Not even death. "Okay, now," I say and take his wet hands in mine.

Later, in the hotel room, he suggests we come back together next time. It takes me a minute to figure out that it's not California he's talking about. He means our next life. I think of how the last six months have been better than the entire thirty-nine and a half years I spent without him and nod my head that's squeezed up next to his.

My hair is still in a tangled braid from swimming in the ocean. Gabriel put it in before we left the hotel this morning. It was crooked from the start, but I love it because he did it and I got to feel his fingers as they weaved and tugged, and I can see my ears, which are shaped exactly like my mother's. I can't look at hers anymore, but I can see my own and remember.

With my peripheral vision, I see us reflected in the mirror. Two people wrapped so snugly around each other that, at a glance we appear as one. I look much stronger like this, with Gabriel's body bolstering mine. It's been hard for me to look at myself since the diagnosis. I keep thinking I see the cancer in every shadow of my face and every underdeveloped muscle. What does it look like on the inside? Some days I picture it as a gray dense fog with the open mouth of a snake slithering through my body, and other times it is the Pac-man character moving swiftly with intention, devouring the dots that are my cells. I'm terrified of this monster. How did it come to be that my own cells decided to turn against me? Was there a gatekeeper who let them in? And was that gatekeeper me?

When we get back home, I have to start chemotherapy. I'm scared, but not as scared as I was before we came here, and not nearly as scared as I'd be if I was facing this alone.

October 28, 2009: Back in Onset now, I'm sitting on the rock next to the Native American woman sculpted out of bronze and taking in the impressive view of the harbor while Gabriel paints a house in Yarmouth. So far, so good on the chemo. I'm still able to eat normally and I haven't gotten sick yet, but he won't let me go to work with him because I'm supposed to rest.

The plaque underneath the statue says that her name is Aquene, which means "Peace" in the Wampanoag tongue. She is the only company I will have today, but I don't mind because I know that as soon as darkness returns, so will Gabriel.

I take a long look at Aquene, at her two braids and the necklace made out of shells, and it inspires a thought. Human beings are like beads on a string, of various colors and designs, but nonetheless connected. Gabriel is vermillion, twisted into a thousand glittering shapes. I am pale green and three-dimensional only. But that's okay. If we were all the same, the world wouldn't be as beautiful or interesting. And it gives me an objective platform from which to view his brilliance.

Oct 30, 2009: This morning while Gabriel was showering, I removed the tape from the knobs on the truck radio and tested it—it works. I don't think there was ever anything wrong with the radio. For some reason, it was there to keep music beyond his reach. I don't know why he was punishing himself, and I haven't asked, but this evening when he returned home, I heard music coming through the open windows of the truck.

October 31, 2009: I love Aileen, Gabriel's mother. She brings a feeling of family to my life. Until I got to know her, I was part of a partnership. Now I'm part of a team. Here's some of the stuff I love about her the most:

- When pondering something important, she places her hands in prayer position with the tips of her index fingers resting above her top lip. Her eyes are Gabriel's, deep. . . brown. . . thoughtful. I can see them filtering and analyzing.
- She smells like Easter lilies.
- She touches people to show affection and has extraordinarily soft skin.

- She sings a lot, like my own mom. (My mother had a church choir type of voice. She liked to sing in Italian, which I'm told I mimicked perfectly as a toddler.)
- She smiles at strangers even when they are not smiling at her.
- She adores Gabriel. It's like electricity, this love, with tangible energy. It engulfs him like a cloud the second she steps into our home.
- Even though I'm all grown up, today she brought me Halloween candy in a plastic pumpkin and it's almost like being eight again, which is a very good thing. I loved being eight. I was smart, but not overly informed. Life was fun every day.
- She never uses the word "sick."
- She listens to my stories about spirit messages from my mom and takes them on faith without trying to disable them.

Chapter Fourteen

Joe Senior & Paige, *the Old-School Catholic & the Heretic*

To one there is given through the Spirit. . . miraculous powers, to another prophecy, to another distinguishing between spirits, to another speaking in different kinds of tongues, and to still another, the interpretation of tongues. All these are the work of one and the same Spirit, and he distributes them to each one, just as he determines.
—*1 Corinthians 12*

"I remember that green dress," Joe Senior asserted confidently.

He was sitting on the end of the bed he shared with his wife, socks and shoes beside him. Every morning he dressed himself, and Evelyn left him alone to do so. He insisted on it. Tucked safely in the back of his mind, that often failed to make sense out of the information presented to him, was his desire to be treated with dignity.

"Your mother bought it for you." He dropped his head into his open hands and fingered the softly textured hair between them. It was almost as thick as it was when he was young, but now as white as a dove. "I can't remember why, Paige," he surrendered.

Joe lifted his head and focused his eyes as if locked on someone else's, though no other physical being was in the room. "That's right!" he exclaimed. "An argument with Chris. You were going to a fancy party. Your mother bought you the dress to cheer you up." He pulled the notebook from his shirt pocket and wrote *green dress, Maria*.

The words were his way of conjuring memories. Without them, he'd have no recollection of the conversation. His system was not foolproof. Sometimes his words sparked recall, other times his eyes saw only scattered letters floating on the page, like islands in the tiniest of seas.

As a younger man, Joe had never believed it was possible to communicate with a person who had passed out of the physical world. His intellect had disabled that notion. Now it didn't strike Joe as odd to be talking to his dead daughter. Dementia played a role in his perception, though not the most obvious one. He wasn't hallucinating or misunderstanding. Conversely, the limitations that his mind had absorbed as truth over the course of his life were no longer accessible. Therefore, the belief system that steered his seventy plus years on Earth no longer stood at the helm. Joe could see Paige standing before him, so he returned her gaze. He heard her speak words, and therefore, politely replied. He didn't stop to think *could this be real?* He didn't analyze it at all.

He noticed the ball of socks in his hand and reached down to slide them on. His balance was precarious; he realized it and sat up. Joe no longer trusted his body. He couldn't expect his equilibrium to respond any more than he could expect his brain to spit out the appropriate word when he commanded it. *Youth is wasted on the young* was once his favorite quote, and how true it had turned out to be. As a young man, Joe had taken for granted the well-oiled machine that was his body. Some mornings he awakened believing he was still a boy, but then he'd feel pain in his back, or his hips and he'd remember: *I'm an old man now.* How had time fled so quickly?

A solution occurred to him. He rolled onto his back and lifted his feet into the air to get the socks on his feet. "Ah, you think I'm clever? Well, you were always a wise guy," he chortled. Still laying on the bed, he scribbled *wise guy* in his notebook. "Yes, I can hear you," he stated. "There's something here." He tapped on his head. "But I can hear. You said *Tell Abby you saw me. She'll remember the dress.*"

He jotted down the word *Abby*. Had Abigail been standing in front of him during the conversation, he could have repeated the message. But to remember Paige's words days, or even hours later, was beyond his ability. He never made phone calls anymore because the buttons confused him. Some days he couldn't remember how to hold it and was surprised when a voice came through the earpiece.

Socks on, his feet hit the floor, and Joe's face grew somber. The shoes were still waiting. He slid his feet into them and stared down at the untied laces. He drew one foot onto the opposite knee and wrapped the shoelaces around each other until they were in the twisted pattern of a barber shop pole. A grin spread across his chapped lips as he let go but fell apart as quickly as the laces. It was like a complex engineering problem, trying to understand what he needed to do to make the laces stay together.

"Ask Evelyn?" he muttered with a scratch on his chin. "You're right, she's very good with thingamajigs." That was his concocted word to label all the objects whose names evaded him. Satisfied, he dropped his foot onto the floor before resuming the conversation with his daughter. "I thought we were bringing you to the—the fishpond. Remember we used to go on the little boat?" He laughed at the photographic image his mind created. "The fishhook in your sister's. . ." He rubbed his head to indicate "hair." It was Paige who cast the line haphazardly and tangled it in Abby's perfect golden tresses. Maria had to cut the hook out with scissors. The event sparked a year-long argument between their girls, not only because Abigail's beautiful hair was damaged, but because Paige had laughed.

"I couldn't help it! I always laugh when I'm nervous!" she'd protested for months.

Joe closed his eyes and watched the images displayed in his mind's eye like an old family movie. He saw himself as a younger man backing the station wagon into the driveway so that he could attach the rowboat to it and drag it down to the Town Hall Pond. He saw the three kids with their poles, fishing hats and brightly colored lures, the cooler filled with bologna sandwiches and plastic sandwich bags stuffed with potato chips and Oreos. They always stopped at Cumberland Farms to buy cold drinks. Sometimes they'd play a game—whoever was quietest from the house to the store won the right to choose soda or a quart of lemonade. Abigail was invariably the winner. Paige always busted out in laughter, and it quickly rubbed off on her little brother.

A chuckle rolled out of his chest at the thought of his wife, Maria, with her thick brunette curls and brooding brown eyes riding shotgun beside him, and serious Abigail in the back seat wedged between Paige and Joey, both in fits of giggles.

"Rosary beads?" Joe suddenly asked. His eyebrows tugged together, and his bottom lip set into a pout. He blinked. "Paige!" he sputtered as his eyes searched the room for his daughter. It wasn't her voice that answered him. It was Evelyn's. She was standing in the doorway watching him with worry embedded in the lines of her face.

Marriage is like a game of roulette, she was thinking. You never know what lies ahead, fortune or bankruptcy, health or illness, antagonism, or friendship. The day they married, she'd imagined Joe as the new head of the household, who would relieve her of the responsibilities she'd juggled alone since her husband's death. She'd had no intention of being the alpha dog, but that's what she was now. The twist was that she liked it. Through this unimaginable role she found out how clever and strong she was.

"It's me, Joe," she offered and took painful strides on her arthritic legs to sit beside him on the bed. A storm was rolling in outside the windows, and with it pain in her joints. As a child she'd been taught that rain on the day of a funeral was a sign that the soul arrived safely in Heaven. It didn't surprise her that the day of Paige's funeral was uncharacteristically sunny and warm. But it'd rained almost every day since.

"You were taking a long time getting ready," she voiced.

"I was talking to Paige," he replied nonchalantly. "She was wearing that pretty green dress. Remember it?" Evelyn shook her head. "And rosary beads. . . on her. . . her. . . ." He couldn't recall the word, so he tapped his wrist.

"Paige with rosary beads?" *The beatnik*, Evelyn thought, *would never wear rosary beads*. It was an unkind thought, she realized, and struck it from her mind.

"She ran off," Joe sighed. "That's her way." Evelyn was surprised by the accurate assessment of his free-spirited daughter. But now his sadness over what Evelyn assumed was her imagined departure was filling the room. "I had a message for her."

Evelyn patted his knee. "What was it?" she asked.

His watery gray eyes momentarily flashed with intelligence, but almost immediately resumed their placid, unfocused gaze. "Tell Maria I'll meet her by the fishpond."

Evelyn's face was like a Venetian mask bearing the exuberant expression of a clown, even though her heart was throbbing. If Joe was at all comforted by the idea that his first wife and daughter were alive, she would never take that away from him.

"Do you mean the pond in Hanson, by the cemetery?" she asked.

"Yes. No, not there. The other side, where the boats go in."

She smiled and knelt beside him to tie his shoes. It hurt her knees to do so, but she did it anyway because it was easier for her than for him.

"Wait," Joe said. He slid his foot out of the shoe and turned it upside down. A quarter fell out, landing on the rug. Evelyn handed it to him unceremoniously.

He slipped it into his pocket with the grin of a schoolboy who'd scored a favorite baseball card. It would be added to his collection of quarters that he'd found around the house and yard since Paige's death. Once he'd even found one in the bird feeder. And this was the third time he'd found one in his shoe. "You think I don't know you, but I do," he said to his wife. "You type fifty-five words a minute. You're Evelyn."

She turned her face to meet Joe's excited eyes. This man, who had once been the greatest intellectual in her life, was giddy with excitement because he remembered her name, and he was waiting for her to acknowledge it. He had no way of knowing the pain he was causing her because his brain no longer stored the piece of information signifying her true relationship to him. Evelyn mulled it over for a minute, considering what words she could summon to correct his mistake. Should she remind him of their first date or the day they went shopping together for living room furniture after he proposed? Or perhaps she could spark his recall by telling him about the spring they planted their first vegetable garden, and the nest of bird eggs they discovered in the forsythia bush. But in the end, she only squeezed his knees with fingers that were curling into hawk-like appendages and crafted a smile on her lips authentic enough to fool anyone, even her husband.

"That's exactly right," she said.

November 11, 2009: It's interesting, isn't it, the things we do for love?

There is a large plastic container next to Gabriel's side of the bed that used to house popcorn, but now holds our change and dollar bills. Every time I toss a quarter into it, I remind myself that it is an act of love. This is our piano fund. The old upright in ill repair that Ben found at a yard sale is all Gabriel has to practice on. The Indigo Lounge down the street has a pianist playing on

Wednesday nights. We used to walk down before the chemo waged war on my internal organs. The owner said Gabriel could audition, and that if he was good enough, he'd give him a night of his own. He doesn't pay much, but the tips are good. Gabriel said that's because Onset is a blue-collar town, and people with less always tip more.

Every time I look at the plastic container teeming with coins, I think of the retirement account I fought over with Chris. All that wasted energy. People take it so seriously, but in the end it's only a pile of cash set aside for a day that might never come. I told Gabriel I'd like him to have my "retirement" money if I die, so that he can buy a good instrument, but he said no. Every time he needs an instrument, he assured me, it finds its way into his life, and it will this time, too.

November 12, 2009: I love watching Gabriel play piano. The notes released in response to his fingers are an expression of who he is. I can't hold onto the notes, store them in a jar on my dresser to take out and admire whenever I choose, but they are, nonetheless, Gabriel.

It's himself that he shares with everyone in the room every time he plays. Visual artists lay down pieces of their soul in splashes of color on otherwise blank canvases. Poets build sculptures out of words that would be no more meaningful than an encyclopedia entry without the human spirit embedded in them. And musicians, like my beautiful boy? They paint the world with invisible ink.

November 14, 2009: It's finally caught up with me. I'm sicker from the chemo than I ever imagined was possible. Can. Not. Write. Today.

November 15, 2009: I'm pretty sure I crapped out an organ this morning. Bodily fluids are escaping through every possible outlet. Gabriel brought me a peanut butter and banana sandwich on homemade bread from the Common Ground Café today, but the smell made me vomit. I'm done journaling until I get past this stage because I don't ever want to read back and remember how bad it was.

December 8, 2009: Almost a month has gone by, and I still can't bring myself to write. I'm sick, sick, sick. And my energy is M.I.A.

December 10, 2009: It started when I asked about the year that he missed jumping off the bridge on the first day of summer. It's such an important ritual to him, something he does for Billy, his dead best friend, so it's hard to imagine anything important enough to keep him from it. Gabriel was completely silent at first, which is unlike him. One of his goals, he's told me, is to wear his life on his arms like his tattoos. Secrets, he says, will kill you in the end.

He looks up from the piano keys he is fingering to meet my eyes. "Remember I told you about the car accident that killed Billy?" His fingers hit the keys savagely, creating an unexpected clamor. Then he says it. "I was driving the car."

He spent a year and a half in prison for vehicular homicide. He wasn't drinking he said, just stupid. The night of the accident they were driving a jeep up the side of a sand pit. The jeep rolled and Billy—who wasn't strapped in—was thrown from the vehicle and crushed underneath it. That's why

Gabriel moved from Falmouth, to get away from all the faces who know the story.

"Am I your penance?" I ask that night in bed, after my brain has absorbed all the facts. I can't help but think about all the puke he's cleaned off the floor because I wasn't strong enough to make it to the bathroom, and the bed sheets soiled with diarrhea that he's had to launder. Until recently, he's been carrying me to the bathroom and holding me on the toilet, so I won't fall off. It's a husky, dry laugh that escapes with his breath in the darkness, not playful like it usually is.

"You're my everything," he says.

Chapter Fifteen

Gabriel's Parents, *the Methodists*

Peace, peace! He is not dead, he does not sleep—he hath wakened from the dream of life.
—*Percy Bysshe Shelley, about the death of his friend John Keats*

The bridges got smaller every year.

The first year after Billy's death they followed Gabriel to the Mount Hope Bridge in Bristol Rhode Island, a suspension bridge spanning the Mount Hope Bay and landing at the foot of Roger Williams University. At sunset, the electric lanterns, painted blue, looked other worldly against the changing sky. It was during that time of day, when the air itself felt magical, that Connor and Aileen Byrne, Gabriel's parents, found their only child leaning against the bridge railing and gazing down at the bay. They understood his intent. The depression was evident to everyone who knew him before the accident. But it wasn't a condition that could be treated with medication. Self-forgiveness was the only conceivable remedy. Remorse was eating him alive.

It took some time to talk him out of his plan. The Mount Hope Bridge wasn't something kids jumped off for the thrill of it. It was the kind of bridge people plummeted from when they wanted to die, and Gabriel wouldn't have been the first to have succeeded at that. Locally, it was known as the place architecture majors, and other students at Roger Williams University, ended their lives when overwhelmed by the workload and someone else's expectations.

"You're my only child," Aileen pleaded, and that convinced him to get in the back seat of their car. Those were the words that shifted his perspective.

Because he was an only child and he'd learned to read when he was four years old, Gabriel spent most of his early childhood immersed in books. That changed one Saturday when, on route to the town dump with his father, he heard Bill Evans playing on the radio. He'd never been exposed to pop or rock music, but he'd heard a fair amount of jazz because that's what his parents listened to.

"How does he do that?" he asked his father from the back seat and saw his father's eyes in the rear-view mirror turn to him.

"Do what, son?" he asked his seven-year-old.

"Make the notes sound like they're crying," he replied.

That was the moment Connor Byrne knew that his child was a musician. "Would you like to learn?" he asked, and Gabriel's serious brown eyes fixed on his own in the small mirror. They were ancient eyes, incongruent with his baby face and pouty mouth.

"We don't have a piano," Gabriel replied. It was the first time that his brain was concerned with not having a musical instrument to play, but it wouldn't be the last. As a child, Gabriel knew when his parents experienced financial strain, not because he overheard them talking about the mortgage payment or an unexpected car repair bill, but because his intuition was sharp enough to feel the energy of their worries. And he understood when his father casually threw out the invitation to take lessons that there was no extra money to pay for them, let alone purchase an expensive instrument.

"I'll figure it out," his father replied. Connor was a resourceful man, who would do anything and everything for his son. He solved the problem by buying a keyboard out of the Want Ads and hiring a local college student to teach him.

And so, Gabriel's piano lessons began. The rest of his musical education was also initiated. His parents bought him cassettes by people like Herbie Hancock, Chick Correa and Keith Jarrett, and made phone calls to local clubs to find out which ones would allow a minor to enter with a parent. Connor brought Gabriel to every jazz bar that he could. Every year they attended the Newport Jazz Festival. Music was the main source of Gabriel's young life. It was all he knew, until Billy.

Billy Spencer moved to their neighborhood in Falmouth when the boys were eleven years old. His parents were able to move their three boys out of a duplex in South Boston due to a skillful young stockbroker named Abigail Delaney, Paige's older sister, they'd discovered at the funeral, who had nearly doubled their portfolio. Billy was the youngest child. He had reddish hair, an impish grin and a bright, energetic mind. He arrived at Gabriel's front door on a skateboard, which was a tell-tale sign. For the entirety of Billy's short life, he was drawn to anything that had wheels and moved fast.

Gabriel received a BMX for his twelfth birthday that he rode for three years before he totaled it by crashing into a tree while racing Billy through the woods. That was the first time the two boys and both sets of parents came together in a hospital emergency room. Within a year, they met again in the very same emergency room after Billy rode his skateboard off the flat roof of a local business and broke his leg in three places. It had been good news to his parents' ears. The desperate phone call they'd received from someone in the parking lot only informed them of their son's plunge from the roof. They'd expected much worse. But fate was cruel in that respect; the night of the car accident they learned of Billy's death in the very same waiting room.

It was during middle school, while the boys were listening to Nirvana's *In Utero*, that Billy decided to take up drums. From the beginning, he played with a startling amount of upper body strength and the same intense energy that he brought to everything else that stirred his interest. Their first band, *Soul Transmigration*, was intended to be a rock and soul fusion, but it never got there because Billy's style, no matter how he tried, was far more *Alice in Chains* than *Tower of Power*.

When Gabriel announced his plan to attend Berklee School of Music, Billy decided to go there, too. He'd never been an academic like Gabriel, so he had to work harder than him to get the grades, but he did it, much to the shock of his parents and teachers. It wasn't a surprise to Gabriel, though, that Billy was accepted to Berklee. He knew he could do anything if he wanted it badly enough. To Gabriel, Billy was infallible, immortal almost, the closest thing he'd ever witnessed to a superhero. This was, after all, the same kid who'd ollied twenty-five feet off a roof and lived to tell the story.

They jumped off their first bridge, the Harvard Bridge that reached over the Charles River, while freshmen at Berklee. They took the leap late on a Saturday night after hearing a story about Harry Houdini jumping off the very same bridge with his hands and feet bound. The water was not as clean as when Houdini dove in. They bobbed to the surface and noticed debris that wasn't discernible from the bridge railing at night, floating on the water's surface. A discarded doll floated alongside plastic soda bottles, car tires and an unidentifiable yellow muck. They scurried out of the water like river rats and were later sent by the school nurse to the hospital for tetanus shots.

Billy's adventurous mind often led him to places that would have been better left undiscovered. At Berklee he hung with the druggie crowd, the kids who justified being chronically high by pointing to all the brilliant drug-addicted musicians who came before them. Curiosity led Billy from alcohol and weed to Percocet and heroin, where he soon found himself trapped. Two months into junior year he was caught with drugs in his dorm room and was expelled from school.

Another year or two went by before he faced his addiction. In Gabriel's view, it was the first obstacle he'd encountered that was stronger than him. It was after Billy cleaned up at a rehab that he turned up again on Gabriel's doorstep, this time on a motorcycle and wearing a shiny gold cross around his neck.

During the drug addicted years, he'd broken trust with Gabriel. "I'm finding my way back," Billy told his best friend.

"Swear it on your life?" Gabriel asked. That was the code of their friendship and had been since they were boys.

"I swear it on my life," he promised.

Billy was steering clear of his user buddies and wanted to re-establish a friendship that had been damaged by his drug abuse and all the behaviors that came with it. Like the time Billy pawned his laptop for Percs, or the time he stole Gabriel's term paper because he hadn't showed up for school in weeks and was about to flunk out.

That was one of the reasons Gabriel had such a hard time accepting his role in Billy's death. He was the good kid, the one Billy's parents trusted. He knew that every time the two of them walked out the door together his parents breathed a sigh of relief.

Billy was clean and sober, but he was still itching for adventure. He tried skydiving and bungee jumping and was saving money to take flying lessons. In the interim, a used Jeep Wrangler sufficed. It was remarkable that there were no crashes while Billy was driving, considering the number of risks he took with Gabriel in the passenger's seat. But it wasn't Gabriel's time to die; it was Billy's, which Billy comprehended intuitively. He often commented that he knew he would die young. For Gabriel, the understanding of why Billy passed over and he didn't came much later. It wasn't until Paige's diagnosis that he realized there might be a reason for his continued existence.

Although he'd never told anyone—not even Paige—the night of the accident it was Billy who insisted Gabriel drive the jeep up a hill that appeared unclimbable and was. In his mind, the accident was entirely his fault. He should have known better. Gabriel walked away with a broken arm and a broken tooth. But what was broken under the surface was much more dangerous to his mortal existence. There was an emotional bleed that he couldn't stop, no matter how much pressure he put on it.

His parents did everything in their power to see him through the grief that was crushing them, too. They hoped that music would be his salvation, but Gabriel turned away from it. The piano in their living room was sold at his insistence. Since he was fourteen years old, he had discovered and celebrated music with Billy by his side. How could he suddenly go solo? In every note, he heard something of Billy, in an E, his scruffy voice, in an A his wild laughter. He refused to listen to CDs or the radio, to the echoes of his friend that he had accidentally killed. He turned his back on Chick Corea and Herbie Hancock, the idols of his youth, and replaced music with silence.

Every day for over four years, even during the time Gabriel was locked away in the Barnstable County Correctional Facility, his parents wondered if they would receive word that their son had died. It might be called an accident, they knew, but the truth would be that he was simply carrying more weight than his conscience could withstand. When, after his release from prison, he announced that he was moving to Onset, his parents understood that he required freedom to live a normal life. But he had no friends anymore. He had cut ties with everyone.

And then he met Paige. Almost immediately, it was obvious that Gabriel's and Paige's lives had woven together like two reeds in a basket. Gabriel phoned and told them that he had met someone who had changed his life irrevocably, and they invited him to bring her down for Sunday dinner. Aileen watched from behind the living room curtain as they walked to the front door holding hands and had to choke back tears at the sight of it. She'd almost forgotten what her son looked like with a smile on his face.

Gabriel hadn't mentioned ahead of time that Paige was a dozen years older than him, but that mattered very little to his parents. During dinner they heard him *laugh*, and that was what resonated. It was the magical sound that caused Connor to meet Aileen's eyes across the dinner table and give her a secret wink. Standing in the driveway of their Cape Cod style Falmouth home that evening with a light mist falling on them and clinging to their hair and sweaters, they waved goodbye to Gabriel and Paige, and for the first time in four years, they felt like their son was going to survive the accident. Aileen let out a sob as the pickup truck pulled out of view, and Connor embraced her while she wept tears of relief.

There had been a time when Gabriel's independent spiritual views were shocking to his parents. They'd raised him in the Methodist Church, the same religion they'd been raised in, and never suspected that he would challenge that belief system. To them, being part of a church community was an essential part of life. To their son, it wasn't. Gabriel was only sixteen when he calmly renounced over Sunday dinner his intention of attending church services because he felt it would be hypocritical. "I don't feel the need to be 'saved,'" he admitted. "I don't believe I was created for the sole purpose of seeing whether or not I can pass a test. If there's a God, I don't believe it's vengeful. I think that idea came from someone's attempt to personify God, a force that isn't a person at all." At the time, his words infuriated his mother.

But when she met Paige, her feelings shifted. It didn't matter anymore whose God she was praying to, hers or Gabriel's. Some power beyond her own had saved her son. Someone had loved him as much as she did, had seen his pain and had done something about it. Every day, she decided, for the rest of her life she would give thanks for that. And she did, even after Paige died, and the time came to scatter her ashes.

Gabriel had already declined the invitation to join them. "We were thinking about Old Silver Beach," his mother threw out the night before during dinner at their Falmouth home. "Remember, we had brunch in the resort there that time?"

Her comment broke the silence created by Paige's absence. Gabriel forked noodles and broccoli in his mouth and nodded his head slightly. The silence was so *loud*.

"Or Truro," his father suggested. Both parents smiled wistfully at the visual the word created.

Gabriel glanced up and wiped his mouth with his napkin. The pain in his chest swelled like a tide, making his heart feel three times that of his rib cage. He could still hear Paige's giggles as he piggybacked her up the sand dune, and her insistence that they roll back down it. He'd relented, of course, like he always had with Paige, and that night back at home they had to wash the sand out of each other's hair.

"Or North Beach in Chatham," Aileen said. "Remember all the birds we saw there?"

"I remember the birds, Mom," Gabriel replied, "I remember everything, but I have no say in this. Base it on your relationship with her, not mine."

Their relationship with Paige had been a good one from the start. Connor and Aileen had visited often at their home, joined them for walks around Onset Village, or swam at the beach near their house. Paige quickly became like a daughter to them, and for her, the relationship was every bit as meaningful. Having lost her mother to cancer and virtually her father to dementia, it was almost like having parents again. After her diagnosis, they played a greater role. In the beginning, they helped with transportation to doctor visits when Gabriel had to work. Later, when she was bedridden, they cooked, cleaned, did laundry and made sure Gabriel was fed.

He forked a piece of vegetarian chicken and glanced up at his mother. "The food is amazing, Mom. Dad, how do you like the meatless chicken?"

Connor put his fork down. "Until about five seconds ago, I thought it was real."

Gabriel laughed and his mom said, "I guess we let the cat out of the bag."

"I'll get used to it," his dad said and took a swallow of wine to wash it down. Gabriel winked at his mom and pulled a small pad of paper from the rear pocket of his jeans.

"What are you writing?" she asked as he scribbled the words *love is a bowl of pasta with fake chicken* in the small notebook.

"I'm trying to finish Paige's list," he explained. "The one on the whiteboard." Some days Paige's *Love is. . .* list was the only way he could keep his mind on positive things.

Aileen smiled at his remark and offered, "We were at a shop in Sandwich the other day that was selling little bird figurines. There was a crane. Of course, I thought of Paige and bought it. It's on the mantel over the fireplace. Can you see it from here?"

Gabriel leaned back in his chair, so the front legs came off the floor, and stretched his neck to see into the living room. "Yeah, I see it, Mom. It's nice," he commented before he let the chair legs come to rest and reached again for the pencil. *Love is a bird on the mantel* he wrote and slid the notebook back in his pocket. His mother's eyes flitted away from his wrist when he noticed her looking at it. A long string of black beads was wrapped around it numerous times. Her glance at his wrist mala reminded him of something. "There's a gift for you in my truck," he said and pushed his chair away from the table.

Aileen turned her eyes to Connor's when she heard the front door shut.

"As well as could be expected," he replied to her silent question regarding his thoughts on their son's welfare. Then Gabriel was back in the house, grasping a bag from the Christmas Tree Shop, a local store located at the base of the Sagamore Bridge.

"Listen, Mom," he said carefully. "You might not want to look at it right now. It's from Paige and was supposed to be for Mother's Day. She bought it months ago, but I forgot until I saw it in the closet yesterday when I was looking for Crazy Horse."

"Why don't you put it in our bedroom," his dad suggested, and Gabriel followed the advice before taking his place again at the kitchen table.

"Tell me what it is," Aileen instructed.

Gabriel glanced at his father first. "Are you sure, Mom?"

She nodded. "That way it won't shock me."

"It's a hummingbird feeder," he said. "You know how she loved hummingbirds."

"She used to tell me when she'd see them," Aileen replied. "I told her that I never see them in Falmouth. I guess she was trying to bring them to me." After a pause she added, "I think Truro is the right place to bring her ashes. What do you think, Connor?"

"The sand dunes in Truro it is," he answered. "You know, tomorrow's Saturday." He nudged his son with his elbow, and Gabriel forced a grin.

"Are you coming?" he asked, even though he knew the answer. His parents might be in Truro by day, but by night they would be in Cambridge.

"Would we miss a chance to see our son play at the Regattabar?" Connor shot back.

It was a club his dad had taken him to as a child. Some of the greatest contemporary jazz musicians had played there, Branford Marsalis, Joshua Redman, and McCoy Tyner. The year Gabriel graduated from Berklee, he and his dad had ventured there together to see one of his favorites, Chick Corea. Now he was substituting at the same venue for the pianist who was double booked in Boston and New York, a lucky break for Gabriel.

"It's the biggest night of the year," his father said, "the one we've been waiting for."

Gabriel didn't reach for the pad of paper this time, but he made a mental note to add to the whiteboard *Love is unconditional.*

December 18, 2009: My sister was right about Gabriel. He is a criminal. But she could not have been more wrong. The whole experience is making me think about judgment, and how we pass it mindlessly on each other. I understand that he was the cause of someone's death, but how could I have survived without him?

Is the human brain wired that way or is it practice handed down from one generation to the next? Regardless of its origin, I think as human beings we can do better than this. We have the capacity to be so much more. If I live long enough to have a child, I'm going to break the chain. We will, Gabriel and me. A person on the outside could look at my life and say that I am a failed journalist, living with an ex-convict a dozen years my junior, and conclude that I am not someone worth knowing. Or a cancer patient who might even fail at that. But I'm more than that.

I think of the pastor at the church, and I remember: I am a blazing light emitting Divine Love into the Universe. Because this is what I choose to be.

Darkness has no power over light. Place a candle in a dark room, and the light will pervade. The darkness has no ability to extinguish it. But to extinguish darkness, all we have to do is flip the switch.

December 25, 2009: It's Christmas morning and I wake up alone. The space beside me in the bed is cold, so I know Gabriel's been up for a while, but I didn't hear him leave. I call his name, but the house remains silent.

This isn't how I thought we'd spend our first (and possibly only?) Christmas together. I'm recovering from the chemo, but my hair is gone. I feel hideously skinny and ugly.

I venture from bed and smell the coffee. It takes a minute to tie a scarf on my head, but my self-consciousness requires it. It's silly, he sees me without it every night in bed, and when I'm half-asleep, I appreciate the feel of his fingertips or his lips on my scalp. The mirror still controls me too much. The Christmas tree lights are on, but there's no Gabriel. Snowflakes are falling gently outside the kitchen window. The world is void of sound, as if the color white has suffocated it. Then a key in the doorknob breaks the silence and I turn, relieved.

"Merry Christmas!" Gabriel spurts, swiping a beanie from his head, and kicking snow off his boots. There's a box in his hands and the top, adorned with a big red bow, is illogically moving by itself. My curiosity is overpowered by my need to feel him in my arms. I push my face into his neck and breathe him in.

Then the top of the box hits the floor, and I look up to see the strangest little face looking at me from the box, a blue-eyed imp-like cat as skinny and bald as me. A startled laugh escapes me. It is a Sphynx, the cat we talked about the day we met. "He's mine?" I shriek and reach for it. The cat curls up in my arms and it's like holding a newborn baby. Instinctively, I wrap my robe around it.

Gabriel nods, his tongue nervously wetting his bottom lip. "You like him?"

"Do you believe in love at first sight?" I throw back. My heart is pounding over the creature in my arms, and I can't look away from his stunningly blue eyes.

"You know I do," Gabriel says, and grazes my cheek with his knuckles, taking away the skinniness and the ugliness and the loneliness all in an instant. I'm actually smiling as we move to the sofa so we can snuggle our new baby, who is making funny little chirping sounds. Now it feels like Christmas.

"He's a rescue," Gabriel explains. "Someone abandoned him, and he almost froze to death. The foster mom was nice about keeping him until today. I thought I'd get back before you woke up, but the roads are slippery."

"It's okay," I assure him. He knows how I hate to be alone now, as if the cancer might gobble me up in his absence. "Does he have a name?"

"It's Crazy Horse," he laughs, "but we can change it if you want."

"Crazy Horse?" I stammer. "Why would anyone name a cat Crazy Horse?"

He shrugs and says, "It kind of fits." The cat does look a little off kilter, but I don't say it because I don't want him to hear. Maybe it's the size of his ears or his eyes. "This could be good practice," Gabriel suggests as he wraps his arms around me, and I nuzzle my head onto his chest. Practice for our own baby, he means. According to Dr. Schuller, it's very unlikely that I will survive for that to happen, but I am more hopeful now than I was ten minutes ago.

Everything feels different now because of Crazy Horse the rescue cat.

December 29, 2009: I know now how our cat got his name. There are paw prints all over the house in the strangest places, on the refrigerator door, the bathroom mirror, even on the blades of the ceiling fan over our bed.

Take a moment to visualize how they got there, and you have decoded the mystifying personality of Crazy Horse.

Aileen has fallen in love with him, even though at first, he scared her. She'd never heard of a Sphynx, and I think conjectured that he was deathly ill because he has no fur to speak of. He is like a peach, covered in the softest layer of down. His face is triangular, like a pixie's. While I fix tea, he hides from Aileen behind a plant and intermittently holds a paw out to get her attention until she seeks him. It's like playing with a child, and it makes her laugh.

Crazy Horse has lifted my spirits, too. I don't focus on myself as much now that I have him. I'm trying to fatten us both. We eat our meals together every day and it reminds me that I'm not the only one trying to regain my health. Aileen brought homemade scones and strawberry preserves to have with our tea while Gabriel and Connor attend an open-mic blues jam. My sweet baby sits in my lap nibbling pieces from my fingers, enjoying it as much as I do.

For Aileen's birthday, I gave her a red floppy hat with the hope that she would give the Red Hat Society a go. The tragedy of Billy's death has made her heart heavy, and I believe that a group of women intent on having fun would help her to heal. Today she is wearing it—as a show of female solidarity—and she brought me a red sequin baseball cap. Now we have our own sisterhood.

Chapter Sixteen

Billy's Parents, *the Pentecostals*

Here lies one whose name was writ in water.
—*John Keats, epitaph for himself*

For some people life is painful even when it's not supposed to be. Their heightened sensitivity serves important purposes, like allowing them to feel another human being's emotions, giving them the opportunity to understand and help them. Sensitivity also allows the person greater access to their own feelings, giving them a greater ability to express themselves creatively. Gabriel was one of those people, as was Billy's mother. Interestingly, given both of their abilities, the word "sensitive" is sometimes used synonymously with the word "medium."

It was this baffling ability that caused Bridget to leave the Catholic Church of her childhood and eventually become "born again." When she was fourteen, still living in Ireland, she made the mistake of telling her priest that she often dreamt of her dead relatives and was able to converse with them. Father Mike suggested she might be possessed by a demon and instructed her to cut off all future communications.

"But how?" she'd pleaded, terrified. "I have no control. It happens while I'm asleep."

"Ask God to take it away!" Father Mike ordered and walked off as if he were frightened to be too close to her.

The dreams continued, even though she prayed about them. Eventually, it occurred to her that only loving words had transpired during the communications, and that she always awakened feeling joyful. Why would it feel like love if it were truly a demon speaking to her? And she had a blasphemous thought: Maybe Father Mike didn't know everything. Maybe *the Catholic Church* didn't know everything.

It wasn't long after moving to the United States that she met a girl who told her she could "speak in tongues" and led her to a Pentecostal Church. The service was nothing like what she was accustomed to. People danced, sang, and shouted as a means of praise and worship. And speaking in tongues was not at all unusual. The Pentecostals perceived it as the entrance of the Holy Spirit into the followers of Jesus Christ. When she shared her secret—the spirit dreams—with the minister, he called them "visions" and told her that she possessed "the gift of prophecy." For Bridget, his acceptance gave her permission to accept part of herself that she had never been at peace with before.

Gabriel had always felt a connection to Billy's mother, even before she shared with him the story of her visions—that were startlingly like dreams he'd experienced as a child. Her life, he realized, much like his, was guided more by spirit than mind. Also like him, she wore her experiences close to the surface. Gabriel could detect her wounds, even before she disclosed them. Billy was the opposite. He was like a tumbleweed. He could be blown here or there and be none the worse for it. Any emotional pain he suffered was hidden beneath a chronic grin.

Some days while Billy pieced together a model race car or helped his older brother work on his Camaro, Gabriel would sit at the kitchen table and sip Irish breakfast tea with Bridget, who always shared with him her current grievances: her oldest son forgot her birthday or her husband's criticism of a meal she'd cooked. Gabriel, a child, could offer little more than an understanding nod, but that was enough. He was quieter, sweeter, and more perceptive than her "ricochet boys," as she called her sons because they could bounce off walls or wooden floors and be none the worse for it.

Over tea, she told him about her childhood in Ireland and her immigration to the United States, where she met Richard, her husband, at an Irish pub in Boston. He'd been scraping by as a musician, sleeping in his car in warm weather and hostels in the winter. It was his voice that she fell in love with, his voice that spoke as clearly of his personality as his boyish face and jet-black hair. His leather motorcycle jacket didn't hide the sweetness of his nature that she detected in his voice as it fluctuated from one note to the next. She'd sit in the pub with her pint of Guinness and listen until he packed up his gear. He was often the only person in the place without an Irish accent, but that didn't deter her interest. So, what if he wasn't Irish? His soul felt like hers.

It was Richard's daredevil grin, prominent ears and musical ability that Billy inherited, but the red hair, freckled complexion and indomitable spirit came from his mother. In 2010, at the age of fifty-eight, and as the mother of three grown boys, Bridget bore the fresh face of her Irish childhood, even if it was marked by laugh lines and worry wrinkles. Her bold personality had been tempered by time and experience. She knew when to hold her tongue and when not to. Life had taught her diplomacy, a gift that had not yet been earned by her youngest son. Billy revolted against anything that tried to constrain him, be it a human being, a law, or an addiction, and he'd displayed his strength in an unyielding manner, like a young horse. If only he could have tamed it earlier, his mother often thought, it might have saved his life.

The phone call that came after the accident was not what awakened Bridget. It was the dream of Billy that preceded the ring of the telephone by several minutes. She'd seen his face as clearly as if he was sitting next to her and peering through the other side of a magnifying glass. She saw the amorphous splashes of freckles on his skin, the ridge of his nose that curved just a bit to the right, his auburn eyebrows, so perfectly formed they might have been plucked, and the surprising depth of his icy blue eyes. The dream had alerted her to leave bed and check on him. She was standing in the doorway to his bedroom, looking for a form under the covers, when the phone rang, and it was in that split second that she understood Billy had passed over. He had been trying to warn her with the dream, to prepare her before she heard the words spoken by a stranger.

It wasn't the first time she'd lost him. Two years prior he'd overdosed on heroin. The overdose stopped his heart, but with Narcan it started again. Ten months later, he lost control of his motorcycle and slammed it into a tree. The motorcycle accident tore the cartilage in his knee, leaving him with a pronounced limp, and injured his shoulder. It was a miracle, the emergency room physician said, that his head escaped collision with the oak tree, even though his shoulder hadn't. To his mother, retrospectively, the two narrow escapes were an alert of what was coming. She believed that Billy was given the opportunity to make things right before he passed over, to heal relationships that had been damaged during the drug-induced years of his life. And if he had to pass over at an early age, who better to be with than Gabriel? For Billy, forming acquaintances had been easy, but establishing friendships had not. Gabriel was his one true friend, the only person he never pushed away, even during the heroin years.

She didn't blame Gabriel for Billy's death. Still, she avoided the Byrnes' because it was too hard to see her own pain reflected in their eyes. They'd lost their son, too. He'd turned inward, disappeared under the surface like a drowning boy.

While the boys were growing up, Bridget had seen Aileen as another pea in her own pod, an Irish girl like herself with an untamed, though intelligent and talented child. They used to spend Saint Patrick's Day together every year. That stopped the year Billy died and Gabriel went to prison to pay for it, even though she knew, as her husband did, that Billy was every bit as much to blame. It was the state of Massachusetts' case, and the state enforced the charges against Gabriel. Still, how could she invite Aileen and Connor over for corned beef and cabbage without stirring pain into the pot? It seemed an unhealable wound for all of them.

The same morning Aileen and Connor were on route to Truro to release Paige's ashes, Bridget and Richard were tending to the wild roses growing along the fence that ran parallel to the road. Bridget saw their Audi approaching. Because they lived on the same street, she often saw them come and go. She'd even noticed Gabriel's truck in the driveway the evening before and had been tempted to walk over. She worried about him, even more since his girlfriend's death. How much tragedy could a young man be expected to carry, especially one as sensitive as Gabriel?

In the end, she decided not to knock on their door, but when she spotted the Audi, she took a step toward the street as she waved to them, hoping they would stop. Connor pulled the car over in front of their house and rolled down the window. Aileen was wearing a red sun hat, a gift from Paige, she explained.

"Gabriel was very appreciative that you came to Paige's funeral," she offered after they indicated the intention of their trip to Truro.

"He was surprised," Connor added. "He's convinced himself that you hate him."

A small cry escaped Bridget's lips. Richard wrapped an arm around her slumped shoulders and answered for her, "That would be impossible."

Aileen peered through the passenger window at Bridget standing in the arch that bridged the walkway and the white picket fence. In stark contrast were deep orange trumpet flowers growing on vines that resembled honeysuckle. Just as Aileen's eyes turned from the vermillion blossoms to Bridget's face, she noticed movement over her shoulder. At first, she saw only one, but within seconds another identical creature had been captured by her vision. They were tiny birds, fluttering next to Bridget's head.

"Hummingbirds!" Aileen breathed.

Bridget bent her neck to glimpse the birds flying fearlessly close to her face, but her mind was on something more important to her. "What I was wondering," she voiced softly, "is if you could ask Gabriel to stop by for tea. I'd like to hear about his music and about his life." A heavier Irish accent was slipping into her voice. Her brogue always thickened with her emotions. Still, the hummingbirds hovered only inches away. Their miniature wings whirred like small engines, and held the Byrnes spellbound. "Without him being around like he used to be, I feel like I've lost two sons," she concluded.

Aileen's eyes immediately shifted to Bridget's. She knew what it was like to love someone like her own child. Her fingers tightened on the vial of ashes in her hand. Paige had been that person to her. *Paige and her hummingbirds.*

"Gabriel has a show in Boston tonight," she said. "Why don't you join us?"

The invitation drew a smile from their faces, and Aileen decided then to buy Bridget a red hat of her own. Perhaps they could wear them to Gabriel's show.

January 1, 2010: None of us are fully aware of our impact on other people's lives. For better or worse, we leave a thumbprint. I've been trying to decode some of the marks left on me. Here's what I've got so far:

My father. When I was a little girl you told me I could fly if I believed it hard enough. Thank you, Dad, for introducing limitlessness to my young mind. Your words empowered me.

My mom. The living embodiment of kindness. You made love an action word.

Abby. You taught me to be smart, to think things through. (I know, I know, this part of me still needs work.)

Joey. Every time I hear your voice, you remind me that innocence still exists in the world. You are entirely naïve, and it fits you beautifully.

Christopher. You are my friend and that counts for so much more than I understood until recently. Even though we never talk anymore, if I really needed someone to be here, a little voice in my head would say, "Call Chris."

Julia & Kim. Silliness and tomfoolery matter; they keep us young and joyful.

Yara & Davi. The most graceful couple I've had the privilege of knowing. Your union is an emphatic reminder that love can indeed last a lifetime.

Arica & Ben. If we are both lucky and brave it is possible to find perfect balance by blending two human beings into one indestructible partnership.

Gabriel. You understand there is no value in holding onto someone with both hands. I am yours, not because you possess me, but because you have no desire to, and because there is no other place I'd rather be. You are my home.

January 3, 2010, Dream Journal entry: Between wakefulness and sleep, I experience an odd dream or vision. I am an insect, crawling underground on the numerous legs I feel scrambling beneath me. There are others, too, nearby. We bang up against each other because there is not much space, but I don't mind that. This is my world, the only thing I know. We move when the soil is warm and sleep when the earth cools down. I have no understanding of why the earth all around me changes temperature and I don't question it. This is life and it is good. Then, for no reason it seems, strange sounds come from overhead, and we scramble. "This way," someone up ahead sends out telepathically, and we march, the tiniest of soldiers, climbing upward. The dirt under my feet is becoming spongy, and it is harder to move. Water is seeping in. Soon it is coming in torrents, and I begin to signal with my thoughts, "It's the end of the world! The end of everything!" and I hear it echoed behind me. But those ahead have better vision. "Keep moving!" they command, and not knowing what else to do, we follow blindly, sure that we'll all be extinguished. Then I see something strange ahead, and I hear cheers. It is light, they say. I have never seen light and it, too, frightens me. I step out of the tunnel and see the expansive universe around me, painted a multitude of colors I have never seen or even imagined. Until now, I thought everything was brown. And then I wake up—with a new understanding. What I've always known was not the whole world, after all. It was only a small part of it.

January 13, 2010: "I met this guy at a hookah bar."

Those were Gabriel's first words this afternoon when he walked in the door. The words make me laugh every time I think of them. They are so very Gabriel, so full of color. What the hell is a hookah bar?????

According to my boyfriend (who visited the place with Ben, our hookah-smoking friend), it is a place where those 18 plus can gather to smoke various flavors of tobacco from hookah pipes.

The guy he met is skilled in henna art. Gabriel says he will take me to him to have my hands done.

I want to smoke from a hookah, too, I tell him, and he frowns at me with his petulant mouth. "Maybe after the PET scan," he replies, "when we know everything is clear." He thinks I'm buying his confident words, but Gabriel's eyes are like a crystal ball. He can't hide his fear any better than I can.

Chapter Seventeen

Ben, *the Jew*

Heaven is under our feet as well as over our heads.
—Henry David Thoreau

I am alone in the woods smoking from a hookah, Ben wrote in his notebook. He stole a nervous glance over his shoulder and laughed out loud. It felt like being fifteen again and getting stoned in the woods behind his house. The same sick sensation tugged at his belly, as if any moment his dad might leap out from behind a tree and bust him. He brought the lai of the Syrian hookah to his mouth and pulled the smoke into his lungs.

"Hell, yes," he released with the smoke, and waited for THC to surround his brain like a swat team. With any luck, it would take his mind off the vial of ashes.

The woods were a perfect place to enjoy the instant peace of mind. Pine trees had littered golden needles that made a carpet for his bare feet, and birds hidden in the branches continued to talk to each other, as if he had not invaded their home. He had a clear view of the pond nestled in the trees, forgotten for the most part by the human race. That small pool of water, like a mirage in the desert, was one of his favorite spots.

He'd brought his kids there once and they'd spent the day exploring the pond and the path that circled it. That night after he'd dropped them off, his ex-wife called and complained that the children could have been bitten by mosquitoes and contracted encephalitis, and who did he think he was risking their health like that?

"Their father," he'd replied. "I think I'm their father." There was a click and the call ended. Within a week, a sheriff served him papers and Ben had to defend his actions in court, not only the adventure into the woods without mosquito repellant, but his response that afternoon to his son's casual comment that Jews are God's chosen people.

"We're all God's chosen people," he'd said. "It doesn't matter whether we're Jewish, Christian or Muslim. It doesn't even matter if you behave or not. God will love you, no matter what, because that's what God is."

It had taken him too long to learn it, but he understood now that to claim any group of people were, physically or spiritually, ranked higher than others was a racist concept, and Ben had no intention of raising racists.

Arica, his fiancée, was as black as the night sky, born in Nigeria. She didn't practice any religion, but she was the most spiritual human being he'd ever met. He'd sensed that about her immediately, back in junior high school when she moved to Cape Cod to live with her father. To Ben's twelve-year-old perception, she seemed to glow. After he made the mistake of telling his parents that his new friend grew up in Nigeria in a Muslim community (even though she wasn't one), they spoke of the shame he brought to the family for admiration of a "Muslim" when there were plenty of "nice Jewish girls." And Ben internalized it, every single word. That was the reason he and Arica weren't more than friends as teenagers, because Ben never dared to cross that line—except once, when he kissed her during a game of Truth or Dare.

He brought the pipe to his mouth again, remembering the feel of Arica's teenage lips during the game that had transpired more than two decades before. He'd gone off to college at Brandeis University in accordance with his parents' wishes, but he'd carried an imprint of that kiss with him. It wasn't all flower petals and angels singing like the poets say. His body was shaky and the roasted chicken he'd eaten for dinner had grumbled in his stomach.

What the Hell *was* that? he'd asked himself afterward. But now—in his mid-thirties—he was pretty sure he knew. It was soul recognition. He knew her. He knew her before she ever stepped into his classroom with hair cut shorter than his and skin so black it made the blackboard behind her look gray. Even then there was a gravitational pull toward Arica, a small voice whispering wordlessly *pay attention—this person is important.*

Ben was a self-professed romantic. He believed in love at first sight, but not because he thought physical appearance was enough to ignite it. It was because he trusted intuition and its ability to lead the right people to each other at the right time. To him, there was something much bigger at work than physical attraction. If Arica was Latino or Asian, would he have loved her? Undoubtedly. If she was German or Arabic, would he have loved her still? Yes, of course he would have loved her no matter how she appeared. It was the glow that would have caught his eye.

Once, when Paige's yoga friend, Yara, was visiting and the women were sipping tea at the kitchen table while the guys watched *Mad Max* in the living room, Ben had noted that the three of them—Paige, Arica and Yara—looked like sisters from the three different cultures and races, one white, one black and one brown. The comment had made them laugh, and after that he'd noticed they'd sometimes playfully use the word "sister" when addressing each other. And Ben liked that. Building a family out of three different nationalities seemed a brilliant idea to him.

Now he scribbled in his notebook: *I came here for you, Paige, because I never took you to the hookah bar like I promised you I would.*

Ben liked to carry a notebook to write down all the things he wished he could say, a habit developed in college. When his parents had asked via telephone how his classes were going, he'd respond, "Fine," and write in the notebook that they could not see: *They suck. I'm in the wrong major.*

"Have you met any nice girls?"

"They're all nice," he'd reply and jot down: *no one remotely interesting.*

"Are you staying away from the students who smoke marijuana?"

His "Of course," was followed by *they're my cohorts and cannabis is my deity.*

Ben hadn't thought of it as a journal. They were simply scattered thoughts recorded in his Economics notebook. With time, it became a habit to carry a notebook with him everywhere he went. It was preventative medicine that replaced the need for Xanax that he'd started taking when he was ten because he'd been having panic attacks in school.

Paige had been interested in his notebook, and after he confessed to her its purpose, she'd informed him that his throat chakra was blocked. Ben had never heard of a chakra, but Paige must have known what she was talking about because after leading him through a series of meditations to clear the blockage, words seemed to burst spontaneously from his mouth, instead of seeking escape through his fingers.

As a way of disempowering the notebook, he once spent an hour with Paige reading his notations out loud while she rolled on the floor of her living room in hysterics.

"You snort like a boy," he remarked because he was annoyed by her response. To Paige, everything in life was laugh-worthy, even the stuff he wrote down because he felt too vulnerable to say out loud.

His comment silenced her. "So, I snort like a boy," she finally replied, "And you cry like a girl, but I love that about you." Ben gasped and that had made her giggle again, which was incomprehensible to him seeing how he was the one who was stoned.

"Why are you laughing?" he finally demanded, paranoia gripping his brain.

"Why aren't you?" she'd challenged. Paige rolled onto her belly and rested her chin on the palm of her hand. "Here's the thing," she confided. "If something makes me feel shitty, I put a spin on it, to transform it. I think that's why God gave us the ability to laugh, so we don't implode. Besides, not everything is as life-altering as you think it is."

But some things are, Ben thought, *like cancer*. Then the thought shot out of his mouth before he could catch it. Paige had cancer and was most likely going to die, according to the prognosis he'd managed to squeeze out of Gabriel. And that was life-altering for her and for the rest of them. He couldn't laugh in the face of her illness. So, how could she?

"How do you measure life?" she quietly asked.

"It's different for everyone," he suggested.

"Right. But how do *you* measure it? For me, it's by the way I feel, by my own happiness. When I see it that way, I remember that time is just background music. It doesn't matter how much time we have, as long as we're happy."

Ben searched for his pen. If he was able to conjure an answer, he wouldn't allow it to shoot out of his mouth, like his last comment. He'd do the sane thing and write it down.

"Seriously, Ben, cannabis is your deity?" Paige quipped in an obvious attempt to shift the mood. "I'd love to see your mother's face if you said that out loud."

Paige had met Ben's mother only once, but that was all it had taken to make an impression. Mrs. Cohen bore the energy of an army sergeant. Although he'd never said so, Ben was clearly scared of her. Whenever she was around, he shaved and dressed more conservatively—even wore shoes, which was a feat for Ben, who rarely wore anything on his feet, even in the winter. Ben always aired the house out, too, for several days prior to his mother's visit. Her car door would slam as she departed and within minutes the sweet smell of marijuana would float through Paige and Gabriel's window.

"Did you pass inspection?" they'd tease. It was a joke, until the next visit. Then he'd go into defense mode. Most of his life he'd tried to protect himself from his parents' judgment. For them, he became a modern-day changeling. For Paige, he never had to.

"There's only so much time to be who you really are once you figure it out," she advised, and gently pried the notebook from his hand. "Can I draw something in it?"

"Knock yourself out," Ben replied, trying to absorb her comment. He hadn't figured out who he was until he was in his early thirties. He often wondered if it was that way for everyone, or if some people were born knowing their path like baby turtles that cracked out of their eggs and headed straight to the sea.

On the inside cover Paige drew a sketch of a dragonfly. She used the indigo ink of the pen to shade its eyes and added a small grin to its unusual face. "Do you know dragonflies are only able to fly near the end of their lives and that's only a few months?" she asked, the pen poised between her fingers. Ben had shaken his head as Paige handed the notebook back to him. Underneath her rendering she had written the words, *it's time to fly!*

After that, Ben occasionally opened the notebook to gaze at the dragonfly and remind himself of its message. Since Paige's departure, however, he had purposefully avoided looking at it. He used a bookmark now, something he never used to do, to be sure he'd open the notebook to the next blank page and not accidentally catch a glimpse of the cartoonish insect and be reminded of Paige's illness and death. He wasn't ready to deal with it. He hadn't even gone to the funeral because he knew that he'd have broken down in public instead of being strong for Gabriel, and he wasn't sure he could ever forgive himself for that.

Ben lit the pipe again and was taking a nice deep haul when a dragonfly came out of nowhere and landed on the words he'd written to Paige. He held the hash smoke in his lungs. Its eyes were blue, like the ones she had drawn with the pen, and for a nonsensical moment, it felt like the dragonfly perched on his notebook was the same one Paige had drawn, magically come to life. It lifted off the page like a helicopter and hovered briefly near his face before it flew off. As Ben watched it journey across the pond, he exhaled the smoke, and slowly regained a sense of balance.

Arica was home cooking dinner for Gabriel, and Ben had assured her he'd return before Gabriel arrived. He glanced at the time on his cell phone. There were still a few minutes to spare. He headed for the water. His feet were callused from going barefoot year-round. They weren't hurt by the sticks and rocks he had to step on to reach the water. He stripped off his clothes and stepped into the pond up to his knees. It felt good to be naked outdoors, as if he'd tossed convention to the ground with his clothes.

But he kept thinking about the dragonfly. If Paige could have seen his face when he witnessed it land on his journal, she'd have laughed, and that brought a reluctant grin to his lips. It felt like sharing one last joke with his friend. There had been quite a few.

His favorite was Paige's insistence that her cat acted stoned because of the smoke drifting out Ben's window. Once she told him she'd returned from the store to find the cat spinning around on the ceiling fan. At first, he'd taken her seriously and asked if Crazy Horse was all right, but then he noticed the smirk. *You make this shit up just to amuse yourself*, he accused, and she released the wild laughter she'd been holding in.

A group of fish found his pale legs fascinating and circled him. Every few seconds a brave one would rush in and nibble at his flesh. If he dropped Paige's ashes in the water, would the fish eat them? The thought was enough to make him question his plan. Would it be irreverent to scatter her ashes in a place where they could be consumed by wildlife? In silence, he watched and wondered what it would be like to live his entire life under water with no other purpose than to live. For animals being alive was enough. Why wasn't it for humans? Why for people was there always acquisition involved? A new job, a new lover, a new house. The list was endless.

If he was a fish, he never would have gone to a college chosen by his parents so he could score a job also chosen by them. If he was a fish, he would have done what made him happy. He had that now, but it had taken him years of discontentment to get there. While working as a restaurant manager he'd taken art classes at the Rhode Island School of Design and had started making sculptures out of metal that he scavenged from junk yards. A seagull crafted out of an old car hood had been his first gift to Arica.

"This is what you should be doing with your time," she said as her doe eyes and elegant fingers explored the bird, and Ben's heart felt like a machine gun firing. He'd been waiting years for someone to say that, for someone to set him free.

Now he was as liberated as the seagull he'd used as a model. When he moved into Arica's small house in Onset, he quit the restaurant to focus on his art. Now he had an internet business where he sold his sculptures and served as an agent for other local artists. Their goal in life was not to acquire physical possessions, but happiness fed by an unlimited flow of freedom. And it worked beautifully. The universe delivered everything into their lives that they needed, even friends with a similar outlook.

He returned to the ashes and used his T-shirt to dry his face. He knew now what he had to do—it was the dragonfly that

clued him in—but first he opened the notebook to the sketch
Paige had drawn. His eyes and fingers trailed across the words
It's time to fly!

They were deliberate steps that led Ben back to the pond.
He released the ashes into the water without another doubt. It
didn't matter if the fish ate the cremation ashes, or even if Paige
somehow saw it happen, because he knew that even if she did,
she'd put a spin on it, she'd transform it. Paige, he understood,
would find a way to make it funny.

There was a lesson he learned from all this, from the
friendships that seemingly end, but don't really, from the
grasping onto the last piece of something he believed to be
sacred when the sacred part had already slipped away. There's
room for grief, but also room for laughter. And it's okay, and
sometimes even essential, to have both.

*January 17, 2010: Jews claim to be God's chosen
people. Christians claim Jews and Muslims will
burn in Hell for not accepting Jesus Christ as their
savior. And Muslims claim Jews and Christians
will burn in hell for believing that Jesus is the son
of God. Hell must be a big place.*

Postscript: PET scan today. Please be good news.

*January 23, 2010: Is there a scarier word in the
English language than metastasis? The PET scan,
scheduled to see how the chemo worked, revealed
the cancer's progression. It didn't stop it and
now it's in my lungs. I found out a week ago, but
I haven't been able to journal about it.*

*If I write it down, does that somehow make
it true?*

*January 25, 2010: Today I went for a walk in
the snow with Gabriel. We ran into Ben and Arica.
I started crying and Ben did, too. Arica's eyes*

stayed dry, they never shifted from mine, and her hands were steady on my arms. She's the best listener I know. My illness is hurting her, too, but she never shows it. They knew about the prognosis because Gabriel went over and told them what Dr. Schuller said, but today was the first time I've seen them since. I used to think in terms of years, but now it is months, and soon it will be weeks. I wonder, dear reader (Gabriel? Abby?), in the depths of your imagination, could you imagine that?

Abby stopped by later and we played Monopoly for the first time since we were kids. She didn't know what to say and neither did I. We were silent and acted intent on winning the game, but I didn't need her to talk. I only needed her to be here. I hope she knows that.

We've made a lot of assumptions in this family, I realized as I waited for Abby to think of the right thing to say because she assumed I expected it. As human beings what we don't communicate is far greater than what we manage to express.

Joe purposefully creates distance from Abby because he assumes she will reject him if she knows the truth about his life. Abby assumes Joe doesn't like her, or that he loves me more because he tells me things. But the truth is he's less afraid of my thoughts because they are more like his; it has nothing to do with love. All three of us assume that our dad has no understanding of us anymore because of his dementia, but he's proved us wrong on numerous occasions. Last weekend he showed up for a visit, and after he left, I found five quarters on the table next to my bed. With my dad those quarters are code for "I love you." They mean he wants to buy me ice cream to make me feel better like he did when I was a child. What a disservice to this man to assume he no longer understands.

Abby assumes that I disagree with all her core beliefs. But that's not true. At the base level we both believe there should be an approach to life that includes treating others with respect and refraining from hurting anyone. We learned these values as children, and I think they are just as relevant to atheists as they are to anyone else.

She's done a remarkable job as my sister. Granted, I've resented her because I felt like she was trying to constrain me, but I understand now it was love that motivated her to take on the role of my savior. I'd hate to pass out of this world without her knowing that I love her just as much but haven't been able to show it without feeling like I was conceding something sacred to me, my freedom.

Chapter Eighteen

Onset Church Group, *the Spiritualists*

dear girl
How i was crazy how i cried when i heard
over time
and tide and death
leaping
Sweetly
your voice.
—E.E. Cummings

They had agreed beforehand to meet at the gazebo, the group of friends and acquaintances who knew each other from church. Two elderly ladies in summer dresses were perched on the bench when Gabriel arrived, one of them holding the vial of ashes in her hand. Four other people were waiting in the gazebo and several others were milling around on the grass, conversing. He inhaled deeply and scanned the skies before he approached them.

Gabriel was wearing his best shirt, one Paige had bought him at a sidewalk sale, and dress slacks, even though he knew the intention was to bring her ashes onto the beach. It didn't matter if the slacks were ruined from sitting on wet sand or walking too close to the waves. Paige would be there. *Where every vial travels, so will I,* she had promised. *And if possible, I'll remind you.* Therefore, he dressed like he was meeting her for a date.

One other person was set to arrive—a well-known medium from the Boston area who had met Paige numerous times at the church and at the wigwam. She was the one who'd given Paige the message that convinced her that her mother's spirit was alive and well. The woman's name was Janice and she had taken a particular liking to Paige. Janice was a breast cancer survivor and had been inspired by Paige's courage during her illness. She had a big personality like Paige, too. Gabriel saw Janice exit her car wearing a purple dress and red lipstick and waved to her. They were all meeting, not only to release Paige's ashes on the beach, but to have a "circle," the contemporary term for a séance, in the hope of receiving a message from her.

The word "séance," thanks to Hollywood and ghost stories, has a negative connotation, an association with the dark side. But it is light, not darkness, that is needed to successfully communicate. It isn't frightening to those who practice it because they understand that all human beings are spirits, whether they are attached to a body or not. It's a conversation of sorts with a person's consciousness that continues even after their body is gone. The idea is that, although the body requires consciousness, consciousness does not require a body.

To communicate with those who have departed theirs, the energy of those in the circle must have a fast enough vibration to merge with those of a naturally higher vibration, due to the lack of density in their form. This is accomplished through positive thoughts and actions, by meditation and living mindfully. Spiritualists are not devil worshippers. In fact, there is no room in their religion for demons or the confines of Hell. They believe reformation is viable for all souls. Life is not about sinning or not sinning, but about learning or not learning. Sunflowers are the symbol of their religion because they always turn toward the light.

Although he'd believed in the afterlife, it had taken time to convince Gabriel that communication was possible across the two dimensions. The first seed was planted the night of the car accident. Before the paramedics arrived, he'd seen a stream of swirling light lift from Billy's body. It wasn't Billy that he saw, the body he was familiar with, but he'd understood on a deep, undisputable level that it was him. And that event had marked the beginning of his journey, although looking back over time he could identify clairvoyant dreams he'd experienced as a child. Meditation improved his vision, and by the time Paige passed over, he was able to see her spirit body standing before him.

He took no credit for his spiritual abilities. In his mind, that belonged to his friend Billy and his other teachers. At the end of each day, he gave thanks to all of his spirit friends who were working, unseen, on his behalf. He understood that, because of their efforts, he reaped the benefits of a greater understanding. But his truth was still exactly that, *his* truth. He had no desire to force it on—or even suggest it to—anyone else.

Gabriel embraced Janice as soon as she was within reach. "Thanks for making the trip down here," he said, and she waved the comment away with a flick of her hand.

"I wouldn't be anywhere else," she replied and greeted each person in the group with a smile. She loved being a medium. It gave her the chance to help people ease their grief. "Shall we begin?" she asked and slipped out of her sandals.

The group followed her to the beach, the elderly lady in a sundress and white canvas sneakers still grasping the vial of ashes. It was a Thursday morning in June. School was still in session, so the beach belonged to them alone. On a sandy stretch in front of the azure water, they sat in a circle. Gabriel's eyes turned upward toward the flawless sky.

"And there it is," he said out loud. "A crane," he added when he noticed everyone looking at him. One man's sea bird is another man's message from the universe. To Gabriel it was the sign he'd been waiting for, Paige assuring him of her presence.

"Did Paige like cranes?" asked the old woman clinging to the ashes with her wrinkled hand.

"Paige loved every living thing," he answered. "But we saw one here on our first date, and after that she was always looking for them. At her funeral one flew over, too."

Gabriel turned his eyes down to his feet, trying to focus on something other than the emotion building like an electric storm in his chest. He never knew when he shared such thoughts if it comforted people or caused them to believe he was delusional. But this was, after all, a group of Spiritualists, people who live for that kind of stuff.

His comment drew excited murmurs from the small crowd. The crane was beautiful to watch, the long white body flying elegantly through the air. To Gabriel, it recalled Paige, her long slender body that she'd moved gracefully through his life.

"Should we hold the ashes until after we're done with the circle, so Paige can be here?" one of the old women asked. Gabriel could never remember their names, but he knew both started with the letter "M": Muriel and Margaret or Marjorie and Mary? He'd never seen them apart. They walked through life like Siamese twins. They might have been sisters, friends, or lovers. It was impossible to tell. It was only obvious that they loved each other. Gabriel was fascinated by the many ways human beings try to define their relationships. To him, what it always came down to was love, which in his mind was indefinable anyway.

"Let them go," he replied. "She's already here."

The first lady—the one in the sneakers—stood first and held her companion's hands to help her up. Everyone followed, except for Gabriel.

"Is it okay if we put them in the water?" Janice, the medium, asked.

"Whatever feels right," Gabriel replied.

Once alone, he placed his hands in prayer position in front of his chest and closed his eyes. He didn't need to see where the ashes were scattered. His time would be better spent meditating, so that he could raise his own vibration. Maybe then he could get a clear picture of her. He wouldn't be able to hear her, but he was hoping Janice would.

He removed the mala from his wrist and lay it across his palm. His thumb and middle finger began their journey across the one hundred and eight beads as he tried to close out the sound of chatter behind him and focus only on his breath. All the while he silently repeated: *om mani padme hum*, the mantra of the Buddha of Compassion.

He wasn't a Buddhist, but he believed in the power of thought, and it was one of his daily goals to live more compassionately. Also, focusing on a positive mantra helped to cleanse negative ideas from his brain, negativity that could slow down his vibration. He could easily identify the difference. When he was vibrating at a higher rate his body felt adrenalized, like endorphins rushing through him after a run. He felt like he could fly. When he was vibrating slower, his body felt weighted to the earth. It was harder to move, and kind thoughts were not easily making their way to the tip of his tongue.

The group returned just as he was reaching the end of the beads his fingers had traveled deftly across, each time accompanied by his mantra. They took their seats, and respectfully waited for him to finish. He smiled when he opened his eyes and saw all their faces turned toward him. Gabriel didn't ask how it went. He could see tears staining the faces of several people, and the two old ladies, who'd known Paige only as acquaintances, were consoling each other. Paige had a way of making an impression.

"Whenever you're ready," he said to Janice, and she nodded her head.

Everyone followed her lead, closing their eyes and opening their hands on their laps. She was quiet for quite some time. Gabriel could hear the waves softly, rhythmically, rolling over the sand while he waited to see if the medium would be able to bridge the gap between Paige and him.

"I'm hearing the words 'beautiful boy,'" Janice suddenly said, and Gabriel opened his eyes. "Would you understand that?"

"Yes," Gabriel acknowledged.

He was beginning to feel Paige's energy. It was light-hearted, almost ecstatic, the same kind of energy Paige had emanated when she was excited. What startled him and made his hands tremble was the stark contrast between Paige's elation and his own heavy heart. He dropped his chin and rubbed his eyes with the heels of his hands.

"I can see her," Janice continued, and became quiet again before she released a small laugh as if she were sharing a private joke with Paige. The gesture instantly lightened the mood in the circle. "Her face is much younger. And her movements — she's like a child, chasing the seagulls. Her feet are lifting off the ground with the wind. She's completely unrestrained, and absolutely thrilled about it. She's laughing — can you hear it?"

"No," Gabriel replied. He dropped his hands away from his eyes and tried to steady himself. All he wanted for Paige was for her to be free and to be happy. It was everything he'd been praying for, yet for some reason, it was hard to hear. Were his tears from relief and joy? Or were they from heartbreak?

Janice was focusing on him. "Paige is pointing to your bare feet. And her hand is covered in paint. She's waving it in front of you, trying to get your attention. I can actually see the paint dripping onto your leg."

"I think — I think I know where she's going with this," he muttered, his voice thick.

"Now I'm seeing green paw prints and a red —" Janice continued.

"Heart," Gabriel interrupted, and Janice smiled.

He was talking not so much to her, as to Paige. She was here to assure him that her love for him had survived physical death. He understood her intent, and he needed her to know it.

"It's a red heart," he said.

February 1, 2010: Today we played with paint. When I tell him how much I loved finger painting in kindergarten, Gabriel dips my whole hand in the red can. We are sitting on the floor of our small kitchen on an old bed sheet, and I am between his legs. It is unfathomable that I am happy and at peace, but I am.

"This moment," he says, "is the only one that matters."

I lean back in his arms and let my head fall on his shoulder, our necks wrapped like swans, and his breath warm on my cheek. Paint is dripping off my hand onto his jeans, but he's not distracted by it. He strains to reach my lips and kisses me. I've lost so much weight that my skin puddles and dark brown bruises circle my eyes, but in this man's arms I am beautiful. I kiss him back with all the love I can muster, imagining filling him with it like pouring water into a vase.

I have left behind the fear of no longer existing. Gabriel has driven the thought from my consciousness like a priest exorcizing a demon. I trust that I will continue, just not in the physical way I am accustomed. But a new fear has been born inside me—being separated from him. The thought is agony that robs me of my breath.

Crazy Horse is my comic relief. He steps on the green paint lid and paw prints sprout like flowers on the floor and countertops as he scurries away. Gabriel is not annoyed by the mess. He's as accepting of Crazy Horse as he is of me. I lean forward and paint a messy red heart on his bare foot with my finger.

"I wish it would last forever," I say, as if it is a masterpiece. That way he would always remember me and how I love him. If I could paint like Michelangelo, I'd cover the ceiling with attestations of my affection, so he could always look up when he needs the reminder, but I can't, so my temporary rendering will have to do.

"I know your love will live on," he says. "Like with your mom and Billy. If their love for us died with the body, they'd have no reason to come back, but they do."

Indeed, they do. This morning while we had our coffee, Billy was making the light blink over the table, letting us know he was present. How do I know it was him? You might not believe it, but I'll tell you anyway. Once at church a medium I'd never met called on me and started talking about someone in spirit tampering with the electricity in our cottage. She said that the guy has red hair and walks with a limp. Coincidence? No way. Billy's here because he wants to ease Gabriel's burden. And you know what? He is. When I get to the other side, if I'm able, I'll do the same.

February 5, 2010: The peaceful contentment I felt a few days ago has evaporated, and now I'm just angry—I'm so FUCKING ANGRY!!!!! Why can't I write any louder than this? There aren't enough expletives or exclamation points to express my emotions. I need to scream in reds and purples. I swore I'd write nothing but light in this journal, but I can't find it. "DO YOU HEAR ME, GOD? I CAN'T FIND THE LIGHT!"

February 8, 2010: Can't do this. Angry and fucked up again.

February 10, 2010: We sat on the deck today in the cold. The sun was painting everything gold, but other than us, the birds were the only ones who noticed.

February 11, 2010: "I'm still jumping off the bridge with you," I tell him in my snarkiest tone. "You promised." We've been planning it all year, practically since the day we met. He doesn't say anything, but I know what he's thinking, that there's no way in hell he's jumping off that bridge with me. I suggested he carry me, but I'm so frail that he's probably scared the impact would break my bones.

February 14, 2010: Valentine's Day. He did it again, made me feel beautiful when I'd been thoroughly convinced that beauty was a privilege exclusive to the young and the healthy. I was napping when Gabriel woke me up with a surprise. The henna guy was in the kitchen waiting to paint my hands. I smiled in spite of myself, and he noticed. I don't want to waste the time I have left on depression and anger, but they are unyielding opponents. It's a quandary, trying not to squander precious time worried about time I will miss later.

We sit in silence, the henna artist, Uday, working and Gabriel and I watching in awe as my hands and forearms transform into breathtaking art. The color of the paste is a deep green, but the art will be orange once the paste is dried and peeled away. "How long will it last?" I ask. I want to be a work of art forever.

"One to four weeks," he replies, "depending on how much you wash them."

"I won't," I say stubbornly and Gabriel laughs. I'm hoping it will last for the rest of my life, which is a possibility. "Does it mean something, the lacy designs?"

Uday looks up excitedly. I've asked the million-dollar question. His eyes are even darker than Gabriel's, a pool of ink against the white sclera. "In my country," he says, "the henna designs on a bride's hands are believed to bring love, health, protection and happiness, both in life and in death."

After he leaves, we can hardly wait for the henna paste to dry so we can tumble into bed. I smell like curry from the paste, but Gabriel doesn't mind. The rest of the day we spend making love and napping. We're like newlyweds discovering each other, and I am happy for the first time in weeks.

Postscript: 8:15: Ben and Arica knock on the door and Gabriel stumbles out of bed to answer it. I throw on sweatpants and wander out to find out what's going on. They never stop by at night without calling first. But it's Valentine's Day, I realize at the same moment I see the bottle of champagne clutched in Ben's hand. "You're engaged!" I exclaim and nearly knock Gabriel off his feet. He hadn't figured it out.

It's all hugs after that and Ben gets misty. It's a good moment, a very good moment. "We're sorry to wake you up, but we had to share it with you," Arica says. "You're our best friends."

In my wildest dreams I never imagined I'd find someone I could feel so connected to, yet I found him—and then we found two friends to share it with. It is remarkable really, how all four of us ended up in the same place at the same time, as if Onset is a gigantic magnet, that pulled us here. If

I could freeze time, I would right now, right here in my kitchen with Gabriel and Ben and Arica. Life can feel so perfectly aligned sometimes. Why can't it always?

Gabriel finds wine glasses in the cupboard and Ben pours the champagne. There's a brief silence while we all search for the right words. I lift my glass.

"L'chaim," I suggest. "Isn't that Hebrew for congratulations?"

"You're thinking of mazal tov," Ben corrects.

"Oh, right—mazal tov. What's L'chaim mean then?"

Ben's eyes skirt to Arica's. "To life," he says tentatively.

Now I understand the awkwardness. "That's even better," I assert, although my heart is cracking, and lift the glass again. "L'chaim!"

Chapter Nineteen

Arica & Ben, *the "Muslim" & the Jew*

I salute the light within your eyes where the whole Universe dwells. For when you are at that center within you and I am at that place within me, we shall be one.
—*Crazy Horse, Oglala Sioux*

Even as the boat lifted with the waves underneath their wedding guests, she could see the cracked dry earth beneath her bare feet and feel the hot wind caressing her skin. She could smell the heady fragrance of Acacia trees, known in her native country as "scented thorn," and hear the kettledrums played by her younger brothers. Nigeria.

Arica's feet first touched American soil more than two decades before. She'd been a frightened child who carried with her a sense of betrayal because her mother had sent her to live with her father. Her mother was the person she was closest to, the one who felt like part of her own body. Being separated from her warm embrace was initially both inexplicable and unforgivable. And her father, she barely remembered.

She'd been a shy child, born with a lanky body that made her feel awkward, and a stutter that kept her from communicating like other kids. In Nigeria, most of the children she played with were neighbors, from families who shared meals with hers. It was a community as tightly spun as a spiderweb. The children didn't tease her for the stutter, although they sometimes spoke for her before she could get words out. Many of these children were Muslim, Islam being the largest religious group in Nigeria.

Arica's parents allowed her to play with Muslims, Christians and children whose families were part of indigenous congregations. The Muslim children would ask, "Are you people of the book?" which meant *are you Jewish or Christian?* And once she informed them that her family was not, the children would play with her. Daily, their religious faith only entered into her activities when it became time for prayer, which they performed five times every day. Arica never minded the cessation of play so that the children could fulfill their duty. When they returned home for Salat al-Zuhr, the early afternoon prayer, and for Salat al-'Asr, the late afternoon prayer, she sat cross-legged in her own home and spoke to God silently. Later in life, she credited this practice with creating what she referred to as "her bond with the Universe."

In Nigeria there was clean water and viable sanitation for only half of its inhabitants. Life expectancy was forty-seven years. Her family lived in extreme poverty and had little chance of changing that. Arica was given the privilege of a new life because she was the oldest. Her uncle had immigrated to the United States before her birth, and ten years later her father was able to immigrate based on their sibling relationship. Arica's immigration was celebrated, but it splintered the family. Her mother and brothers on one side of the world, she and her father on the other.

In Nigerian the name Aiyetoro means "Peace on Earth," which was a fitting name for Arica's father. He'd left Africa in order to give his daughter a better life but was only able to see his wife every four or five years, whenever he saved enough money to journey to Nigeria. Aiyetoro befriended people quickly with his wide grin and smiling eyes. Communication was not a problem because English is the official language of Nigeria, although colloquialisms often confused him. When this happened, he would reach for the person's hands. That was his way of saying *I understand what you are saying is well intentioned. We are friends.* Touch, he discovered, speaks all tongues.

In the United States there were new obstacles. Arica was the only black child in her new school and was nearly a foot taller than all the boys, which drew taunts from them and increased her stuttering. Within a month of living in America she had acquired several valuable skills: 1) to choose her friends carefully, 2) to control her emotions in order to avoid additional teasing, and 3) to don a poker face when she couldn't.

Aiyetoro made a living fishing off of Cape Cod. By American standards, their Wareham home was a cottage. By their standard, it was a mansion, a sublime blessing. Arica's parents had taught her that there is a Benevolent Force in the universe, and that of utmost importance was the need to be aware of and give thanks for her blessings. Arica learned to silently offer gratitude while putting groceries away, preparing food and eating it, after learning something in school that had once appeared un-learnable; when extra cash somehow flowed into her father's pockets just in time to buy much needed shoes or winter coats; while watching the sky change color in the late afternoons, when a new friend cured her loneliness. Because she was persistently focused on her blessings, the happy child grew into a happy adult—one who was grateful for her parents' selfless decision to send her to America.

On this summer evening, she was standing next to Ben on the stern of a boat, dressed in traditional Nigerian wedding clothes and wearing a coral headpiece, necklace and anklet. A justice of the peace was reading the inside cover of Paige's journal, which Gabriel had photocopied for the occasion.

"Who are we to each other?" the woman asked.

They'd leased the boat used for the canal blues cruise, and now it was carrying fifty of their relatives and friends. Arica's mother, who had crossed the ocean for the marriage ceremony, stood beside her and Gabriel stood beside Ben.

"The human race is like an immense spiderweb," the justice of the peace continued. "If I was to draw it as a mural it would look like an enormous mandala, a great wheel spinning slowly, untraceably. In my mind's eye I see us all bumping up against each other with our arms and legs reaching."

Her best friend's words were building a knot in Arica's throat, but she would not reveal that emotion to the group. She swallowed hard and turned to face her family and friends, then calmly completed Paige's journal entry that she had memorized. "Where would I put God in my imaginary drawing, at the center of the wheel, or surrounding the parameter? Maybe God is the 'in between,' the energy that binds us to each other."

The day had begun drearily, rain pounding the streets of Onset. Flowers drooped from the water's weight; birds hid in the trees. But now the sun was filtering through the clouds and a rainbow was forming. It reached across the Cape Cod Canal, a kaleidoscopic replica of the Bourne Bridge—with Arica poised at its center.

Ben caught Gabriel's eye and nodded toward it. "Paige," he softly said. They'd been waiting for a sign that she was present.

Arica was still addressing the small crowd. "I extend my arms to all of you standing here with us, each of whom is here out of love. It is a powerful combination, all of us here together with the same purpose. In my mind and in my heart, I extend my arms over the vast ocean to my brothers. And we acknowledge our friend Paige's spiritual presence. As she noted in her journal, we are all touching in one way or another."

It was Ben's turn to speak. He was thinking about how he met Arica when they were children and were friends throughout high school, then met again as adults. Regarding Paige's metaphor, the connection between them had been there the entire time. Even in their separate lives their fingers had touched.

A couple of years back, he'd awakened with the thought of Arica perched on the edge of his brain as if they had just spoken, even though years had passed since they'd seen each other. He Googled her name and discovered that she was living in Onset.

An hour later, he was standing on the sidewalk in front of her cottage when Arica stepped out the door wearing a dress that reached her ankles. Ben had forgotten how tall and slender she was, *like a string of licorice,* he'd said in seventh grade. She was the one he realized in that moment, the one he had always intended to be partnered with.

"How do you measure life?" Ben said to the wedding guests. "That's a question my friend Paige asked me once. I didn't have an answer, but I think I do now. Today I measure my life by the amount of love in my relationships and by how much freedom and joy I receive from them." His eyes were filling up. He tucked his chin into his chest until the emotion settled like dust after a storm.

Gabriel touched his shoulder and offered an encouraging nod.

"To Arica's parents," he continued. "I need to thank you for loving her so much that you made it possible for her to live here, even though it was a sacrifice for you. I want you to know that I'll do the same. I promise you that I will always do what is best for Arica. If you hadn't helped her to immigrate, we wouldn't be here today exchanging wedding vows. In fact, I believe every person here with us played a role in our union."

Even people who weren't present played a role. The dead intertwine with the living. Not only Paige, but his grandparents, dead for twenty years, continued to influence his life. Ben turned to face his parents. He understood it was their family history that gave rise to their deep-seated fears. Ben, an only child, was born on American soil after his parents emigrated from Israel. His birth certificate read: Binyamin, which was written as בנימין in Hebrew. The name Benjamin, like many of the perspectives that made up his personality, was the Americanized version, not the one used by his parents.

"Ema and Aba," Ben began, using the Hebrew words for mother and father. "Thirty-five years ago, you blessed me with the name Benyamin, which means *strength*. It took me a long time to find mine, but I have it now. Thank you for reminding me with this name that the strength I seek is inside me. Always your instinct has been to keep me safe, and you have. You've been trailblazers who found a path for your child. All the generations that come before us, their beliefs and their values, trickle down to become—like America—a melting pot in each new generation. I am who I am because I am your son, and because of my own unique experiences.

"We've not always agreed, but that is because our points of reference are different—we have had dissimilar life experiences. I can't give you mine any more than you can give me yours. But we can do something better than that, we can allow our love for each other to be greater than our differences. By choosing to stand here with Arica and me today you have taught me that lesson."

Ben and Arica faced each other, hands clasped and exchanged marriage vows before Mrs. Cohen stepped forward, holding the Talmud in her hands, and greeted the wedding guests. She kissed Arica's cheek and whispered, "bat Yafa," Hebrew for "beautiful daughter" before she read the Sheva Berachot, the seven marriage blessings, out loud in Hebrew. At the conclusion, it was so quiet that only the waves could be heard lapping against the walls of the boat. Few understood the words, but all understood the tone. Ben's father ceremoniously poured a glass of wine, which he handed to Ben. The newly married couple drank from the glass. Ben wrapped it in a cloth napkin and then stomped on it in accordance with Jewish tradition.

Cries of *mazal tov!* and *Congratulations!* rang out, breaking the silence and shifting the mood from ceremony to celebration. Waiters circulated with trays of champagne.

Gabriel was leaning on the railing as the crowd dispersed, moving like a herd toward the stairs that led to the buffet table. "I'll leave you two alone," he said to the bride and groom when it was only the three of them left on the stern of the boat. He'd known ahead of time that their intention was to release Arica's vial of ashes after the ceremony.

"Please stay," Arica pleaded. "We should be together."

"All of us," Ben reiterated and held up the bottle of champagne his fingers were clutching. Gabriel nodded his assent and Ben poured the liquid into four glasses. The fourth one sat untouched on the railing. Arica lifted her own and said "L'chaim!"

"To Life!" Gabriel cried, before Ben removed the vial from his jacket pocket and handed it to his new wife. She touched her lips to the glass vial then removed the top and let the wind sweep the ashes into Onset Harbor.

February 15, 2010, 3:35 a.m., Dream Journal Entry: I'm sitting on the end of our bed with Gabriel beside me and I feel good, remarkably good. It's a strange new freedom. There's no anxiety, nausea, pain or fatigue, only Gabriel and me. I keep telling him that—everything is perfect. Somehow, I'm not sick. His eyes are admiring the henna tattoos on my hands and forearms, the color vibrant against my fair skin. "We're the same," I note, "with our arms tattooed."

He laughs. I look down at his arm and notice the tattoo snake has moved up the tree, and immediately understand why. He has gained wisdom.

"I'm proud of you," I tell him, and his arms slip around my waist to pull me against him. I can smell his skin and feel his warm breath on my neck.

I notice pomegranates growing on the tattooed tree on his arm and they are bleeding musical notes instead of juice. "See?" I say, "Just like I told you. You can make music out of anything."

He lays my hand on Crazy Horse, who is sleeping beside us. Immediately, I feel the cat's vibration in my core, deep and thick like notes from a bass guitar. "How about this?" he says and touches my hand to the scarf tied to the bedpost. A high-pitched whirl of sound seems to be coming from inside my ears. I nod and he smiles. "Even this?" He has the tattooed snake from his arm between his thumb and index finger and places the wriggling creature on my palm. The vibration from its body is rhythmic, a drum beat that feels primal, like ancient African music. I have always been afraid of snakes, but suddenly I understand their beauty, and how their existence is orchestrated with the rest of the pulsating universe.

"Yes," I acknowledge, and Gabriel places the tiny squirming creature back down on his own skin, where it resumes its slow journey up the tree trunk toward the light—that I can see now glowing over the top of the tree.

"I'm proud of you, too, Paige," Gabriel says. He reaches behind his back and pulls out a long string of beads, a rosary I think at first. It too, has a cadence, more like an engine than a drumbeat. "It's a mala, from Tibet," he says and wraps it around my wrist. "For your birth day. In every bead I've placed a prayer, in every bead a wish for you."

"It's not my birthday," I protest.

"I know," he replies.

I want to ask what he means, but I have a sudden sensation that I have to leave. I look over my shoulder and see myself asleep in the bed with Gabriel curled up behind me. The "me" that is sleeping looks lifeless, with hollow eye sockets and only a thin coat of hair, though the me that is watching is not sick at all, and my hair is long again; I can feel it grazing my shoulders. I'm wearing the emerald-green dress that my mom bought me. The alarm clock says it's 3:33.

"I'll ask you when I wake up," I sputter because I can feel the pull toward my physical body strengthening.

My comment makes him laugh. He kisses my cheek and I awaken. His arm is around me, just like it was when I watched us from the end of the bed. The clock on the bedside table says 3:34. Gabriel is spooning me in his sleep, but I can still feel the impression of his lips on my cheek.

February 28, 2010: Gabriel has been seeing my dead relatives in our house. At first, he denied it, but I recognize the expression on his face when he sees clairvoyantly. He says there are spirit lights around me all the time, but I've only seen them a couple of times when I woke up to use the bathroom during the night.

Gabriel sees the lights with his physical eyes, and forms. But with his third eye he can see individuals. Today he described my mother perfectly, right down to her fuchsia lipstick, thick black hair streaked with gray and the beauty mark under her eye. He said she was smiling at him and wrapping her arms around me. She's waiting for me to transition, I understand, although he tried to suggest that she's here to give me strength. Perhaps. But her true purpose is to lead me home.

March 3, 2010: "What if I hadn't found you?" I ask him. "That day on the bridge. What if I hadn't gone looking for the wigwam that day?"

"You're missing the point, Paige," he says calmly and holds the straw to my mouth. I haven't left our bed for I don't know how many days and don't know if I will again, but I don't admit that to him. He is feeding me Ensure to keep me alive.

"How so?" I ask.

"I would have found you," he responds. "Even before I found you, I found you."

In my dreams, he means. I push his hand away. I want to write down his words before I forget. My memory is getting worse. And I'm losing the energy to journal.

Postscript: he comes back and lays beside me on the bed, careful not to touch my abdomen. It is comforting, the feel of his worn jeans against my bare legs and his toes grazing mine. "You understand, don't you?" he asks after we lay in silence for a while. "I found you, not only because you needed me, but because I needed you. You healed me, Paige. You healed my heart."

March 7, 2010: My sister called Gabriel and asked him what his plans are for when I become too much to care for. They thought I was sleeping, but I heard the conversation and I know what she said by his response: "She's staying here with me." After that she either asked him about his job obligations or maybe even offered money. He indicated that he's not worried about money. I am, but I won't voice it. Gabriel hasn't worked in two months, and he's barely left the house. He's been playing his piano a lot, though. Sometimes

I hear it in my dreams and think I've passed over. Tonight, he's auditioning at the Indigo Lounge down the street. I'm making him. He needs music to be waiting for him when I no longer am.

March 16, 2010: Hospice has been called in. I have a nurse who visits every day. She reminds me a little bit of my sister. She has the same porcelain complexion and stormy eyes. When the nurse smiles, I see Abby at age 12 or 13, back when she was more carefree and was my role model for absolutely everything. I thought I'd learn just from being around her how to outgrow my tomboy status, to walk gracefully, speak in captivating tones and enter a conversation without being rude.

"Will I look like her someday?" I asked my mom. To me, Abigail was as flawless and elegant as the Waterford crystal vase my grandmother sent from Ireland before I dropped it on the dining room floor, and it smashed into a million pieces.

Every human being is irreproachably beautiful. It's tragic how we all try to look like someone else, the Hollywood elite, models on jeans ads or even our big sisters, as if this exquisite container we navigate through life could ever be generic. I no longer wish to look or be like anyone else. I only want to be me in this body for as long as I can.

The nurse's name is Teresa, and she is one of the kindest people I've ever met. I tell her she must have been named after Mother Teresa and she chortles.

Today she told me a story about children receiving education in Tibetan monasteries. She said they gather outside every morning to sing a song of praise to the rising sun. I tell her it's the most beautiful thing I've ever heard, and Gabriel smiles his agreement, though his smile is looking worn these days. The visual in my mind is so clear—a group of little angels singing thanks to God for life itself—that I fall asleep dreaming of them with Gabriel's hand still stroking my head.

In my dream I visit the Lake of Turquoise, one of the four holy lakes of Tibet, without losing my conscious awareness of his hand.

On waking, I tell Teresa that when I pass, I want to stand on the roof of the world, to visit Tibet. She nods with lips closed tight, understanding my intent. "Do you think that can happen?" I ask. I know she won't lie. Teresa is chronically honest.

"I'll make sure it does," she promises.

Chapter Twenty

Teresa, the Hospice Nurse,
the Higher Powered

I have been all things unholy. If God can work through me, He can work through anyone.
—Saint Francis of Assisi

Some of us visit Hell—spend a prolonged time there even—before we find our footing and make our way toward Heaven. Teresa was a recovering crack addict. Once upon a time, Hell had been her neighborhood.

Now her time was devoted to people with terminal illnesses. It was a crooked path that led from one place to the other. Nothing of significance in her life had been a straight line. But every twist and turn were necessary. As a result, she had something to give, particularly to those standing in the doorway between this life and the next.

Material objects don't matter much to those waiting to pass over, but a strong pair of hands to lift them and a lighthearted smile matter a great deal. Every morning she fell to her knees and asked her Higher Power to keep her away from her drug of choice and any other substance that might lead her back to it. And she asked one more favor before she gave thanks for another day and another opportunity to grow her own spirit, that her words and her actions be guided so that she might help someone else.

As a child, she had no intention of growing up and becoming a hospice nurse. What she'd really wanted was to be a singer. Graced with a voice that could silence a room, there was a delicacy to her tone that could overpower even a crowd of misbehaving boys. She was the only daughter of seven children in a family raised by a single mother. *Thank God*, she often thought, she wasn't the youngest. Had she been, she wouldn't have had the strength to muscle all her brothers. Her childhood was survival of the fittest.

Teresa grew up in South Boston, better known as "Southie" by its residents. Her mother worked, but still relied on food stamps to keep her family alive. Thanks to the WIC program, there was usually milk, cheese, peanut butter and cereal in the house. At the end of the month when the pot was empty, her mother would shake the coins out of the ceramic pig Teresa made for her in girl scouts and send one of the kids to the store for a loaf of bread. They could always make sandwiches from the WIC cheese.

Teresa only knew Paige for two months, but they became unexpectedly close. Paige was the only patient she ever confided in regarding her addiction. It was toward the end when it was difficult for Paige to drink. The conversation was sparked by Paige's suggestion that she must have been named after Mother Teresa.

"I'm not a saint, Paige," Teresa objected. "I'm a recovering drug addict, and I did a lot of bad things for drugs."

"All saints have obstacles," Paige softly replied. "It's what makes them strong."

"You don't understand," Teresa argued. "I was a terrible person."

Paige was slow to respond. Was she judging her? Teresa wondered, "We all have reasons for doing the things we do," she finally said, "reasons that aren't obvious to the rest of the world. Sometimes not even obvious to us."

Teresa's body froze, her fingers stiffened on the needle she was preparing to slide into Paige's vein. They'd been acquainted for such a short time, yet Paige *knew* her. And her words reminded her of her purpose for living. Bringing joy to a person who is in constant pain and preparing to say goodbye to everyone they hold dear is, for those who can bear it, an immense privilege.

A decade earlier, Teresa had been someone's angel of death. In an abandoned crack house in Brockton, she'd been sharing a pipe made out of a soda can with a guy she'd just met when he'd dropped dead. She'd been pacing on the frozen strip of grass between the crack house and the street when the paramedics arrived, having used the guy's cell phone to call 911. The cell phone was stashed in some bushes so she could later trade it for a rock. After they loaded the dead addict into the ambulance, one of the paramedics grabbed the arm of her coat. "We'll be coming for you next," he'd hissed through his teeth. "You hear me? You're next."

Before he climbed into the driver's seat and slammed the door, he reached into his pocket and dropped a business card at her feet. After the ambulance drove away with its lights flashing, she picked it up. On the card, scribbled in black ink, were the words *Alcoholics Anonymous* with a telephone number scribbled underneath.

She was craving a cigarette, but the pack was inside the house. Or maybe in the dead addict's pocket. She couldn't remember his name, even though he'd told her a dozen times when she'd met him an hour earlier. "I'll do whatever you want, just fuck me up," she'd said when he'd approached her curled into a ball on a bench in D.W. Field Park.

On the streets Teresa was known as a "rock star," someone who exchanged sex for crack. He'd led her to the abandoned house with so many shingles missing that snow coated the floor that was littered with used up lighters and rusted spoons. The guy was nice enough to get her high before he made his demands, and he died before they were fulfilled. Teresa was glad about that as she stood outside trying to decide whether to go back for the cigarettes, and no matter how hard she tried, she couldn't feel guilty for it. *She'd be next*, the paramedic had said, and the only emotion that thought stirred in her was relief. Life as an addict was unbearable. She wanted out.

No one was watching. Those who'd wandered out to see why the ambulance was in their neighborhood had crawled back into their holes. Just another dead addict. Teresa breathed on her hands for warmth and noticed the business card still between her fingers. She crumpled it up and dropped it on the frozen ground before she headed back inside. The pack of butts was on the floor sitting on a patch of snow splattered with blood from the guy's nose and mouth. She snatched it, trying not to look at the pools of red that looked like tattoo art. Then she noticed a piece of paper slipped in between the cigarette box and the cellophane covering it. It was another business card, identical to the one the paramedic had given her. He must have placed it there, knowing she'd be back. *Self-righteous prick.* But then she had another thought—the most pivotal thought of her life. She'd heard that at AA meetings they let anybody in the door, and they give out free coffee. They don't care if you smell like a dead animal or if you're strung out. *Hot coffee in a warm room* was the thought that led Teresa inadvertently to sobriety.

She used the stolen cell phone to call the 800 number and the woman on the line told her where to find the closest meeting. It was within walking distance, so she walked over and waited on the front steps for it to start. And it wasn't as bad as she'd imagined. No one made judgmental comments or appeared to be talking about her from across the room. People were kind. They asked her how she was and gave her hot coffee and a small book with all the meetings listed in it. "Sit up front," one guy suggested. When it was her turn to talk, she told the whole room full of people that the guy she'd been with that afternoon had dropped dead while they were smoking a pipe. People expressed sympathy and patted her shoulders. One woman even hugged her, even though she smelled like she hadn't showered in a month, because she hadn't.

"Keep coming back," they all said at the end, and Teresa had, at first for the coffee, but soon for the companionship, and by the time she'd attended a dozen meetings, it was because she wanted what they had—a peaceful mind and a normal life.

Just when she concluded that life was over, it began.

The woman she chose as her sponsor was a nurse who worked at Children's Hospital in Boston. Her name was Kelly, but everyone called her Kiki because she was once a nightclub singer and looked like Kiki Dee, the pop singer from the '70s. Kiki was a single mom with three kids at home. Still, she managed to stay sober and take care of other people's sick children. And she smiled a lot. On the streets, smoking crack, you don't meet many happy people, but in AA, you meet lots of them. They are Phoenixes risen from their own ashes, grateful to be breathing air and mingling with the human race. *You don't know what you've got until it's gone*—so goes the saying. But for clean and sober addicts the truth is you don't know what you've got until you're so close to losing it that you can feel the hollowness in your chest and belly. There's an unnatural echo about your own life that alerts you it's about to end.

Nursing wasn't Teresa's first act of humanitarianism. Once, during Kiki's vacation, Teresa accompanied her to Mississippi to join Habitat for Humanity in building someone's home. The high she got from hard work was contagious. It didn't cost anything, other than the price of the plane ticket, and after that every time she felt bad about her life, she would visualize herself standing on a ladder, hammering nails. There was a priest working on the project who told her about his experiences working with orphans in Tibet and Africa. When he told her about Tibet, he called it "the roof of the world." If she was interested in volunteering, he said, he could get her a plane ticket. It was too early in sobriety, she told him, to be away from her meetings.

"The orphans aren't going anywhere," he replied and gave her his number.

Two years later Teresa flew to Tibet and spent eight weeks tending to a vegetable garden planted by the orphans with the assistance of two Buddhist monks, cooked meals, washed clothes and tended to the children. In her spare time, she taught English to the monks, and in return they taught her about Buddhism. In Tibet, she realized the value of medical training. When she arrived home, she began the process of applying to nursing schools. She didn't know that she would someday be a hospice nurse. She'd envisioned herself working with children, like the precious little ones in Tibet.

It would be her quest in life, she imagined, until one day she received word that her father, the same person who'd walked out on her family when she was six years old, had been diagnosed with a malignant brain tumor. Teresa headed to Gloucester, where her father had (unbeknownst to her family) lived and worked all those years as a fisherman. And the experience changed her perception of life. He was dying already, confined to a bed and filled with remorse. It was the monks she credited for her decision to visit him for it was they who taught her the importance of living compassionately. Like Gabriel, *Om mani padme hum* was her mantra.

Her recollection of her father as an oversized human being didn't match the shrunken man nearly lost in the sheets of the hospital bed. He looked right at her when she entered the room. The guilt draped in his eyes was as visible to her as the color of his irises—that was identical to hers. When she couldn't conjure any magical words from her throat that would make the pain go away, she instead reached for his hand.

Then something unplanned happened. She started to sing. It was an Irish ballad her father had sung to her as a child, a song that hadn't crossed her mind or her lips for at least two decades. Ironically, it was a song about a homecoming.

Shake hands with your Uncle Mike, me boy, and here's your sister Kate. And there's the girl you used to swing down by the garden gate.

His Irish eyes awakened, opened wider so they could get a clear picture of his grown daughter whom he hadn't seen since she was a little girl. His cracked lips pursed before they parted and allowed two little words to escape, "Forgive me."

Until that very moment, Teresa had blamed her addictions and her resultant dysfunctional relationships on her father. He had left her with a hole that she believed she could only fill with substances. But that day Teresa realized that her addictions were not about him. They were about her self-perception, about her own belief that her father's desertion was due to an inadequacy in her. And she had mimicked this role in every relationship she'd ever been in.

Teresa touched his face and nodded her head to convey her forgiveness, but she didn't stop singing. *Shake hands with all your neighbors and kiss the colleens all. You're as welcome as the flowers in May to dear old Donnegal.*

There was healing power in her vocals, and she finally understood that. Maybe it was the very reason she was born with the ability. That day, and most days after that, Teresa used her voice to lull terminally ill patients into peaceful slumber. She was a bird singing in a cage, one she had willingly entered. It turned out that she didn't have to sing for the whole world, after all. Her small audience was more than enough. Bringing peace was more fulfilling than applause. That became her mission in life, to merge love and music and use that divine alchemy to transcend the most difficult of moments.

After her patients died, she didn't always attend the funerals, but Paige had been special to her. Under different circumstances, they would have been best friends. Teresa didn't have any close friends, other than her sponsor. Like Paige, she had a multitude of acquaintances, but her thinking—like Paige's—was too unconventional. People were intrigued by her, but they didn't dare draw close enough to really know her.

Teresa chose a periwinkle blue sari-like dress, the most colorful piece of clothing in her wardrobe, to wear to the funeral. She knew it was what Paige would have chosen. After the service, she waited until she was sure all of Paige's family and friends had taken ashes before she introduced herself to Arica. They had met several times in passing at Paige and Gabriel's house, but she'd appeared differently then, dressed as a nurse instead of a friend. Arica hugged her and handed her the last vial.

She knew exactly what to do with the ashes.

March 19, 2010: Anxiety is eating me alive. I can see my liver now, swollen like a melon. I imagine it pulsating until it explodes, and I wonder if it will be pain or fear that ends me.

Gabriel paces the floor like a mad tiger until Teresa arrives, angel of mercy that she is, and ups my doses. Maybe now I can sleep. Thank you, God, for Ativan. And for Teresa.

March 20, 2010: "Are you afraid?" I ask from the darkness. He's in the chair beside the hospital bed, but his cheek rests on the pillow next to mine. I can't see much in the dim light, but my fingers take him in. His warm flesh, the line where his hair starts, his thick brows and the cartilage of his nose, his eyelashes fluttering under my touch like hummingbird wings. The question quickens his breath, but Gabriel, unlike every other person I've ever met, never hurries to provide an answer. He allows the question to swim through his brain first. My index finger trails to his lips and feels the hot air exhaled from his body. He is so alive, and I am so not. He closes his mouth around the tip of it and I feel the damaged tooth, the sharp ridge that after nearly five years is still not completely smooth. I sense his fear and his pain like it's a living creature perched on that broken part of him.

He pushes his face closer, nudging against mine like Crazy Horse does. His breath smells like the orange he consumed, and I want to taste it. I want his mouth on mine, but that would make it harder to breathe. "I can't acknowledge it, Paige," he mutters. "If I do, I'll crumble. It'll be an avalanche."

In the silence that follows his admission, he presses his head into my neck, his arm reaches across my chest and his untamed hair tickles my chin. "Okay, beautiful boy," I tell him. "Put it away for another day." I stroke his hair until his breath deepens as he falls asleep and it's the last thing I remember of yesterday, of what I think was yesterday. The days are starting to blur as nauseatingly as being on a carnival ride that never seems to end.

March 22, 2010: Sometimes love is a decision, for instance, standing in a pet store with a wad of cash burning in your pocket and gazing through the plexi-glass. You understand that whichever puppy you take home you will soon be head over heels in love with. But first you must choose. You decide that upon this little dog that you don't yet know you will bestow your love.

The hospice workers are kind of like that, too. They make decisions to help people when those people are still faceless. They walk in the door understanding that they are going to get to know you and be there with you as your body dies. It's a grueling job. They aren't robots desensitized to death. Some days I notice Teresa's shaky hands and wet eyelashes.

With Gabriel, there isn't a moment I can point to and say, "that is where I chose to let go and let love have its way with me." I think I always loved him. I could say he was the man I was waiting to love, but I think it would be more accurate to say he was the man I was loving and waiting to meet.

Chapter Twenty-One

Gabriel, *the Pagan*

I prefer to their dogma my excursions into the natural gardens where the voice of the Great Spirit is heard in the twittering of birds, the rippling of mighty waters, and the sweet breathing of flowers. If this is Paganism, then at present, at least, I am a Pagan.
—*Zitkala-Sa (Red Bird, Sioux)*

The first day of summer for Gabriel arrived later than expected. It was a Thursday and, inexplicably, the church bells were ringing. After Paige's funeral, the rain had started and didn't stop for what felt like weeks. It kept him home, imprisoned with loneliness. He had lined up houses to paint and had anticipated using that work to keep his hands and mind busy, but the weather ruined his plan. And then it was cold, even when the sun shone brightly, too cold to be summer, even though technically it was. When he awakened to the sun pouring through the blinds and the sound of church bells ringing, he knew it was the day.

Gabriel understood as well as anyone that June 21 marked the first day of summer on the calendar, but he didn't feel restrained by that. When it came to the actual experience— the *feeling* of summer—the calendar was usually wrong. He'd learned a long time ago, back when Billy was still alive, not to accept something as truth just because everyone else did.

He was still in bed when the visuals started to pummel him. *Paige on the bridge that first day watching him with curiosity in her eyes. Paige sitting cross-legged in a circle at the wigwam. Paige on the front steps of their cottage wearing a red scarf so she'd attract hummingbirds. Paige throwing the remote control at him because she misunderstood something he said and thought he was talking about another woman.* His thoughts were the one place he could always find her. He tried to groan the pain out of his chest. His own heart called forth the images of her, but invariably those images sunk their teeth into him. They were a double-edged sword.

No regrets, he reminded himself because his brain was spitting out a familiar message. *You should have let her jump.* The coffee pot was gurgling, signaling it was ready. He'd set the timer on it the night before. He took a couple of deep breaths and asked for assistance, like he did every day, *guide my steps, make them holy,* before he swung his feet onto the floor.

Crazy Horse was lying in the middle of the living room floor where the hospital bed used to be, watching Gabriel with his enormous blue eyes. Like Gabriel, he wasn't quite sure what to do with himself without Paige. Unless he was eating or using the litter box, he stayed in the spot he had last seen her. "Come here, buddy," Gabriel said and lifted the cat into his arms.

A whiteboard, approximately one foot wide by four feet long, was attached to the wall next to the countertop that held the coffee pot. At the very top in red magic marker letters were the words *Love is. . .* There were at least a hundred entries on the list that Paige scribbled each time a thought occurred to her. She'd intended to fill it from top to bottom, and to leave it behind for Gabriel as a work of art constructed of observations and messy handwriting, but she wasn't able to complete it on her own. The last entry in her handwriting was *a cat named Crazy Horse.* After that, the handwriting changed to Gabriel's fatter, more legible script. When Paige passed over there was still eighteen inches of white space that he was determined to fill.

He reached for his mug, one of a pair with mermaids painted on them that they'd bought at a coffee shop in Falmouth and poured the coffee. Paige's mug had been in the same spot since the last time she'd used it, he realized as his eyes skimmed the list. The last entry he'd made the night before. *A Janice Joplin song that reminds me of you.* As he tasted the brew, he could still hear her voice singing along out of key. It sounded perfect to his musically trained ears — not because it was perfect, but because it was uniquely Paige. He picked up the magic marker and wrote what he intended when he arose from bed. *Keeping a promise.*

The words reminded him of another promise he'd made, to stop by and visit Mrs. Spencer. When he saw her at Paige's funeral it was nearly impossible to make eye contact. Even though it wasn't her intention, her presence defeated him. But ever since the gig at the Regattabar, he'd been feeling more comfortable with the idea of keeping the Spencers in his life. Every time he felt like he couldn't face Billy's parents, he'd recall the picture of his mom sitting beside Mrs. Spencer, wearing floppy red hats and smiles of encouragement.

He knew Billy wanted him to re-establish a relationship with his mother. Some mornings he'd awaken to the smell of Irish Breakfast Tea, even though no one was drinking it. He figured that was Billy's way of nudging him, Billy's way of making things right. And who was he to dictate the proper course for healing? Billy's perspective was much clearer than his own. He could see all the people involved and how each of them was affected. He understood why the accident occurred, why he passed over and why Gabriel didn't. When they were children, Billy used to demand *do you swear it on your life?* Gabriel always replied, *swear it on my life,* and that meant it was a done deal. Even though Billy was in spirit now, Gabriel trusted him. And he'd do the right thing because he'd promised both his own mother and Billy that he would. But first, he had to keep his promise to Paige. Tomorrow there would be time to heal wounds. Today had a different purpose.

"I swear it on my life, Billy," he muttered as he carried his coffee to the table and placed Crazy Horse on the floor, then slumped into a chair. The house was quiet, too quiet. Not empty, but quiet. He knew better than to believe that he was alone. Vision is imperfect in nature; intuition isn't. He gobbled a bowl of granola and blueberries, sharing the fruit with the grieving cat that had leapt onto his lap.

"Life will go on, you know," he said to the cat, and Crazy Horse touched Gabriel's nose with his own. "You don't believe it either, huh?" he added, and kissed its head like Paige always had. The cat immediately started to purr. "See, here's the thing," he went on as if speaking to a human friend, a confidante. "My brain believes it, but my heart doesn't." He wondered if the cat's chest ached like his.

He gently placed Crazy Horse on the floor and entered the bedroom to find a pair of shorts to throw on. On the dresser was a single item that used to belong to Paige, a half-empty bottle of perfume that was now Gabriel's most prized possession. Anytime he needed to feel like she was beside him all he had to do was close his eyes and take a whiff. Someday, he knew, he'd have to let go of the physical possessions that held Paige's presence and trust the nonphysical instead.

Ten minutes later, Gabriel was closing the door behind himself on route to the Stone Bridge. A flier for the annual Onset Blues Festival was stapled to a telephone pole in front of his house. Last year he'd gone with Paige. Focusing on the memory, he could recall the feel of her fingers laced through his as they walked there together. She'd been wearing a long skirt that swished around her ankles with each step and her toenails had been painted bright pink. How small she'd seemed to him that day, even though they were the same height. It was her frame that was tiny. Even her long slender fingers felt diminutive in his hand.

But her spirit was much bigger than her body. Through the course of the past year, she had slowly revealed that truth to him, and he would always think of her that way, unfolding a layer at a time like a peony in a garden.

"I know who you are, you know," Paige had said during that walk to the blues festival. "You're the man who can make music out of anything."

"Put that on my tombstone, would you?" he'd replied. "It makes me sound magical."

Laughter rolled out with her breath. "Ah, but you are. You're a magic man," she said.

Funny, he thought now, he'd never thought of himself as anything special, let alone magical, until he met Paige. Often, during the four years leading up to their meeting, he had deemed himself someone not worthy of life. He'd had no aspirations of falling in love. That territory was far too dangerous as it held the possibility of another loss. But when they met that first day on the bridge, love was right there waiting for them. Even after they were a couple, he'd had doubts. He'd never questioned the depth of his love for Paige—or hers for him. What he'd relentlessly asked himself was if he deserved it. Did he deserve to have her love, to have a normal life, to be happy? Until very recently, the answer had been "no." He'd felt like a thief, holding in his hand a ruby that belonged to someone else.

Now he understood that their meeting was orchestrated by someone far wiser than himself, someone who knew he could never let go of the past without diving straight into the present. The relationship was granted to him, not in spite of his past, but because of it. It was a gift of love, not forgiveness. He hadn't been judged or punished for his actions. He'd been doing that to himself. The Creator had a plan to alleviate his pain and to make him useful.

Gabriel often thought about Paige's vision of the human race as a great wheel with everyone connected by their hands and feet, and he took comfort from it, even though one of his hands was empty now. She'd left an indelible mark on the map of his life. His imagination saw it as a crease across his palm where her fingers once were. A fortune teller might glimpse it and call it his love line. But it was much bigger than that. It was a lifeline that stretched over time and space. Their relationship was part of his soul's evolution, and not even death's greedy hands could pull that from his grasp.

He stepped onto the Stone Bridge, passed the window boxes at its base that were overflowing again with red geraniums, and recalled the last time they'd ventured there together. It was an unusually warm day in March. The window boxes were barren, though a few small birds hopped in them and feasted on the seeds of last year's flowers. Paige was so sick he had to drive her in his pickup truck, even though the bridge was less than a half mile from their home. She'd lost so much weight that he effortlessly lifted her onto the railing and held her there with her legs hanging over the water.

"I know you won't let me fall," she'd said, but her tiny body was trembling in his arms. When he'd called her on it, she'd replied, "It's like being on a Ferris wheel. It's scary to be up high, but at the same time you trust that you're safe."

"You're trusting me with your life?" he'd teased, trying to get her to smile.

"Don't be ridiculous!" she'd spat back. "I trust you with more than my life. I trust you with everything I am."

After the car accident, Gabriel had been quite sure that no one would ever trust him again. But Paige had proved him wrong about many things, most importantly his value as a human being. Because of her, he didn't need to toss himself off the bridge like a bag of trash.

This year, this time, it was for Billy and for Paige. It was driven by love, not remorse.

Gabriel used his upper body to lift himself onto the railing of the bridge, crouched like a monkey with the concrete scratching the skin of his toes, and his eyes taking in the fluorescent shimmer from the sun on the rippling water. He was conscious of the cool air coming in through his nose, traveling into his lungs and then exiting, warmer from its journey through his body.

He popped the rubber stopper off of the vial and shoved it in his shorts pocket. *I have to do it like she would*, he told himself. *No tricks or acrobatics. Just completely in the moment.*

It was a Thursday morning, so there was traffic on the bridge, people headed toward their jobs at Stop & Shop or the greeting card factory. People were living their lives as if the world had not stopped revolving, even though for Gabriel it had. He ignored the cars passing by in a near rhythmic interval and the faces staring at him through the windows as he stretched into a standing position. Even if he stepped off the railing and stopped traffic, took the time to explain his intention, he knew most of them would continue to gawk at him as if he were a freak.

Not many people understand that it's possible to perform acts of love for a person who has crossed over to the spirit side of life. Most people Gabriel had met thought that once a person's body was dead, they no longer existed. He considered himself privileged to be part of the lucky few who'd discovered otherwise. That knowledge, he understood, was something else to be grateful for.

Gabriel straightened his spine and unfolded his arms like bird wings. The sun was warm on his bare skin and the soft breeze licked at his face. He imagined the saltwater rushing up his nostrils, and the entire world being green for that one magical moment when he hovered there before swimming to the surface, as if he were a creature of the water, not the land. His palm was covering the opening of the vial so the ashes wouldn't blow out prematurely.

Halfway down, let go he told himself and deliberately stepped off the bridge. It was the closest he could come to taking her with him.

March 26, 2010: Gabriel reminded me of one of Silver Birch's teachings. What we call death is actually a second birth, a rebirth to Spirit. Now I understand the dream I had. The mala was a spiritual gift for my journey home, my birth day. Teresa helped me find some online, and we ordered one for Gabriel. People use them to meditate by moving the fingers from one bead to the next with each breath and mantra. They are also worn as reminders to live mindfully.

According to Gabriel, there are people in the Spirit World waiting excitedly for me to be born, just like there were people on Earth waiting for me during my mother's pregnancy. It makes me think about what I'll say to them when I get there and look back on this life. I've made my share of mistakes, but I think that's part of being human and figuring out how to live. It took me thirty-nine years, but I finally did. When they ask me what I learned in this lifetime, I already know what I'll say—that love is the most important thing in the universe, maybe the only thing that really matters.

I had a conversation with Aileen about the mala I ordered for Gabriel. "After I pass, give it to him," I say. "Tell him I'll be wearing mine, too, like in the dream. In every one of the 108 beads I'll place a prayer, in every bead a wish for him."

Later, I asked Gabriel to take care of my body after I leave it. It will be cremated and he, more than anyone else, will know what to do with the ashes. He is the one who knows me. I love many people on this Earth, my dad, my brother and sister, Aileen and Connor, my friends—even my ex-husband—but there is no one I trust like Gabriel. He's the one who accepted me exactly as I am with no desire to change or influence me. And that's ironic because he is the one who has changed and influenced me the most.

Instead of agreeing to take control of the ashes, he suggests small vials be filled and given out at the funeral. That way every person in my life can take a part to a place that was significant in our various relationships (a dozen vials, he suggested and that makes me wonder: who will claim them and where will they set them free? And will I be able to watch?). I want my funeral to be a coming together of everyone I have ever loved. A reminder of the great web that connects us all.

"Every relationship should be honored," Gabriel says. "The universe places people in our path for a reason. You won't know the reasons until you get home. Just have faith that it's so."

I wish I could see with his vision. Once, at the wigwam, Gabriel received a message from his spirit guide who said that his power animal is an eagle, and that is where he gets both his impressive perspective and his clairvoyant ability.

But I don't need his vision to know why the Great Spirit placed him in my path. He came because I was going to pass over and couldn't do it alone. The Great Spirit sent me one of His angels with the name Gabriel so that I would recognize him as such. It was all part of a Divine Plan.

Chapter Twenty-Two

Abigail & Jim, *the Catholic & the Agnostic*

Look within, thou art the Buddha.
—Buddha

The cuckoo clock in the living room was striking 8:30 when Jim entered through the front door, briefcase in hand, and saw Abigail sitting in front of the baby grand, randomly striking the keys with her index finger. Her other hand grasped a glass of wine. The visual struck Jim as odd because she'd never learned to play, but what alarmed him was the resignation on her face.

Positioned on the piano was a photo of Abigail's mom and dad on their wedding day. Jim's eyes were drawn to it as he approached his wife, and for the first time he realized that he and Abby were significantly older now than her parents had been when the photograph was taken. Maria's thick dark curls plunged down her back in stark contrast to the pure white lace veil falling gently over them. She beamed, her eyes focused on Joe, who stood by her side, handsome and proud, and looking like he'd just won the lottery.

Abigail didn't turn to face her husband, although she must have heard him enter. "What's the matter?" Jim asked gently. He was wondering if she'd taken the sleeping pill. Lately she'd been taking them every night, but she knew better than to drink wine at the same time. When his hands touched down on her shoulders, she looked up at him, and he realized she'd been crying.

"I made a mistake," Abigail eagerly confessed, and turned her eyes back to the white keys spilling like moonstones under her fingers.

"What mistake?" he asked and kissed her hair that looked and smelled like honey.

"You understand why I did it, don't you?" she threw back. "He claimed her, and he wasn't one of us. He was just some guy. Some guy she met on a bridge."

"Do you mean Gabriel?"

"When we were little girls, Paige and I were so close, Jim. We were best friends. I don't know what happened to us." She stared into the wine as if looking for the answer there, and then swallowed the entire glassful.

"Did you take a sleeping pill?" her husband asked.

Abigail distractedly nodded her head. "You wouldn't believe it, if you read her journal, the things she wrote." She was shaking her head at the thought of it. New puddles of tears swelled and then poured from her eyes.

"You mean bad things?"

"No, not bad things. Beautiful things. Things I didn't know. She wanted to have a baby with Gabriel. She never told me. I know what it's like to have that within reach and then have it snatched away. But Paige never told me about it. Why didn't she?"

It was the most intimate conversation they'd had in years, but Jim was disconcerted by the fact that she'd taken a sleeping pill and washed it down with wine. He could see the open bottle on the kitchen counter. It was closer to empty than full.

Abigail reached for a massive book on the piano next to the photograph of her parents, the family Bible that she'd inherited at Maria's death. Jim watched her drop it onto her lap and stroke the leather cover with her fingertips. They looked small and defenseless against the weighty book. She was searching again, Jim presumed, for spiritual guidance. Sometimes at night he'd awaken and find her kneeling beside the bed.

As she opened the book carefully, respectfully, to a page that contained her family history, it brought to mind a report he'd heard on the radio while driving home. A pastor in Florida was planning to gather as many Qur'ans as possible and burn them in a bonfire on the upcoming anniversary of the 9-11 terrorist attacks. His intention, he'd said, was to send a message to the Muslim world. *What kind of message?* Jim had wondered. *And how spiritually motivated could it be?* Now he considered his wife's reaction if someone tossed her family Bible into a fire. What kind of message would it send to her? *We care so little about what you hold sacred that we'd happily extinguish it.* The visual his imagination created made his chest throb.

Jim didn't believe everything in Abby's Bible any more than he believed everything written in the Qur'an, but what did that matter? In his view, it was the freedom to believe that was sacred. He watched his wife finger a lock of Paige's hair that their mom had adhered onto the page with Scotch tape nearly forty years before. "She hated that her hair was brown," she said quietly. "I always envied it because I wanted to look like our mother, like Paige did. Look at Joe's. Have you ever seen hair that beautiful?"

Under the lock Maria had written, *Joseph Junior, age 1 year 2 mos.* "It looks just like yours, sweetheart," Jim noted.

"I used to get mad when he'd cut it off. I thought he was doing it for attention."

"We all have demons," Jim remarked. "Things that make us believe we're not good enough the way we are."

"It's only hair. Dead cells," Abigail stated. "Why do superficial things make us so crazy?"

"Maybe in Joe's eyes his hair is too feminine. It reveals something about him that he'd rather not show, even though what he's trying to hide is really a good thing. But no one would ever take him for a linebacker any more than they'd take me for a pianist."

"Is that your demon?" Abigail asked after a respectful pause.

Jim snorted as he took the Bible from her hands and placed it back on the piano—the biggest and most painful thorn in his side. "One of them," he admitted.

"Paige loved Gabriel," Abigail said. "She truly loved him. Did you know that?"

Jim nodded carefully. To him, Paige's love of Gabriel could not have been more obvious than if she'd tattooed his name on her forehead.

"I didn't," Abigail admitted. "I think I saw him through my eyes instead of hers. We've always had different lenses, Paige and me." Her words were beginning to slur. "What if he was right, Jim? What if he was right all along?"

"Right about what?" Jim asked.

"That it's possible for him to see Paige. I'm not saying I believe it, but. . . maybe. If that's true then maybe she can see me now, hear the things I'm saying?"

For Abigail, Jim knew, those words were a huge concession. Thoughts flooded in, phrases he'd always wished he could utter, but had held back. For once he let them out. "You don't have to be the right one all the time any more than you have to be the strong one. All you have to be is yourself. That's enough, Abby. That is so much more than enough."

Her eyes fixed on his as if to ask, *could that be true?* Could she really drop the bundle of responsibilities from her back, the ones crippling her mind and emotions with their impossible weight?

"There was a phone call earlier," she murmured.

Jim crouched next to her and sandwiched one of her small hands between his. He understood that whoever had called, and their conversation, must have set her grief in motion. "Who was it?" he asked when she didn't offer the information.

"Teresa. Do you remember Teresa, the hospice nurse?"

"Yes, of course. Paige loved her."

"She called because she wanted us to know that she'd sent her vial of ashes to a friend in Tibet, a Buddhist monk. She said

Paige told her she wanted to go there and 'stand on the roof of the world.' I'd completely forgotten about that. Remember how she used to talk about traveling to Tibet when she was in college? A pilgrimage she called it, even though she wasn't religious."

"Paige was always spiritual, even if she wasn't religious. I don't remember the pilgrimage story. I do remember her mentioning that she wanted to spend time in a monastery but didn't know if women were allowed."

Nervous laughter escaped Abigail in a hiccup. "When she was little, she wanted to be a priest. You should have heard her when she found out she couldn't be one because she was a girl. Sometimes I think that's why she didn't stay Catholic."

"She couldn't stand the injustice," Jim concurred.

"I should have remembered that story. It felt odd to be hearing it from a stranger."

"You couldn't have remembered everything about her," he said. "Come on, I'll help you to bed." His hands gripped his wife's waist and pulled her into a standing position. She held tightly onto his shoulders as they stood, still embracing.

"Would you do it for me, take care of me, like Gabriel did for Paige?" she asked.

"Abigail, you have to know that," he replied.

She pushed her face into the warmth of his neck. "I'd do it for you, too. But Jim, there are things I need you to tell me."

"You know everything about me," he said. *That's a lie,* he immediately realized.

"Are there things about our life you'd do differently if you could? There are," she added before he answered. "I know there are. I can see it in your face that you're not happy."

"That's not because of you," he offered gently. "It's because of choices I've made."

"I feel that way, too. I thought that was part of life, you know, being an adult? I thought everyone felt like that. I mean, who could be happier than us? We have everything."

He grinned at her comment and nudged her toward the stairs. Jim had known for a decade that a good income plus an upscale home does not equal happiness. The "American dream" was lacking in depth and vision. Joy and a sense of security, he realized, came from something much deeper and stronger than dollar bills and real estate, a place that is ironically harder to reach when overly focused on those very things.

They were halfway up the stairs, Jim supporting Abigail's weight, when he offered, "Paige found happiness and that's a good thing, Ab. Don't be hurt by that."

"It's not hurting me," she countered. She slid off her silk robe and crawled under the covers. "It's confusing me. I thought I had everything figured out."

"No one has everything figured out." He pulled the blankets over her.

"Not even me," Abby conceded, and it made her husband laugh. "You know, Teresa mentioned an orphanage in Tibet. She volunteered there once. That's how she met her friend, the monk."

"Pretty interesting life she's led," her husband answered. "I wonder how she ended up working in an orphanage and now as a hospice nurse."

The corners of Abigail's lips turned downward as she pondered the enormity of a human life, how one step led to the next and then to the next. It was difficult to imagine what kind of circumstance might have led to such a selfless existence.

"I don't know," she finally answered, "but she really made an impression on me. I think I'd like to ask Joe if it would be okay to send the money from Paige's retirement account to the orphanage. I think Paige would like that."

Jim was silent. They didn't need the money; that much was true, nor did he have any desire for it, but Abigail had practically waged a war against Gabriel over it. She had assumed he would try to claim it, even though he'd never said anything like that. To Abigail, Jim intuited, it wasn't about the money. It was about who had the right to possess the last piece of Paige. Of course, the truth was that no one ever had, or ever would, possess Paige.

"I know what you're thinking," she said. "That's the mistake I made, blaming Gabriel. I thought he took her from me. I need to find a way to make it right."

"Let's talk about this tomorrow," Jim suggested and kissed her forehead. An awful lot had been said that he needed time to digest.

"Tomorrow we'll start over," Abby said. She let her heavy eyelids close, but her lips were smiling. "Like Paige did. She didn't have to die to be reborn. She just decided to."

Jim discarded his suit jacket and shoes and crawled in bed beside her. The papers in his briefcase didn't seem as important as they usually did, certainly not more important than holding his wife, who had no idea that her words had sprung the lock on his cage. Maybe with a little effort they could spring the lock on hers. "Hey, Ab," he softly asked. "Are you still awake?" What he was about to suggest was making his heart race, but he had to say it, at least once.

"Mm hm," she muttered with her eyes still closed.

"What do you think about us having a baby?" He held his breath and waited as she rolled over to face him. Her eyelids were heavy. Sleep had already taken its first step, erasing the worry from her face. She looked like the girl she had been when he'd first seen her at the Rathskeller.

"I've been thinking about it, too," she said, "but I'm forty-three now."

"Maybe it's still okay. I'm forty-six. I'll be retired by the time she graduates from college, but so what?"

"She?" came out of Abigail with a laugh.

"Yeah, she," Jim said. "That's the way I picture it."

"You picture it?"

"Of course. I picture lots of things," Jim finally admitted. "Hey, let's call in sick tomorrow and go to that little restaurant in Southie for breakfast. Remember we used to sit there for hours and talk about all the stuff we wanted to do?"

"Do you think it still exists?"

"I know it does. I drove by it the day I picked up Joe at the airport."

"I could miscarry again. There's no guarantee. Especially at my age."

"Abby," Jim said gently and ran his thumb across her small bottom lip that was still as pink and soft as a rose petal. "If there's one thing I've learned in the past ten years, it's that nothing precious ever comes with a guarantee. We could try. Or we could adopt." Her reference to the orphanage had strengthened the idea.

The word startled her at first. They'd never spoken it before. But for some reason, it didn't seem as impossible to swallow as she'd always assumed it would.

"A baby, Jim—can you imagine?" she suddenly gasped. "That would be like a miracle. Let's go to the restaurant in the morning and talk about it."

"We'll make a plan," Jim agreed then laid back to listen to Abby's breath deepen as she sank into unconsciousness, and to ponder how quickly a miracle can be set in motion. It wasn't an action that preceded it, only a slight opening of the mind. Adrenaline rushed through his veins, creating a euphoric feeling that began in his center, somewhere around the solar plexus, and bled out to his fingertips. He remained still so he didn't miss a second of it until his own eyelids began their surrender, and he floated into a dream.

He could see his own bare feet balanced on the railing at the Sandwich Boardwalk. The sun was bearing down and below him the green water was turbulent, but nonetheless beckoning to him. Beyond the boardwalk, on the beach, his father was waiting, walking Mojo. He couldn't see them, but he understood that they were only temporarily out of sight. Someone was holding his hand. A quick glance revealed Abby by his side, her golden hair long and billowing in the wind. She was leaning forward, her body poised like a cat about to pounce. What was waiting in the water below? It made no difference, Jim realized in a flash, right before he stepped off the edge. They were moving forward in unison, and that was what mattered.

They were jumping.

March 29, 2010: There is a sacred secret I've learned over the past year: It's never too late to be who we really want to be. It only takes a split second to recreate ourselves. After four years of not touching a piano, Gabriel reclaimed his right to be a musician. And I couldn't be more proud.

March 31, 2010: I am asleep when Gabriel leaves for the Indigo Lounge and am desperate when I awaken to realize he's gone. It's his first gig—I have to be there. I drag my body out of bed and it is a painful trek to the bathroom to brush my teeth. How did I get so old so fast? I call Arica and ask if she'll help me. She arrives with Ben almost as soon as I hang up. I'm grateful to have loyal friends. Two days ago, they knocked on the door with a pan of vegetarian lasagna, Gabriel's favorite, and I can relax because I know he doesn't have to eat cereal. Why didn't I teach him to cook? I guess because when I was still capable, I believed I'd always be here.

Arica helps me tie the silk scarf on my neck, the one Gabriel won on Ebay when my hair was falling out, and I leave a note for Aileen and Connor, who are due to arrive any minute, before Ben carries me down the front steps. I ask Arica to bring the walker. Even though I've never used it, I don't want to be carried into the lounge, especially because I'll know half the people there. They're townies, like us.

We enter the bar and the crowd parts like the Red Sea to let me make my way up front like an old lady with my walker. Who could ever have imagined me, the wild child, using a walker? Someone swiftly slides a chair behind me once I stop moving and gratitude floods through me.

Gabriel feels me and his eyes dart toward mine. Linger there, worried. I nod confidently and try to smile, but I'm filled with emotion at the sight of him poised over the instrument. He turns back to the piano and his fingers strike the keys.

The notes bleed like pomegranate juice. I am pure consciousness. Me. Just me, and that is more than enough.

Chapter Twenty-Three

Abigail & Gabriel, *the Catholic & the Pagan*

God can be realized through all paths. All religions are true. The important thing is to reach the roof. You can reach it by stone stairs or by wooden stairs or by bamboo steps or by a rope. You can also climb up by a bamboo pole.
—Sri Ramakrishna

Months had passed since the funeral and Abigail had read the journal several times before she called Gabriel. "How've you been?" she asked, as if talking to an old friend.

There was a long pause before he replied, "Lonely. But I'm okay. How 'bout you?"

"I'm not sure how to respond, to be honest. There's a lot to say. I'm calling because I'd like to return the journal to you. And there's something else I want to give you—that Jim and I would like to give you."

"What is it?"

"It's a surprise. Would it be all right if I came by with it on Saturday?"

"You remember how to get here?"

"Of course," Abigail said. "Did you learn how to cook yet?"

Gabriel laughed and Abigail caught her first glimpse of the man her sister had fallen in love with. His voice was raspy, yet had a rich, warm tone. Why hadn't she noticed before? "Do veggie burgers count?" he threw out.

"Absolutely not. Jim could teach you if you'd like," she offered. "I mean, it was his idea, and he is a fabulous cook."

"That's really nice of him," Gabriel said. "I'd love to learn. Tell him I said thanks."

"Thank *you*, Gabriel," she breathed into the phone. "I'm sorry I've never said that before. I owe you an apology—"

He interrupted her. "Trust me, Abigail, you don't owe me anything. We only know what we know. You know what I mean?"

"Not really," she answered. "But maybe you could help me to understand."

"I'll see you Saturday," he replied.

When Saturday arrived, Gabriel was sitting on the deck in a shady spot provided by the enormous maple tree—the one that would soon turn gold and make the backyard look like a postcard beckoning people to New England—when he heard Abigail's car crunch across the seashells that made up his driveway. She was alone as she stepped out of her SUV and for a split second her appearance shocked him. He'd never seen her with her hair down, and she was wearing shorts with sandals. But it wasn't her casual dress that knocked the breath out of him; it was how much she looked like Paige. He'd trade years of his life to see Paige pull in the driveway one more time and approach him where he was standing on the deck waiting for her.

Abigail walked toward him bearing a smile and clutching Paige's journal in her hand. He waited, following her lead before he stepped into her personal space. The last time they were face to face, at Paige's funeral, her energy was angry and resentful. It pushed him away, silently but powerfully. This time she opened her arms to hug him, and he stepped forward to allow it. With his arms around her waist, he had to hold his breath to stop the emotion from moving from his chest to his eyes. She even felt like Paige. When they stepped away from each other and Gabriel took a breath, the aroma of the journal nearly knocked him backward. It was the henna from Paige's temporary tattoo. That scent would forever remind him of making love on that Sunday afternoon with the snow drifting outside and sticking to the bedroom window, creating a white curtain between them and the rest of the world.

"Have you ever read a book that changed your life?" Abigail asked as she placed the journal in his hand. He brought it closer to his nose to breathe it in.

"Many times," he admitted.

"How interesting," she said and looked at Gabriel for a long moment as if she'd never seen him before. "It was a first for me." He smiled and invited her inside. "Thank you for sharing it with me," Abigail added as she stepped over the threshold into his home.

"You're welcome," he replied. "I'm glad it helped."

"It's the henna, right, the smell?"

"Yeah. I hope it'll last a while." He moved from the kitchen into the bedroom that was adjacent to it and gingerly placed the journal on the bedside table before he returned to her side.

"Gabriel," Abigail began and then paused before she continued. "I've been thinking, and I'm hoping we can be friends. I know we had a rough start."

"Some friendships have odd origins," he replied with a shrug.

"Paige never told me that you were jumping off that bridge when you met her."

"Maybe she thought you wouldn't approve," he suggested.

"Without a doubt, that's what she thought. And she was right."

Gabriel's eyes darted to hers. He was leaning against the kitchen counter with his legs crossed in front of him. "You didn't think I was good enough for your sister. I understand that. For a long time, I didn't think I was either. But now I do."

"Now I do, too," Abigail said. She was facing the bedroom door and could make out some eight by ten photographs of Paige over the bed. She turned back to look at Gabriel, still standing awkwardly in the kitchen. "Can I go in to look at the pictures?"

"Sure," he replied. "I took them before she got sick, except for the last one."

On the way into the bedroom, Abigail noticed other photographs hung in the living room: a young guy with auburn hair, wearing torn jeans and a mischievous grin, and straddling a motorcycle; an elderly couple that might have been Gabriel's grandparents, the old man holding the frail hand of his wife, her skin like rice paper; the neighbors whose names Abigail could never remember, wearing brightly colored African clothes and toasting with drinks on the stern of a boat; a woman opening a gift box that contained a bright red hat while perched on the same sofa the picture hung above—Gabriel's mother. Even if Abigail hadn't met her before, she would have recognized her. She had the same soulful eyes as her son. There were pictures of Paige too; one of her snuggled against Gabriel with his arm extended while he took the picture and another of her holding their cat near her face.

"This is all your work?" she asked.

His tongue wet his lips nervously and one shoulder moved slightly, almost apologetically. "The only way I've figured out how to hold a moment in my hand."

All the while Crazy Horse crept behind her, sniffing at her heels and shifting his nervous blue eyes over her body as if he were decoding her identity. Gabriel figured the cat was trying to determine if it was Paige, returned after an extended absence. He lifted him into his arms and kissed him between his ears. Soul mates, he understood, come in all shapes, sizes and colors. And right now, Crazy Horse had a better grasp on his own feelings than any human being did.

Abigail suddenly noticed the cat and locked her beautiful eyes on his. Her fingers reached tentatively toward his strange, triangular face and he nudged her with his nose. "Ah, you're friends," Gabriel told her. "That means he likes you."

Abigail reached for him, and Gabriel noticed the surprised expression in her eyes when Crazy Horse squeezed his head underneath her chin and began to purr, as if she hadn't considered it a possibility that the cat might actually like her.

Gabriel scrambled to pick up clothes off the floor as he trailed behind Abigail and the cat into the bedroom. If Paige were here, he knew, she would scold him for their house being a mess with her sister visiting. He'd made a point of washing the coffee cups and wiping down the kitchen table and counter tops, but he hadn't expected her to venture into the bedroom.

Abigail moved closer to the photographs of Paige over the bed, resting her weight on the headboard to see them up close. Paige was in various yoga poses, the last of which showed her in tree position with her hands in prayer over her head. An electric blue scarf was tied around her hairless head, and she was smiling serenely. That was after the chemo, Abigail realized, and then noticed the same scarf Paige had been wearing tied around the bedpost next to her hand. Her fingers reached for the silk material and brought it to her nose. Emotion welled up inside of her—it smelled like Paige, fresh and clean, like citrus.

"Her perfume," Gabriel noted. He hesitated only momentarily before he stepped toward the dresser and grasped the half-empty bottle. "Why don't you keep this?" he suggested. "Then you can smell it whenever you want."

Abigail was startled by the gesture. "Oh, I don't know. . ." she murmured.

"Please. I'm sure she'd want you to have it. Would you like copies of the photographs, Abigail? I can make them for you."

"Abby. You should call me Abby, like Paige did. And I would very much appreciate that."

He nodded his head silently. "Coffee?" he suggested.

Abigail followed him into the kitchen, glancing one more time at the pictures over the sofa and wondering about the people whose images Gabriel had captured—was the young man on the motorcycle Billy, his friend that died in the car accident? He looked too young and carefree to have passed from this world already. But so was Paige. And that was Gabriel's loss, too, not only hers. Grief has a way of making people feel entirely alone, as if they're the only one dealing with the anger and emptiness of being left behind. She'd noticed something lately, that the more she talked about Paige with other people who loved her, the less alone she felt.

A framed print next to the kitchen table caught Abigail's eye. She moved closer to it so she could read the words while Gabriel poured coffee into the two mermaid cups.

Lord, make me an instrument of your peace;
where there is hatred, let me sow love;
when there is injury, pardon;
where there is doubt, faith;
where there is despair, hope;
where there is darkness, light;
and where there is sadness, joy.
Grant that I may not so much seek
to be consoled as to console;
to be understood, as to understand,
to be loved as to love;
for it is in giving that we receive,
it is in pardoning that we are pardoned,
and it is in dying that we are born to eternal life.

"That's the peace prayer of St. Francis," she observed.

Gabriel smiled. "Yeah, it's there to remind me of how I want to live my life. I'm afraid I'm not very successful at it. Do you take your coffee black?"

She nodded absent mindedly. "I always thought St. Francis wrote it, but somebody told me recently that it's never been proven."

"What difference does it make who wrote it?"

"I don't know if it's even Catholic," Abby stated solemnly.

Gabriel replied, "I've always thought it could be broken down into two words: *bring love.* In every situation in life, bring love to it. To me, it doesn't matter who said it. It's just a great thought."

Abby didn't respond at first. She was reading the prayer again. "You know something?" she finally offered. "That prayer is hanging in my kitchen, too."

Gabriel laughed. "Who would have thought, the two of us trying to get to the same place?"

"Maybe there's more than one way to get there," she said softly.

"Maybe," Gabriel agreed and handed her Paige's mermaid mug before he led her outside onto the deck. They sat silently at first, Gabriel in his lounge chair and Abigail occupying Paige's.

"No wonder she loved it here so much," Abigail commented. "It's breathtaking. You used to sit here together?"

"In good weather, every day. Paige liked it most in the early evening, I think because that's when the birds seem to like it most. And there's something magical about the light when it changes. Right now, from the corner of my eye, you look just like her sitting there in her chair."

"Most people say I look like Joe and that Paige didn't look like either of us."

"Only because your hair is lighter," he responded without turning to look at her. "Your eyes are shaped the same. Honestly, I don't think you're as different as you both seemed to think."

"That's what Bowman said about Joe and me the first time we met. Do you know who Bowman is?" Gabriel shook his head. "I guess he's like my brother-in-law. Joe's partner."

"Oh," Gabriel said with some surprise in his voice. "That's great. You met him."

"You need to meet him, too. He's very sweet. They're coming for Thanksgiving. Maybe you could join us? Bowman says he'll try to talk Joe into moving back here. Of course, I love him for that. He's an investment broker, so we have a lot to talk about."

Gabriel smiled. It was a lot to take in, Abigail talking happily about Joe's lover as if he were part of the family. He understood that by opening her heart to her brother, she'd made her family two people stronger instead of shrinking it. *It only takes one small act,* he was thinking, *to begin the healing process.* Like Paige used to say. The road ahead was forking for him as well, as it had after Billy's death, and he could choose either route, to live defensively, steering clear of the other loved ones left behind, or to live affirmatively and dive into their lives. This time he was taking the plunge. He wanted to know Paige's family the way she'd known them. He'd make it a point to be at Abigail's house for Thanksgiving dinner.

"It's a funny thing about Joe," Abigail offered thoughtfully. "I used to worry about him all the time. I thought he was lost. As it turned out, he wasn't lost at all. He was only afraid."

"Yeah, it's funny how we all have our own universe that our minds have created, and we assume everyone else is living in it. But they're not. They're living in their own."

Abigail laughed. "I agree with you that Paige was living in a different universe from mine. By the way, she got her dark hair and eyes from our mom."

"They look a lot alike," he agreed.

"Have you really seen her, Gabriel, my mother?"

He nodded. "You didn't think she'd leave Paige to pass over alone, did you?"

She shrugged.

"She was a devoted mom when she was here, and people don't change that much when they die. They leave the body behind, but they're the same person. My friend Billy—that's his picture hanging over the sofa—he was kind of a punk when he was alive, and he still is."

Abigail wrinkled her brow. "What do you mean?"

Gabriel took a breath as if he was about to begin a story, but then sighed it out instead.

"You can say it," Abigail assured him. "I won't laugh, or lecture. I just want to hear."

"Well, Billy died in that car accident—you know about it if you read Paige's journal." He glanced at her, and she nodded. "I didn't deal with it well. I didn't know how to. I'd killed my best friend. The weight was so heavy I could barely move. Then, then he started showing up."

"Do you mean you saw him?"

"Not at first. Well, many times at the place I used to live in Falmouth I noticed a patch of color floating around me. It was cobalt—almost purple, and it occurred to me that it could be him, but I didn't know. Then he started messing with the lights. I'd wake up in the middle of the night and the light in the bathroom would be blinking. At first, I figured the light bulb was dying so I replaced it. That night even with the new light bulb it happened again, then in the kitchen when I got up the next morning. I told myself there was something wrong with the wiring in the house. A couple of days later I was having dinner at a restaurant with my parents and the light over our table started blinking right when we talked about him. When I went to the bathroom, it happened there, too. That's when I ruled out coincidence. After I got home, I said out loud, 'hey Billy, I know it's you.' A couple of minutes later the living room light blinked. He does it here, too. Paige and I used to joke about it."

"I wish she'd do that to me," Abigail said.

"She won't if she thinks it will scare you," he explained. "Most people get freaked out because it's not what they expect. That's why people on the spirit side try to work with us in ways we can handle. As human beings, we're big into words. We're so big into words that we forget it's not the only way to communicate. When someone passes over, most people can't hear them anymore, so they try other ways. They might play a song on the radio at just the right time and the hair will stand up on your arms because part of you understands what's happening, that someone you lost is trying to let you know they're with you. Or you'll suddenly smell pipe tobacco, even though no one's smoking, and it reminds you of your grandfather—"

"Or perfume?" Abigail threw out, thinking of the citrus scent on the bridge in Venice.

Gabriel nodded. "She'll find a way, but just so you know, it'll still be hard, Abby. People have said to me that dealing with loss must be easier because of my abilities. It's not."

Her eyes were on Gabriel, on the fine lines under his eyes and around the corners of his mouth, more pronounced than the last time she saw him—maybe because she hadn't really looked at him before, or maybe because it reflected the grief he'd been suffering since Paige's death. It reminded her of the lines on her own face that she'd been so focused on covering with makeup that morning.

"What was it Paige wrote that you liked to say?" she pondered out loud. "Shake it off your shoulders and be free of it?"

A bit of laughter escaped him. "I learned a lot about myself reading that journal. Paige noticed things about me that I never did."

"She suffered so much. I keep thinking that maybe she shook off her body and was free of it."

He drank half the coffee in a slug. Several minutes passed before he spoke. "I know she did, Abby, but still that part is harder for us than the one who's leaving. Know what the last thing she said to me was?"

"No idea," Abigail replied.

"She said, *watch for me.*" He shook his head and laughed roughly. His eyes were on the water and the sunlight making a path across it, not on Abigail. "That was her way of reminding me that she'd still be here. I needed her to tell me, even though I was the one who told her. She threw it right back at me, you know?"

Abigail sighed and thought about it, Gabriel's words that were throbbing with pain, but nonetheless offered a message of hope. She had misunderstood so much about both of her siblings, her own flesh and blood, and about Gabriel. Perhaps she'd misunderstood other things, as well. A flash of movement in the street drew her eye.

"Look who's here!" she exclaimed, her eyes darting excitedly to the side of the house, where a moving van was pulling into the driveway. "It's Jim. He's got your surprise."

"You mean he's moving in?" Gabriel threw out playfully and Abigail laughed for the first time ever in his presence.

Jim stepped out of the moving van, ducking so as not to hit his head, and waved his big hand at them. They moved over to the railing to welcome him. "Hey, Gabriel," he said, "we heard you were looking for a piano."

April 1, 2010:
Gabriel,
This ratty torn journal is my gift to you. I hope it will help you to remember me and to remember us. Mostly, I hope it will help you to remember you.

We are what we choose to be. You're the one who taught me that. You, like everyone else who chooses to be, are an angel of light.

When I was little, my dad used to say, "Be the best Paige you can be." I thought he was asking me to behave, but I've come to see it differently. Now I think he was advising me to be myself to its fullest capacity. That small piece of information is like a pirate's map leading to treasured happiness. So, I'll let that be my last request of you—be the best Gabriel you can be. Bring your light out into the world to heal this planet and its worn, disbelieving, and lonely inhabitants.

Turn it all into music.

Always,

PaigeE

FICTION

Historical fiction that lives

Recent bestsellers from Roundfire are:

The Bookseller's Sonnets
Andi Rosenthal

The Bookseller's Sonnets intertwines three love stories with a
tale of religious identity and mystery spanning five hundred
years and three countries.
Paperback: 978-1-84694-342-3 ebook: 978-184694-626-4

Birds of the Nile
An Egyptian Adventure
N.E. David

Ex-diplomat Michael Blake wanted a quiet birding trip up the
Nile – he wasn't expecting a revolution.
Paperback: 978-1-78279-158-4 ebook: 978-1-78279-157-7

Blood Profit$
The Lithium Conspiracy
J. Victor Tomaszek, James N. Patrick, Sr.

The blood of the many for the profits of the few. . . *Blood Profit$*
will take you into the cigar-smoke-filled room where American
policy and laws are really made.
Paperback: 978-1-78279-483-7 ebook: 978-1-78279-277-2

The Burden
A Family Saga
N.E. David

Frank will do anything to keep his mother and father
apart. But he's carrying baggage – and it might just weigh
him down. .
Paperback: 978-1-78279-936-8 ebook: 978-1-78279-937-5

The Cause
Roderick Vincent
The second American Revolution will be a fire lit from
an internal spark.

Paperback: 978-1-78279-763-0 ebook: 978-1-78279-762-3

Don't Drink and Fly
The Story of Bernice O'Hanlon: Part One
Cathie Devitt
Bernice is a witch living in Glasgow. She loses her way in her
life and wanders off the beaten track looking for the garden
of enlightenment.

Paperback: 978-1-78279-016-7 ebook: 978-1-78279-015-0

Gag
Melissa Unger
One rainy afternoon in a Brooklyn diner, Peter Howland
punctures an egg with his fork. Repulsed, Peter pushes the
plate away and never eats again.

Paperback: 978-1-78279-564-3 ebook: 978-1-78279-563-6

The Master Yeshua
The Undiscovered Gospel of Joseph
Joyce Luck
Jesus is not who you think he is. The year is 75 CE. Joseph
ben Jude is frail and ailing, but he has a prophecy to fulfi l . . .

Paperback: 978-1-78279-974-0 ebook: 978-1-78279-975-7

On the Far Side, There's a Boy
Paula Coston
Martine Haslett, a thirty-something 1980s woman, plays hard
on the fringes of the London drag club scene until one night
which prompts her to sign up to a charity. She writes to a
young Sri Lankan boy, with consequences far and long.
Paperback: 978-1-78279-574-2 ebook: 978-1-78279-573-5

Tuareg
Alberto Vazquez-Figueroa
With over 5 million copies sold worldwide, *Tuareg* is a classic
adventure story from best-selling author Alberto Vazquez-
Figueroa, about honour, revenge and a clash of cultures.
Paperback: 978-1-84694-192-4

Readers of ebooks can buy or view any of these bestsellers by
clicking on the live link in the title. Most titles are published
in paperback and as an ebook. Paperbacks are available in
traditional bookshops. Both print and ebook formats are
available online.

Find more titles and sign up to our readers' newslett er at
http://www.johnhuntpublishing.com/fiction

Follow us on Facebook at https://www.facebook.com/
JHPfiction and Twitter at https://twitter.com/JHPFiction